Line of Sight

David Whish-Wilson lives in Fremantle, Western Australia, where he teaches creative writing at Curtin University. He is the author of short stories and the novel *The Summons*, published in 2006.

davidwhish-wilson.com.au

ALSO BY DAVID WHISH-WILSON

The Summons

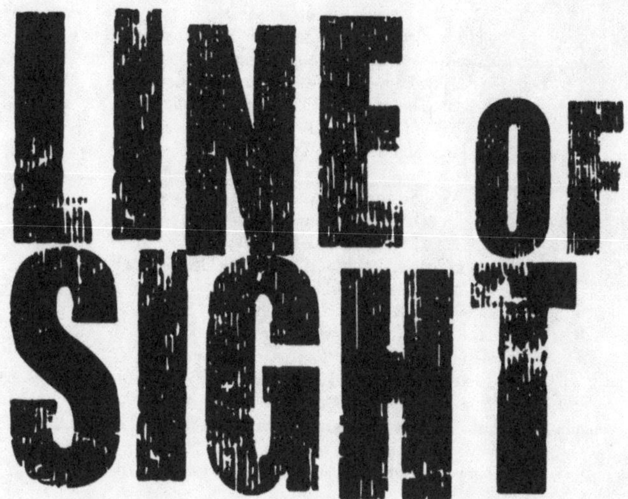

DAVID WHISH-WILSON

VIKING
an imprint of
PENGUIN BOOKS

VIKING

Published by the Penguin Group
Penguin Group (Australia)
250 Camberwell Road, Camberwell, Victoria 3124, Australia
(a division of Pearson Australia Group Pty Ltd)
Penguin Group (USA) Inc.
375 Hudson Street, New York, New York 10014, USA
Penguin Group (Canada)
90 Eglinton Avenue East, Suite 700, Toronto, Canada ON M4P 2Y3
(a division of Pearson Penguin Canada Inc.)
Penguin Books Ltd
80 Strand, London WC2R 0RL, England
Penguin Ireland
25 St Stephen's Green, Dublin 2, Ireland
(a division of Penguin Books Ltd)
Penguin Books India Pvt Ltd
11 Community Centre, Panchsheel Park, New Delhi – 110 017, India
Penguin Group (NZ)
67 Apollo Drive, Rosedale, North Shore 0632, New Zealand
(a division of Pearson New Zealand Ltd)
Penguin Books (South Africa) (Pty) Ltd
24 Sturdee Avenue, Rosebank, Johannesburg 2196, South Africa

Penguin Books Ltd, Registered Offices: 80 Strand, London, WC2R 0RL, England

First published by Penguin Group (Australia), 2010

3 5 7 9 10 8 6 4 2

Design by Tony Palmer © Penguin Group (Australia)
Cover images: Ian Sanderson/Getty Images; Comstock/Getty Images; Jeff Spielman/Getty Images
Typeset in 12pt Adobe Garamond by Post Pre-Press Group, Brisbane, Queensland
Printed and bound in Australia by McPherson's Printing Group, Maryborough, Victoria

National Library of Australia
Cataloguing-in-Publication data:

Whish-Wilson, David.
Line of sight / David Whish-Wilson.
9780670073740 (pbk.)

A823.4

penguin.com.au

for Shane

When the truth which had been confined to literature emerged harsh and tragic within the context of everyday life, and could no longer be ignored, it seemed as if it were a product of literature.

Leonardo Sciascia, *The Moro Affair*

The babysitter had never seen Ruby Devine dressed so glamorously. 'A friend of mine made it,' Ruby said. 'He's one of the best designers in Perth.' She kissed the girl on the cheek. 'Come in – Rebecca's upstairs watching TV. She won't bother you, she's got school tomorrow.'

Ruby led the babysitter through to the kitchen, where she'd laid out a meal for her. 'Just heat it up when you're ready. And there's a Bogart film on tonight. I'll wait by the car. I won't be late.'

The babysitter was already in her bikini when the doorbell rang. She put on her jacket and jeans and went to answer it. Ruby was searching through her silver mesh handbag as she entered.

'I took the wrong keys,' she said, nervous now.

A man in a trilby was waiting by Ruby's Dodge Phoenix, staring out over the river. Ruby turned her away from the door before heading upstairs. When she came back down she gave the girl another kiss on the cheek.

Now the babysitter could have the run of the big house. Now she could swim in the heated pool. The place was like nothing she'd ever seen. She heard the car start with a growl as she locked the door behind her.

Tuesday, 25 November 1975. Six months since Ruby Devine had been shot four times in the head with a sawn-off .22. But that wasn't the beginning of Swann's troubles. They'd started a few weeks before, when his teenage daughter ran away from home. He'd been looking for Louise in the small towns of the Great Southern when news arrived that the queen of vice had been murdered.

The story was all over the airwaves. Ruby Devine killed in her Dodge Phoenix on a fairway of the South Perth golf club. Left there on display. No effort made to hide her body. Even the ABC was calling it a gangland hit, the pundits yapping about the city's loss of innocence. At petrol stations on the long drive back to Perth Swann was asked by pump attendants and truck drivers if he'd heard the news. None of them knew he was a policeman. If they had they mightn't have asked.

Before the news was days old the rumour was that Ruby Devine had been murdered by police. Swann heard it voiced in cynical asides all over the city.

'They'll never find who did it,' a newspaper seller with prison tatts on his forearms said. 'Bastards know how to show no bruises.'

'They'll find someone, mate,' the man behind Swann chipped in. 'Just won't be the one that did it.'

The newspaper seller turned out to be right, because six months later the investigation had gone nowhere. The CIB had no leads. Nothing at all.

But what did they expect, Swann had asked, when the same people who'd killed Ruby Devine were leading the investigation?

The church bells were ringing over the Supreme Court Gardens. An hour late now. Swann waited at his table in the packed courtroom. Fans whirred overhead. The chatter was amplified in the chamber of polished floors and panelled walls. The only remaining seat was the leather chair where the royal commissioner would take his place.

Swann's suit was neatly pressed, his hair combed, his shoes polished and his tie straight. He leaned into the table and drummed his fingers to stop them shaking. The memory of his daughter felt like touching a live wire. The court was crowded with journalists and members of the public, but he didn't want to look. Many were there to support him but some had the rapt look of voyeurs.

Swann had spoken out against the so-called purple circle of corrupt police, who profited from organised crime in the state, and the word on the streets was that he was a marked man. An assassin might already be in the room, waiting for his chance.

The day he'd driven back to Perth after hearing of Ruby Devine's murder, he'd gone straight to the crime scene. The seventh fairway had been cordoned off from the narrow road that ran parallel to the Kwinana Freeway, thick with commuters ogling in the rain. There were no detectives present but he showed his badge to the two uniformed constables, who let him under the tape and into the tent built over Ruby's Dodge. They walked him through the day's events, pointing out by torchlight the blood spatters on the inside roof of the car, the fact that a single cartridge had been located on the front passenger floorpan, just beneath the seat.

Judging by the sprays of blood across the car's interior, Ruby's killer had shot her once from the passenger side, then calmly got out, walked around to the driver's side and shot her three more times before departing. There was no word yet on the time of death.

Swann left the golf course and drove to Central in East Perth, to the CIB offices. Because he'd been away from the city for some seven years, a couple of the younger detectives on the night desk didn't recognise him and he needed to explain himself before Casey would emerge.

Right away, Swann's suspicions were aroused. Detective Inspector Donald Casey, head of the Consorting Squad, who had no reason to be wary of Swann's interest in the murder, was blunt and hard-headed in response to his questions, more evasive than he needed to be. The two of them had served as detectives in Kalgoorlie some ten years before, and both had known Ruby Devine well. But that didn't seem to matter to Casey, who told Swann straight out, in front of the other detectives, to piss off and mind his own business.

It was five minutes past ten when the Right Honourable Justice Partridge entered the courtroom. He was a short man with a straight back and a poker face. He stood at his bench and raised his gavel, regarding the room with clever blue eyes. Partridge was a Victorian and a retiree, but beyond that Swann knew nothing about the elderly man beating his gavel on the bench.

'By command of the Governor, I hereby open the Royal Commission into Matters Surrounding the Administration of the Law Relating to Prostitution, in this state of Western Australia, in this month of November, in this year of our Lord nineteen hundred and seventy-five.'

Partridge nodded to the Counsel Assisting beneath him. QC

Adrian Wallace pushed out his chest and placed a hand behind his back, silks glimmering in the light. He cleared his throat and nodded at Swann, whose hands had stopped shaking. He was ready.

'I request that to begin the proceedings Superintendent Keith Barlow appear before the commission.'

There were groans of frustration in the gallery. Most disappointed were the journalists in the front row, pencils at the ready. Swann too slumped. This wasn't a promising start.

Barlow passed close and smiled as he came to the stand in full uniform, presenting his formal dress cap in both hands. The badge on his cap shone and his sleeve buttons were polished. His hair was oiled and parted down the middle. His green eyes sparkled like fish scales as he took the oath.

QC Wallace waited until the bible had been returned to its place beside the stenographer. 'Superintendent Barlow, could you please describe your current rank in the West Australian police service?'

'I have recently been appointed Superintendent of Central Perth Police Station, uniformed branch.'

Wallace nodded. 'Thank you, Superintendent. My next question goes to the reason we are here, specifically the allegations raised by your colleague, Superintendent Frank Swann. These are of course familiar to anybody who reads the papers or watches the television or listens to the radio. What do you, as a fellow superintendent of the uniformed branch, make of Superintendent Swann's assertions that there exists a core of corrupt police in the West Australian service, and that these unnamed persons are somehow responsible for Mrs Devine's tragic death?'

'Well, I will say from the outset that these allegations are entirely false. In my current role I have thoroughly examined . . .'

Swann watched Barlow as he crafted his response. The man was known in the service as the smiling assassin, someone who collected dirt and informed on his colleagues to those higher up, ingratiating himself and improving his chances of promotion.

'Of course, it's the first law of policing that before motive can be established the quality of the information needs to be determined. In this matter, given the recent history of Superintendent Swann's, shall we say, problems . . .'

Swann looked to Partridge in the hope he might intervene, and was surprised to find that the judge bore unmistakable signs of pain. His forehead was troubled, the same colour as his wig, and his eyes were locked in a hard focus on Wallace.

'Superintendent Barlow, would you please explain for us the reason Superintendent Swann came to insinuate himself into the Ruby Devine murder investigation, given that his position at the time was . . .' The QC glanced at his notes. 'Superintendent of Albany Police Station, a small shire of twenty thousand souls some five hundred kilometres from Perth?'

Swann watched the lines around Partridge's eyes harden at the question, although he allowed it. Barlow, on the other hand, was eager to continue. He stiffened his back and placed both hands at his sides.

'Mr Wallace, I wasn't aware of Superintendent Swann's interest in the murder of Ruby Devine until I received an angry call from one of the investigating officers of the CIB, Detective Inspector Donald Casey. Superintendent Swann had had a long association with the deceased, although I'm not privy to the exact *nature* of their relationship . . .' Barlow let the insinuation hang for a moment. 'Except to say that Superintendent Swann was once himself detective in charge of Vice.'

It took only the briefest glance at the judge for Barlow to see that he was laying it on too thick. He took a deep breath, composed himself. 'Needless to say, I was immediately concerned. Superintendent

Swann was at the time on special leave due to the disappearance of his daughter. It was assumed he was recuperating rather than concerning himself with an unrelated murder investigation.'

Wallace nodded patiently as Barlow paused to sip from a glass of water.

'I was even more alarmed to hear that Superintendent Swann was involving himself because of a rumour that his daughter had been seen in the company of Mrs Devine some time before her death. Detective Inspector Casey gave me assurances that this rumour was precisely that, a baseless piece of gossip.'

Barlow's voice became louder as he worked the rich vein of anger that plagued him as an administrator. He was twenty years older than Swann but had only just been made superintendent, and he wasn't going to waste this opportunity to make his loyalties clear.

'I ordered Superintendent Swann to desist from his inquiries and return to his official duties, but he point-blank refused. It was at this time that I requested he make himself available for a psychiatric examination.'

Swann saw that the judge's eyes had begun watering in the sharp morning light. He glanced around the courtroom but nobody else seemed to have noticed. All eyes were fixed on Barlow.

'. . . repairing the relationship between the uniformed branch and the CIB . . .'

Partridge seemed to be barely holding it together. His bright hunter's eyes caught Swann's gaze and held it. He cleared his throat and tapped the microphone with a bony finger. 'Thank you, Superintendent Barlow.' His voice was surprisingly loud. 'Your statement has been recorded. We will now adjourn until —'

There was another groan from the crowd as Partridge gathered himself out of his chair, reached for the gavel and struck it once, twice, before retreating to his chambers in a swish of red silk.

Swann reclined by the pool and waited for Marion to phone. He had been living in the hotel for a month and his wife generally called at five-thirty, but it didn't look like she was going to ring today.

It had been a long afternoon watching the fix come in. Ever since the commission's terms of reference had been announced he'd been expecting to wear it, but he hadn't expected the purple circle to be so obvious. Their aim was to convince the judge that he was unstable, unreliable or of bad character, and that his testimony was worthless. Witness after witness, each of them from the upper echelons of the force, had gone straight for his weak point – the rumour that he'd had a nervous breakdown following the disappearance of Louise, the revelation of his affair with a younger colleague, and his separation from his wife.

At this rate it was going to be a very brief royal commission.

He whirled the slurry of cracked ice around in his glass, took another mouthful of whiskey and dry. It was also clear they'd be taking advantage of the fact that the commissioner was an outsider. While to the public the appointment of a judge from over east looked like an attempt at impartiality, Swann knew better.

The Counsel Assisting, the po-faced Adrian Wallace, was familiar to Swann. He was known around town as a bad drunk and a frequenter of gambling clubs, but there were rumours too. As an ambitious young public prosecutor a decade ago he'd presided over a rapid increase in convictions for major crimes, which had led to his promotion to Crown Law's Chief Prosecutor. The rumours tied him to the equally illustrious careers of several CIB detectives, in court cases where the evidence was scant, to say the least, manufactured with a nudge and a wink when verbals had failed to work. Swann had heard that with the help of Wallace the purple circle could stitch up anyone they wanted.

Wallace's appointment as Counsel to the royal commission told Swann what to expect over the coming days.

He topped up his drink from the bottle of Jameson beside his sun-bleached recliner. The dry ginger had run out but he was beyond that now. He stood and looked at his wristwatch, fished around in his pocket for a ten-cent coin. The shifts at Central changed at five, but he always gave Terry time to snoop around. Six o'clock was the hour they'd arranged, every night that Terry wasn't out on patrol.

Swann felt like a fool calling from a public phone, but the rumour was they'd put a team onto him. That meant his phone was probably bugged. He'd had a Telecom mate check the line in his hotel room, and while the test showed a wireless signal emitting from the phone, there was no warrant for surveillance on record. But that meant nothing. Casey's detectives didn't bother with warrants.

Swann dropped the coin into the slot and dialled. His fingers were clammy with sweat. He let the phone ring three times then hung up. He retrieved the coin, wiped his fingers on his trousers and counted down a minute on his wristwatch. He had to be careful about using the line in his hotel room, but he also had to be careful of appearing paranoid, now that he knew their plan of attack.

That they were going to paint him as an unreliable witness explained the death threats, and the two break-ins of his room – it had been trashed, and documents stolen. It also explained the barrage of phone calls, hung up as soon as he answered, the damage done to his EK station wagon parked in the lot, the pistol shots fired in the street late at night. Swann knew that the more he complained, the more he would look like the delusional fool they wanted him to be.

But he wasn't going to fall for any of that. The harassment of suspects was an old game. He'd played it himself. You bullied and put the fear in them, slowly drove them crazy. You followed them around and tipped out their garbage bins, broke into their houses to let them know you could frame them, but in such a way that couldn't be proved.

Swann redialled. Terry answered on the third ring, as Swann knew he would. He imagined him in the small windowless tea-room in Traffic, with the cluttered noticeboard and the worn lino floor and the dirty coffee mugs in the chipped enamel sink, smoking a cigarette and holding the door closed with his boot. That guys like Terry Accardi still looked out for Swann was what kept him going. Terry was one of a number of neighbourhood kids Swann had encouraged to join the force, every one of them a certain type – brawlers with brains.

Swann could see their potential because he'd been the same.

'There's nothing on the radio about the royal commission,' Terry said. He had the clipped voice of a copper already, a measure of how well he was fitting in, taking on the mannerisms of his older peers. Terry was twenty-two now, had done three of the five years he needed to get down in uniform before he could apply to become a detective. Then would come his real test of character.

'There won't be. It's looking like a whitewash. Any progress on the ballistics?'

'I heard another vanload of rifles have come in, but no matches yet.'

'Any new rumours?'

'Oh yeah. Word's out that now the commission's on, anybody caught talking to you is for it. Posting out in the sticks for starters, if it's verbal. Dismissal if it's evidentiary.'

Swann couldn't help smiling. The pleasure young Terry took in the way he pronounced 'evidentiary'.

'Said to come from up top, Barlow and the others. Nothing on paper, of course.'

'How's the rumour being treated?'

There was a moment of awkward silence before Terry answered. 'They don't know you like I do.'

'Yeah, well, keep out of it, but listen.'

'No worries. Nobody knows we're mates.'

Terry hadn't needed to say it to make it clear. There were plenty of good cops, honest cops, both in uniform and the CIB, but there was also the code, something drummed into every recruit from day one, the defining difference between the cop and the crim. To Terry's peers it looked as though Swann was going against the code, big-noting himself by turning on his own, weakening them all by bringing on the royal commission. What Swann hoped Terry understood was that he had little choice.

'How long are you on nightshift?' he asked Terry.

'Another couple of weeks, then I'm not sure. I'm going to try and get up there tonight, if they're called out. They've got to get sloppy some time.'

The first whispers of police involvement in Ruby Devine's murder had surfaced with the news of her execution, then hardened into belief after word got out about her tax debt and threats to name names. The secrecy that cloaked the investigation only reinforced the rumours of CIB involvement, but officially the gossip was blamed on Swann's inquiries – an excuse, he knew, for the way he'd been nobbled.

Immediately after he started asking questions the counter-rumours appeared – he'd had a nervous breakdown, he'd had an affair with a younger colleague, Marion had kicked him out . . .

Only one of these stories was true.

'I checked the missing persons register for yesterday,' Terry was saying. 'Nothing there.'

'Stats from the dayshift?' Swann asked.

'A rape in East Vic Park. Two skinheads bashed a bog kid down in Rockingham, used a star-picket – brain trauma. Pack of bogs attacked some skinheads in Hay Street, one broken arm and a fractured skull. Plenty of domestics. A stabbing at the blacks' camp in Coolbellup. Some old Slav killed and ate his son's carrier pigeons in Spearwood, charges dropped. The usual.'

'Thanks, Terry. Tomorrow.'

Swann hung up and walked past the pool, noticing for the first time the old barbeque in its murky depths. Punctured mattresses and broken bottles and a single blowfish down there too, the blowie darting about its filthy aquarium, looking up at him with angry black eyes.

He lit a cigarette and checked his watch. At six-thirty he had a meeting with Reggie Mansell, and the state of Reggie's nerves meant he wouldn't wait if Swann was late. Reggie always feared the worst, which was probably the only reason he was still alive. He'd taken to carrying his passport and enough cash to last him a month in Bali, Hong Kong or Kuala Lumpur.

Swann knew this because Reggie had urged him to do the same, should things deteriorate.

But it was too late for that.

Harold Partridge leaned back in his plush leather armchair and loosened his tie. While his tea steeped in the pot, he cast his eyes over his office. Sherwood-green walls with heavy velvet drapes. A landscape in muted colours depicting, he had been told, Bluff Knoll, which to him resembled the crags of the Scottish Highlands that he and Margaret had first seen on their honeymoon, back in 1925. A display case containing a small club that resembled a shillelagh, gifted to the first governor of the Swan River colony, James Stirling, by native tribesmen in 1830. Afghan rugs on the polished hardwood floor, and a butter-coloured leather couch on which sat a chain-smoking Wallace.

Partridge cleaned his eyeglasses with a tissue while his personal assistant poured tea into three cups.

'Two sugars, please, Carol,' he said quietly.

'I remember, your Honour,' she said. 'Although you used to prefer coffee, with cream.'

'Doctor's orders, I'm afraid. Blood pressure.'

'And your headache – is it better?'

Partridge nodded, smiled. 'All fine, thank you, Carol.'

She placed two mounded teaspoons in his tea, one in her own and handed him his cup. 'Best cure for a headache there is, in my opinion.'

Wallace looked quizzically at them both. 'You know each other, then?'

'Carol worked as a stenographer in the Victorian Supreme Court when I was first appointed,' Partridge said. 'That would be, what – fifteen years ago, Carol?'

'Your memory's as sharp as ever, I see.'

He gave a quick laugh. 'We missed you,' he went on. 'One day you were there, the next you were gone.'

'Yes, I was swept off my feet. As you say, one day I was Carol Bleaney, the next Carol O'Halloran. One day Anglican, the next a Catholic. One day a girl from Doncaster, the next a married woman from Doubleview.'

It was Carol who'd met him at the airport on the weekend, apologising for the taxi they took to his hotel – his personal driver had called in sick. He remembered her as a talkative young woman, but middle age and motherhood seemed to have softened her features and quietened her somewhat. Having briefed her as to the nature of his recent illness – a simple case of influenza complicated by old age – he'd allowed her to take charge of his affairs at the hotel. She'd been most helpful: fielding his calls, organising his paperwork, even sourcing painkillers when his supply was depleted.

Sipping his tea, he resisted the desire to close his eyes. His arms were heavy and his neck ached, but not nearly as much as his head. He felt worse than he had yesterday, despite the pills Carol had administered at lunch. He was grateful that she didn't seem to mind the silence that settled over the room, a balm to his nerves after the day in court. It was flattering that the government had offered the services of the main room of the supreme court for the duration of the commission, but its hard surfaces and sharp edges made for an acoustic nightmare. Every scrape and creak carried harshly from the floor, along with Wallace's voluble declamations. He was clearly a man who admired the sound of his own voice, and the silence now seemed to make him uneasy.

The QC looked relieved when a knock on the door gave him the opportunity to stand up. He retrieved a typed list from his paralegal, which he handed to the judge.

Partridge read over the names of the next day's witnesses. They were exclusively senior members of the CIB and uniformed police, some of them retired.

'I notice Superintendent Swann will not be speaking tomorrow,' he commented.

'No, your Honour. I wanted to fully establish the context —'

'Who will be appearing for Superintendent Swann, Mr Wallace? Is he known to you?'

'Superintendent Swann will be representing himself.'

'May I ask why? Every one of the witnesses today was represented by a police union barrister.'

Wallace stroked his moustache and considered his reply. 'Your Honour . . . the union has refused to represent Superintendent Swann in this matter.'

'Oh? And why is that? He's a serving member of the police force, isn't he? Albeit on sick leave.'

'Yes, he is.' Wallace drank his tea in loud gulps, wiping his lips with a folded handkerchief, avoiding eye contact.

Partridge waited until the silence forced Wallace to meet his eyes. 'Well?'

The QC made an uncomfortable face, lit another cigarette and exhaled before answering.

'Your Honour, by now you will be aware that Superintendent

Swann is regarded by his peers with a mixture of pity and contempt. He hasn't any evidence to support his allegations. If he had, it would already have been reported to a public well versed in such rumours, equally eager to believe —'

'Rumours of which kind, Mr Wallace?'

'Are we really to deal in rumours here?'

'Humour me, please.'

Carol, who had been staring down into her teacup, stood, her eyes wide. 'I'll just go and re-boil the kettle,' she said, taking the silver tray.

'Yes, do. Thank you, Carol.'

Wallace waited until she'd left the room before replying. When he spoke it was with a lack of enthusiasm. 'The rumours, you have to understand, are legion.'

No career-minded Melbourne barrister would behave in such a fashion, of that Partridge could be sure. It was equally certain that no Melbourne barrister would dress so informally while still in chambers. Wallace had changed out of his courtroom suit into flared trousers and a broad-collared shirt, unbuttoned over his chest.

'As you are aware, Mr Wallace, I'm new to your state. I would appreciate your take on the relevance of Superintendent Swann's allegations regarding prostitution in Western Australia, as understood by the man on the street.'

Partridge drank his tea and listened to Wallace recount with reluctance the 'common knowledge' of the Perth citizenry vis-a-vis prostitution, which suggested a long history of corrupt liaisons. The QC's eyes remained directed at a point beyond Partridge's head, and the judge looked instead at Wallace's discarded courtroom suit, hanging off the door like a marionette.

Wallace stopped talking, stubbed out his cigarette and looked pointedly at his gold wristwatch, stroking his sideburns and moustache. The man's unwillingness merely confirmed what Partridge had suspected – that not only was the QC acting under instructions other than his own, he was protected.

He arrived on the evening plane from Sydney. He remembered November as a time of hot mornings and cool nights, the southerly blowing strong off the ocean, but outside it was still hot and smoky. He could see the burning hills beyond Kelmscott, where he'd lived as a boy. He'd started a few fires himself back then, with his elder brother. Now he lit a cigarette as he waited in the queue for a taxi.

He expected to stay no more than a week. He'd told his wife he'd be away for a month, because after the job he intended to head north for some fishing with a mate he hadn't seen in a decade. They would hire a boat in Dongara and make their way up the coast to the Abrolhos Islands, where the Spanish mackerel were thick this time of year.

He watched the smoke of the fire through the smoke of his cigarette and thought of the boyhood fire that had got out of hand – he'd only survived because of the blue-rock cave he and his brother had colonised. It was low and cramped but they'd made shelves for their canned food and firewood and porn. The mouth was hidden by a wax bush that burned away in the fire. They cowered inside while it roared down to the foothills, where they heard parked cars explode in the heat.

They decided to hide until it was safe to return home. In the meantime they ate cold baked beans and masturbated until some torches found them out, and then were ordered down the hill to be interrogated by the firemen. His brother had talked their way out of that one, and it wasn't the first time. He was later killed in Vietnam by a captured claymore mine that was used against his company. They never found his body because he'd been turned into a red mist.

The taxi queue wasn't moving. He looked at his watch. The plan was to stay on the boat and troll offshore for mackerel and kingfish, hopefully shoot a few sharks that could be lured to the boat. He hadn't taken a holiday in years, and a few weeks' fishing was just what he needed. This was going to be a high-profile killing and it wouldn't pay to leave the state too quickly.

He didn't anticipate any problems with the job; he knew the person concerned. The only difficulty would be the lack of sleep while he kept an eye on his man. He'd been cutting down over the past weeks, to the point where he only needed a few hours a night. To keep his resilience up he decided to quit the queue and walk into town, wire himself a car along the way.

Bistro Gregorio was on a quiet corner across from the Esplanade. As he'd done since he was a child, Swann paused to watch the seagulls spooling around the street lamps, hunting moths, haloed by dust and the purple night.

He kept to the darkness as he entered. Reggie was at his usual place by the toilet door, away from the windows but within nodding distance of the bar, where Greg had already poured Swann a neat Jameson. He slid it ironically down the counter.

Swann pointed with his chin to the record player set up behind the bar. 'Haven't heard this before.'

Greg winced. 'It's Herbie *Hancock*. You know, jazz fusion.'

Swann took a mouthful of whiskey to hide his smile. He liked to bait Greg but he had to be careful, sensitive as the man was. Greg was a piano player, occasionally tinkling the ivories over by the fire. He used to play a lot of Oscar Peterson, Nat King Cole and Duke Ellington, although lately his tastes had veered towards the modern, something that seemed to have made him prickly and defensive. The last time Swann was in here a drunk had asked Greg the same question – 'Who's playing?' – and when Greg said, 'Chick Corea,' the man wondered aloud whether they were playing those instruments or hitting each other with them. Greg had flat out refused to serve him another drink.

Swann and Reggie never ate in the bistro, but it was private and quiet and Greg was the last barman in town who poured large measures straight from the neck. Swann took his whiskey over to Reggie, who pushed out a chair so he could join him in observation of the front door.

Reggie was a strange bloke but Swann was used to him. He no longer noticed the bright orange hair that grew like an exotic weed on his great spherical head, or the large blue eyes that watered constantly in their pouches. Reggie had the creamy skin of a child, and during the harsh summer days could be seen slouching about town in long sleeves and a lady's drooping hat. He was a rich boy from Dalkeith, and his one remaining affectation from his time as a lawyer was the range of dicky bows in eyesore stripes and comical spots, all from fine English tailors. His shirts were gravy-stained, his belts crimped and twisted, his trousers too small and his shoes scuffed and cambered with age, but his silk dicky bow was always clean and shining beneath the third of his chins.

'Getting any sleep, Reggie?' Swann opened, as always.

'Not since last Saturday, on the couch at Mother's after a bottle of her cooking sherry.'

'How is the old dear? Did it work with her licence?'

'Yes, it did. Thanks for that.'

Swann had had a word in the ear of a clerk at Traffic, and so somewhere out there was a 93-year-old with a renewed licence and a powerful Brougham. He was glad he wasn't driving as much these days.

'Quite a performance from Barlow today,' Reggie said. 'I thought they'd take a more subtle approach. Then I saw this.' He tossed the evening paper on the table, headline up: ROYAL COMMISSION TO FIND SWANN MENTALLY UNSTABLE.

Swann held out his hand, palm down. It shook only slightly.

'Good,' said Reggie, although he didn't sound convinced.

After Louise's disappearance, after the murder of Ruby, after Swann had broken off all contact with Helen, it had been Reggie who sat there night after night and listened. And when, frustrated by the lack of investigation, Swann started making statements to the media to try to provoke a response from Ruby's killers, he and Reggie had decided to work as a team, constructing a campaign of insinuation to keep the issue in the public mind.

For a while it had worked. A superintendent of the West Australian uniformed ranks making public allegations of police corruption caused such a furore that eventually the government was forced to call a royal commission. Witnesses had come forward who'd initially stayed away, followed by others claiming they had been told by certain police officers to keep quiet. But Swann and Reggie's optimism that justice would be done had faded with the announcement of the commission's terms of reference.

Swann flipped the newspaper over. 'It's not far from the truth, anyway. You call them?'

'Sure. I called the subeditor. Asked him what happened to the notion of "without fear or favour". The mighty fourth estate.'

'And?'

'He told me he'd been pressured on what line to take by the new editor, the Victorian bloke they brought over. Reckons they've been warned by the premier and the police minister, *and* Barlow – no more tit. They publish anything beyond verbatim material from the commission, it's no more mother's milk from the police.'

'No more tales of crime and punishment, eh? Half of that paper comes straight from Barlow's mouth.'

'And every second headline.'

Greg had turned up the music. Swann gave him a nod of thanks but the barman looked sceptical.

'I'm starting to feel like a voodoo doll.'

'When it comes to self-pity, Swann, you're not in my league.'

There came now the inevitable pause whenever they met in the bistro. The two of them weren't what could be called friends, and Swann had no idea what Reggie thought of him personally – a bit rough around the edges, perhaps, a bit tight around the mouth, a copper to his boots. But Swann admired the ex-lawyer because he was without doubt the most stupidly courageous person he'd ever met – and he had met a few.

Reggie's secret was a vast network of insiders, spread throughout every institution you could name. Swann had his own stable of informers but the quality of the relationship was different. He'd learned long ago that some people had a need to snitch to someone more powerful. It was the classic master–slave relationship. When they informed to Swann they put their lives in his hands, fulfilling some urge that went way beyond self-interest.

Reggie's people worked along different lines. He had been to jail to protect some of them, had been bashed and shot at and had turned down bribes, and everybody knew it. Everybody knew that if you had something to say – something important, on the record or off – then the quiet, crazy, brave Reggie was your man.

'Got anything on the judge?' Swann asked.

'He's clean as far as I can make out. A straight arrow, right back from his student days.'

'How will he play it, then?'

'No angles. Father and father-in-law were both judges. He's an institution man, born to it. Never rocks the boat, never controversial, never puts a foot out of place.'

'That's why all the clichés, eh?'

'Exactly. Smooth as a river stone.'

'I get the picture. But *Partridge* and *Swann* . . .?'

'Birds of a feather?' Reggie forgot himself and smiled, showing his bad teeth. He immediately plugged the hole with a mouthful of whiskey. 'He's just retired from the Vic Supreme Court. He's all they had available.'

Swann shrugged. He nodded to Greg – two more for the tab.

'Anything from your boy in blue?' Reggie asked.

Swann shook his head. 'Two thousand registered Anschutz rifles in Australia. They've located two hundred-odd so far. Not exactly a rush job.'

'Interviews?'

'Nope.'

'So Jacky's still the only suspect? What a joke.'

Jacky White had been Ruby Devine's lover. The 21-year-old was interviewed after the murder and cleared, according to Terry, then she immediately disappeared. A cue for Casey and his detectives to fix upon her as the prime suspect. The rumour was she'd been murdered herself, buried in the Gnangara pine forest.

The calling in of the Anschutzes was nothing more than a ploy; the .22 used to kill Ruby had almost certainly been unregistered and since destroyed. Police interviews had focused on witnesses who'd seen Ruby's Dodge from the safe distance of the freeway. The dead woman's financial dealings, her threats to name names, had gone unexplored.

Swann had given up expecting to hear anything interesting out of the CIB. Whoever had killed Ruby knew they were safe. It was written all over the crime scene. She had been shot in cold blood and her body left on display as a message to others. Others who knew what she knew.

Finding out what Ruby Devine had known was what Swann and Reggie were all about.

Reggie took a Craven A from Swann's packet. His teeth were hurting again – Swann could tell by the way he sipped his whiskey but didn't swallow, letting it soak into his gums. And there was something else bothering him.

'What is it, Reggie?'

A grimace in reply. Reggie inhaled deeply, looked up at the ceiling. 'Bad news, I'm afraid. It could be more misinformation coming out of the CIB, but it seems Helen's going to appear at the commission. Like I said —'

Swann raised a hand. 'It's all right. I expected it.'

That was a lie and both of them knew it. Swann had hoped against hope that Helen would be kept out of the commission, but that was naïve considering their tactics so far. Despite the anxiety spreading through him – he could feel every pulse in his neck, wrists, temples – he eyed Reggie evenly and tried to laugh it off. 'So I had an affair with the woman. She wants to tell the world about it, that's her business.'

His thing with Helen hadn't been much, and it hadn't been for long, but because it was connected to Louise's disappearance it weighed on him worse than guilt. The last time he'd seen his daughter was the night she caught him leaving Helen's house. She'd been waiting outside, for what he couldn't tell. When he came out Louise was so angry she wouldn't talk to him. The next day she was gone. He assumed she'd run away to punish him and he'd ended it with Helen the same day.

He had never lied about the affair, so his enemies had little to gain by publicising it. Unless of course Helen had been got at, was going to lie herself. He could tell by Reggie's silence that this was what he'd heard.

Swann put his glass down and stood up. 'Okay,' he said, 'let's get this done.'

In an empty driveway on Rawson Street in Subiaco, sheltered by hedges of jasmine and grevillea, Swann and Reggie sat in the warm dark with the windows of the EK down, smoking and waiting for the CIB. The engine ticked as it cooled.

Two weeks before, Reggie had been contacted by a schoolteacher who lived across the road from a brothel belonging to Pat Chesson, one of three green-lit madams in the city, and Ruby's main competitor. She had since taken over all of Ruby's brothels and refused to speak to Swann, claiming she was too afraid. But she didn't appear afraid whenever he approached her. Instead she had the look of the cat that got the cream.

Reggie had dropped in to interview the teacher. She told him she'd often seen detectives calling into the brothel at night, and yes, she could remember their faces. She thought it suspicious due to the length of time they stayed inside, and because they always seemed to be inebriated when they left. When she complained to Pat Chesson about the noise, two detectives appeared only minutes later and threatened her with arrest for being drunk and disorderly, even though it was the detectives who were clearly drunk.

Reggie phoned Swann to tell him this, and Swann, taking the call in his hotel room, had written down the details, added the woman to their list of potential witnesses.

A few days later Reggie called again to say the teacher was frightened and angry that he'd betrayed her to the CIB. She'd had a visit from two detectives who knew exactly what she'd said to Reggie. They told her to keep her mouth shut.

Reggie went back to her and got a positive ID on Casey and Detective Sergeant Webb, the consorter in charge of Vice. It was pretty clear what had happened. That was when Swann got his phone checked.

A few nights ago they'd put it to the test. Reggie called Swann and told him he'd bumped into a friend who claimed to have seen Louise in a flat in Nedlands, not far from the university. The two of them parked in bushland opposite the address and waited for three hours, but nobody came.

That the call wasn't responded to meant one of two things – either Swann's phone wasn't bugged or Casey knew the sighting couldn't have been legitimate.

Tonight they would find out for sure.

Reggie rolled up his shirt sleeve and scratched at a sunspot on his forearm. 'Who the hell put a blowfish in your swimming pool?' he asked.

'Same bastards who tipped the garbage bins into it, sank the HMAS barbeque. Casey's clowns. Don't know where they got the blowie from, though.'

'I'll say it again, you're always welcome to bunk at my flat.'

'Understanding types, your neighbours, are they?'

'My neighbours could do with the excitement,' he chuckled. 'And while we're on the subject of pools, Clive Lloyd and Viv Richards were taking a piss off their penthouse balcony into the hotel swimming pool, last time the Windies were on tour. Clive leans over to Viv and says, "Jesus, mon, the water's cold." Viv says, "Yeh, mon, and deep too!"'

'Here we go.' The urgency in Swann's voice wiped the smile off Reggie's face. They sat deeper into the bench seat. An unmarked white HQ Belmont, the generic plainclothes sedan, cruised past with the siren off but dash beacon flashing. Swann looked at his wristwatch. Eighteen minutes since he'd taken the call from Reggie in his hotel room. It was fifteen minutes from Central to where they were parked, with sirens on.

Seconds later, another vehicle of the same model appeared. Swann was able to make out the driver talking on a dash-mounted handset. Then another, and another, all of them silent and converging at the same corner. Reggie grabbed the binoculars and the two of them climbed out of the station wagon and stood behind the hedge.

Four, then five unmarked cars at the crossroads, blocking each of the access roads. The detectives remained in their cars, headlights illuminating the gnarled peppermint trees and verge, all of them waiting for something. Someone.

Swann saw the tan Statesman just before he heard its low growl, cruising down the side street in low gear.

'There he is.'

Reggie passed the binoculars and Swann focused on the Statesman, whose driver's door was opening. Detective Inspector Donald Casey set his feet on the asphalt. Wedged into one of his boots was a pistol.

'He's got a throwdown in his boot,' he told Reggie.

Casey climbed out holding a cracked shotgun and stood in the park lights of the nearest HQ.

'Looks like they're planning an execution. I can see Hogan there by the Statesman. Sherving. Chaney. Webb. All armed.'

Casey stood a good head taller than the others, shirt untucked beneath his jacket. He was listening to Detective Sergeant Sherving, who was looking grimly at the shotgun in Casey's large hands.

'I make that Dominic having a ciggie over there by Webb,' Swann said. 'And Kader – that's his curly hair. The ones in the car look like Gannon, Hocking and Donnelly.'

Detective Sergeant Hogan was head of the Fraud Squad, too senior to be out on a call like this, as were all the others. The fact that ten high-ranking detectives had turned up within minutes to put the fear into a pair of imaginary witnesses told Swann that whoever pulled the trigger on Ruby Devine hadn't acted alone.

'Gannon's gone to knock on a door. Wait . . . Christ, should see his face. Like a puckered arse. He's going back to Casey now.'

Ten CIB detectives, while not one had bothered to attend the call about his daughter – this told Swann that Casey knew where she was. What made him feel sick was that if Casey was so sure Louise couldn't have been in the Nedlands flat, then almost certainly she was dead.

'He's got the news. Get down.'

The last thing Swann saw before he ducked was Casey's disgust at registering that there was no 87 Rawson Street.

Partridge finished his breathing set with a long, weak exhalation, closed his mouth and opened his eyes. His head felt light and his pulse was faint but at least the pain behind his eyes and the tightness in his chest had gone.

This was just as well; he had a lot of work to do. He climbed off the bed, tightening the belt on his dressing-gown, and sat again at the table, before the neat piles of papers, photographs and reports. He took up the photo of Ruby Devine made famous by the newspapers – Ruby in the same cinnamon-coloured satin gown she'd worn the night of her death. Only here she was happy, smiling for the camera, holding out her dress to exhibit its flow and sheen.

The rest of the photos had been taken after her death. A picture of the seventh fairway, where her body had been found in her Dodge Phoenix, not a kilometre from where she lived. Ruby slumped across the driver's seat, her right hand fallen to her side, her left hand placed modestly on her lap, and her heavy breasts thrust forward in her low-cut gown. A close-up showed blood seeping from her right ear, down along her jawline and across her chin; her eyes were in shadow and her mouth was closed. She looked peaceful in death.

Next came pictures taken at the mortuary. Her head had been imperfectly shaved, with patches of longer hair remaining on her pale neck. Each of the four bullet holes was visible in the lower back half of her head, marked with thick black texta: 1, 2, 3, 4. Partridge had seen photographs of such 'bowling ball' executions before, and recognised the powder burns around the bullet holes. One in particular betrayed the intimacy of the firearm; the woman's skin was overlaid with the square imprint of the sawn-off stock, forced into her neck before the bullet was fired.

He opened the accompanying coroner's report and noted the stated occupation of Mrs Devine was 'housewife'. He noted the fatty deposits discovered in her right aorta, the substantial amount of blood found in her stomach, the diamond in an upper right tooth, the fact that her skull was found to be 'exceptionally thick' – fifteen millimetres, compared with a normal skull, which was less than ten millimetres. He let his eyes drift across descriptions of the implants found in her breasts – written up as 'plastic bags' – the analysis done of her dress, then pages and pages of statements by witnesses who'd driven past the vehicle during the night. There were recurring mentions of a Bogart film televised earlier in the evening, the red brake lights of the Dodge, the reverse lights, the car moving backwards and forwards on the fairway, two people talking in the front seat.

He read the statement of Devine's lover, Jacky White, who had been asked by Ruby to leave the house after their poolside barbeque dinner on account of a 'big business meeting' taking place that evening. Ruby had told Jacky that the man coming to see her would solve all her problems, but he didn't want to be seen by anyone, not even Jacky; he wanted to remain a 'silent business partner'.

The reason for the late-night business meeting, according to Ruby Devine's lawyer, was the large bill she had received from the taxation department. She was in the process of appealing it but didn't hold any real hope of success. The sticking point was the 73 000 dollars in a trust fund that Ruby claimed wasn't hers. She refused to disclose who the money belonged to, or to whom she had made regular payments over the years. To reveal the names would mean certain death, she claimed, an explanation which the taxation department would not accept as mitigating circumstances.

Partridge finished his reading. Unable to dispel the grisly images, he picked up the tourist brochures on the bedside table. He had no measure yet of this city, the most isolated in the world, according to one brochure, 3000 kilometres from the next, far across the Nullarbor. This place of mysterious light, in particular the light off the river, which in the early evening had reminded him of a line from a poem – 'reality is a sacred apparition'. But the captivating quality of the light wasn't what had given Perth its status as the City of Lights, he read – it was so named because in 1962 the astronaut John Glenn, in orbit around Earth, had noticed that the people of Perth kept their lights on as he passed overhead, later describing how the bright cluster there amid the great darkness had given him courage, had cured his loneliness, and wasn't it perfect that the inhabitants of the world's most isolated city and the lonely astronaut had comforted one another?

Even through the double-glazed windows of his fifteenth-floor room, Partridge could hear the round-the-clock construction going on – the result of the latest mining boom. When he'd looked out his window this morning he was greeted by the sight of gouged foundation pits and high-rise concrete shells, and cranes like masts across the horizon. It was a vision of great ugliness compared to the photographs lining the walls of the room, sepia shots of Perth when it was all sandstone colonial and weatherboard shanty.

He couldn't begrudge the city its eagerness, however, nor the people their excitement. Although it did amuse him to read that when the French sailed up the Swan River in 1801 it was summer, the place dry and infertile, and they had rejected it as a potential colony, whereas the English, out of pure good fortune, explored the river in winter and found fresh water and other 'pleasant aspects'.

There but for the grace of God, Partridge mused. And yet here I am, a century and a half later, like some latter-day Ovid cast upon the fringes of Empire, lulling myself to sleep with parochial legends of settlement and starvation, failure and pestilence, and wars against the blacks, in a place where as recently as my father's day every second person was a convict.

How much more benign his homeland across the desert appeared to him now. And at last – wasn't that the first tug of darkness calling him down into his body? And wasn't this perhaps how the astronaut had felt, floating across the dark vacuum of night, his eyes on the lights below until he too had lost all feeling in his body, except for a vague sensation of weight, and of sinking, and then of falling . . .

Nobody trusts a cop who drinks alone. Swann lifted his Emu Bitter and took a long draught, meeting eyes with the sideshow clowns across the room. Everybody knew who he was and what he was about; nobody wanted to see him there, nobody wanted any trouble.

The bar was a weatherboard annex tacked onto a derelict hardware store off Roe Street, not far from his hotel, not far from Central. It was illegal but had existed at least as long as Swann had been a cop, and was known as the beer with no pub. It was tolerated because it gave cops off the nightshift somewhere to drink, and the hookers and taxi drivers and queer crowd from the clubs on James Street somewhere to come down.

The place was full of smoke and tinny laughter, but also a rising panic. The night was sliding away. They were rolling towards the sun. Swann could see in the punters' eyes the recognition of an unwelcome day. The bar had all the atmosphere of a school canteen. Bare concrete floor, hosed out at dawn. Scavenged tables and chairs. Stained and sunken plaster ceiling. Leaking bin by the door. The smell of piss from the outhouse by the back fence.

The barman's possie was a milk crate by a bathtub full of beer and ice. He looked at Swann with the cold malevolence of a poisoner. There was a good reason for that – Swann had put him away thirteen years ago. They were roughly the same vintage, but the other man's face looked like it had been poached in spirits and left in the sun.

He'd be grateful for this job, Swann knew. He could drink all night and sleep on the floor during the day. He could bitch with Pat Chesson's hookers and wash under the tap out back. He could gather dirt and feed back to whichever Liquor and Gaming D was letting him run the place.

Swann lit a cigarette to hide his disgust at being here, again. Reggie was home snoring, no doubt, on the couch. Swann had tried everything to get to sleep but even his last resort of a hot bath had failed to work.

It was the same every night. Unable to knock himself out for those hours between two and dawn, he'd inevitably end up here or one of the other illegal clubs on the block. Because if he failed to get to sleep, the horror of what might have happened to Louise would hit him like a punch to the heart. He would see her naked and strangled and buried in the dirt, or bound with gaffer tape and weighed down with rocks, rotting in some scum-covered swamp in the outer suburbs. Even worse, he'd see what she'd gone through before she died. What had been done to her, the fear and despair she would have felt, her last words, calling out his name, but Swann not there, never there, her eyes wide and his chest tight and fists clenched.

Then he would know that sleep was impossible and he would get up and drink. By day, too, the images of his daughter never left him and he was driven out in search of her, telling himself there was still hope, that he would find Louise, slouched against the wall in a makeshift bar, there amongst the barely living.

He glanced around at the other drinkers. What made it worse was that this was the life his stepfather had lived, had envisaged for him too. Swann thought of the times he was called to some back-alley Fremantle sinkhole where Brian was passed out, having been gone for days – days that Swann counted as blessings. His mother would send him out to find her husband, to guide him home or go through his pockets for his pay packet, what was left of it.

The idea that Brian's prediction for him was coming true deepened Swann's self-disgust, made him want to flip the table and break things, just like he'd done as a kid, wild and violent and resentful, devoid of better feelings.

He unclenched his jaw, put another cigarette in his mouth and lit it, taking a long draw. He felt leached of everything good he had ever done. During the daytime, he was still more or less himself, optimistic by nature, in spite of everything, a man who generally liked people and was liked in turn. People spoke to him, looked him in the eye, shook his hand, told him to keep it up, keep going. And he needed that support in order to go on, needed the encouragement of strangers, ordinary people who knew what he was up against.

It was four o'clock and soon the sun would be up, and Swann was glad of it. At this hour he felt even more out of place in his scuffed leather shoes and suit trousers. He wasn't much older than the people around him but he looked like he belonged in another century. It was all big hair and earrings and platform shoes now, and that was just for the men. The drugs had changed everything, the drugs and the music.

Right now in the bar an AC/DC track was spinning, something he recognised because of his daughters. All the kids were into the band. It was the kind of thing he'd have been into at their age too – it had that blue-collar rock'n'roll spirit that he loved. He'd grown up on Johnny O and Jerry-Lee and Johnny Cash, but he didn't mind the Negro music that Sarah, his middle daughter, was tuned into. Blonny, the youngest, was more into the charts, KC and the Sunshine Band, Skyhooks, the Bay City Rollers, which she listened to on his old footy transistor when she couldn't get past her sisters to the record player.

The image of his daughters squabbling over the turntable made him wince. Louise, being the eldest, usually won out over the other two, leaving them resentful and brooding. But now, just like their mother and father, they were missing her, not understanding why she wasn't there. At fifteen and thirteen, Sarah and Blonny had taken their sister's disappearance hard. They were struggling at school, having been uprooted from Albany to return to Fremantle, to their old home by the biscuit factory, closer to where Louise was last seen alive. Both girls wanted Swann to move back home, but no matter how much he explained that he needed to be away to search for Louise, Sarah and Blonny didn't get it. The truth was that he didn't want to put them at risk, that it was safer for them if he lived elsewhere, something he couldn't tell them because it would only make them worry more.

Swann tried to avoid downing the last of his beer. He had a bad headache and his chest was thick from smoking too much. If he paced himself he'd be sober enough to manage a plate of something at Roy's.

Turning on his stool he saw Donovan Andrews in the doorway, dirty silk shirt open to the waist. Catching sight of Swann, the man hesitated, but his momentum carried him over the threshold and into the bar.

For such a good snitch, Andrews was a pretty average actor. He continued with his ritual of blowing kisses to a pair of Pat Chesson's girls snuggled in the corner, but the light had gone out of his eyes. He faked a smile for Swann, accepted a shot of gin from the barman and necked it, making a show of not being able to find his lighter as a pretext for bolting. Swann leaned across and flicked his zippo.

Andrews sucked in the smoke without meeting his eyes. He stank of marijuana.

'There you go, mate,' said Swann in his most reassuring tone.

'Thanks. Some bitch jus' stole my lighter.'

'True love, was it?'

Andrews laughed a little too loudly, anxious to humour him. 'Eh? Oh, yair. You got me.'

As soon as Swann had gone public he lost his stable of snitches, except for the few who he owned, would always own. And he owned Andrews; that is, he thought he had until Andrews failed to keep their last few appointments.

But Andrews wouldn't leave now unless he was dismissed. He squirmed and fidgeted but kept playing the easygoing bludger with a laugh like a concussion grenade, the raconteur of stupid jokes and criminal capers, someone you didn't take seriously. The whole time Swann had known him, Andrews' rep was as a drug hoover and ageing cocksman, whose dick was like a faulty compass needle that pointed him from one disaster to another.

All of this was to Swann's advantage. As long as Andrews was a party boy he was welcome in any circle, from the upper-crust crowd in their riverside mansions to the rough-arsed hoons in the outer suburbs. Andrews had given Swann some crucial information over the years, things he'd overheard in nightclubs and alleys, sharing a joint or taking a piss, pretending to be passed out on the back seat of a speeding V8 headed to another bikie clubhouse.

Swann leaned towards him to stub out his cigarette. 'See you at Roy's in fifteen,' he muttered, before standing to go. As he left he eyed the barman, who was seining ice from the bathtub with blue fingers and even colder eyes.

Roy Pickett had been an army cook until he was wounded in Tobruk and shipped home. Instead of opening another greasy spoon or milk bar or offal pit like those on the Terrace, he set up a barbeque joint on Riverside Drive, modelled on a New Orleans clam shack he'd seen in a magazine. It was still there thirty-five years later, and so was Roy, at all hours, grilling steaks and split chickens on the range, blackened steel tongs hanging on the wall like implements of torture.

The sun was ripping up over the blue mountains and flooding the diner, reflecting off the orange formica and shining steel. Roy stood at his post in a pillar of light. He raised his eyebrows to Swann as he entered and nodded towards the booths out the back, hidden from the street.

Andrews was already there, slumped with his back to the wall, looking miserable. He started up even before Swann sat down. 'Mate, I'm sorry about last week —'

'Last month, last fortnight *and* last week.'

'I couldn't come. I've done what you said finally. Got myself a job. Full-time pearl diver. Washing dishes down in Freo, getting trained up as a kitchenhand. My nerves have been bad, I'm just holding on as it is. Trying to get a stake together, me and this girl . . .'

Swann watched as the words came pouring out, felt them on his face like the steam from a pot boiling over. Andrews' hands were fluttering and his eyes were wide and mad. Swann waited for the silence that he knew would follow – so big and empty he could walk right in.

Swann owned Andrews because he'd broken him. When it happened in an interrogation, neither party was ever the same. Swann learned things about Andrews that the man hadn't known himself until that day.

He had arrested him for bringing in a Filipino girl to work in a Kalgoorlie brothel. He caught him at the airport with the eighteen-year-old, who couldn't speak English and whose visa didn't hold up. As soon as he got Andrews' to the interview room he knew his story wasn't going to hold up either.

He was familiar with Andrews from previous charges, but this new scam was way out of his league. It didn't take much to work out he was just a charmer paid to grease the wheels and deliver the product. But it was a dirty business, as Andrews had learned, and Swann quickly identified something he could work with – a sense of shame. Some kind of bond had formed between Andrews and the girl during their journey. All the money in the world couldn't hide the fact that she had been tricked, didn't know what she was in for.

But Andrews wouldn't say who'd set the game up. He baulked at that. It was late at night when Swann interviewed him. He wanted Andrews alone so he sent the uniforms away. Seated across the table, he worked on Andrews with his open hand, the way he'd been trained, the way it had always been done. Every time Andrews lied he slapped him hard; he must have slapped him a hundred times. Swann could see in his eyes that they were heading into strange territory. Andrews was afraid, on the verge of breaking, but wouldn't give the name – his life depended on it.

It wasn't hard to figure out. A Kalgoorlie brothel full of imported sex slaves would never go ahead without at least a nod from Kalgoorlie CIB. The desert city was too small. Nobody would be that stupid. And Swann, now a Perth Consorting detective, knew the okay would have to have come from Casey, Swann's counterpart in Kal. They had once been partners there but no longer talked, ever since Swann had requested a transfer back to Perth so that he could be honest in peace.

Andrews wouldn't give Casey's name because Casey would kill him.

By the time Swann eased off on Andrews he'd already gone too far. The man was calling for his mother, his eyes gone somewhere else. Back to when. His fingers gripped the edge of the table, his neck was rigid. He ground his teeth. He didn't stop howling until he was asleep like a snotty-nosed child, face down on the desk, while Swann paced the room, sick at himself.

Knocking around career crims was standard procedure. You couldn't get them to speak without a bit of violence, something Swann had always been told was the difference between justice and the law, although there was a line he never crossed – you never forced a confession out of an innocent man.

Andrews wasn't innocent, but knocking him about filled Swann with shame. He was just the sort of kid who shouldn't be in the game, who wasn't made for it, and Swann had gone and broken him. What made it worse was the pleasure he'd felt, the kind he'd seen on the face of his stepfather when he was laying into his mother. Or into him.

Swann felt so bad afterwards that instead of putting Andrews in a cell or dumping him on the street, he took him to Roy's for breakfast. At the very booth they were in now. The interrogation had had a curious effect on Andrews; it hadn't made him angry. Swann gave him the lecture, trying to guide him away from the life, and to his surprise the kid responded.

Swann got him a job as a mechanic's apprentice, which lasted until Swann moved to Albany, when Andrews had gone back to his old ways.

Their breakfast arrived to break the silence. Bacon and egg roll for Andrews. Steak, egg and chips for Swann. Two cups of strong, sweet tea. Roy not looking at either of them as he put the plates down.

Andrews was spent from his rant. Relieved to be spent. More calmly, he confessed, 'I saw Jacky. Two days ago.'

Swann took a sip of his tea as though this news was nothing, but his heart was racing. 'You sure it was her? Where did you see her?'

'Bus station. Coming off a bus.'

'Did she see you?'

'Nah, hid myself. Want nothing to do with Jacky. I knew you'd want me to follow her, but like I said, I've got this new girl and —'

'Was she alone?'

'Far as I could tell. Nobody met her or anything. She had on dark glasses and a truckie's cap but it was her all right.'

Swann nodded his permission towards the bacon and egg roll. Andrews swooped on it, began to unwrap the wax paper and spread it over the table. The sun was well up now and traffic was beginning to drone. Swann was sober and hungry, just as he'd hoped. His plate lay steaming in the brightness. But first he drank his tea, sweet and hot in his throat and belly. Best cup of tea he'd ever had.

It had been a long walk from the airport but now he could sleep. A pity his hotel room smelt musty. He had a keen sense of smell and could tell that the previous occupant had been a smoker and a dog owner. A woman. The shooter wouldn't be making the same mistake. He'd handle as little in the room as possible.

He had one pair of shoes, with featureless rubber soles, a suit and a hat and sunglasses. A change of shirt and underwear. He kept a 9mm pistol in a holster under his suit and a folded knife in the pocket of his trousers. He'd left a pair of swimming trunks and a towel in the car he'd stolen on the way into town, a Valiant that he'd torch on the day he left for Dongara.

He stripped off his clothes and laid them on top of his army bag. Got under the shower and let the cold water run over him. He didn't use soap or shampoo, and his hair was buzz-cut and easy to manage. He didn't go in for disguises on operations like this – there was a certain level of protection that could be taken for granted.

He had left the stolen Valiant a block from his hotel and walked to Kings Park, for old time's sake. An easterly was gusting as he climbed the path that rose above the Swan River, announcing his slogging steps and giving eerie voice to the stands of zamia palm that grew into the limestone bluff of Mount Eliza.

When he reached the terraces of the botanical gardens, he turned along the cliff that followed the river, silky under the moonlight and vast across the southern plains. Its banks glowed with the phosphorescence of jellyfish stranded by the tide. It smelt of rotting seaweed, sour mud and blowfish carcasses.

He found himself paused on the edge of the cliff, crouched over the ribbons of light that flowed in every direction. From there he could see right to the Indian Ocean, lying beneath a blanket of mist, an arc of horizon under the cartwheeling stars.

Below him on the foreshore a magpie clan began the pre-dawn chorus, soon joined by wattlebirds and honeyeaters and the studied cadence of a mopoke owl. He was only a foot from the cliff edge. At its base spread the concrete apron that followed Riverside Drive and the old brewery. He closed his eyes and felt the downward pull of the earth . . .

Out of the shower, he lay on the bed without towelling himself and closed his eyes. He felt the water dry on his skin, listened to the metronomic ticking of the clock beside him. Taking his flaccid penis in hand he meditated upon the face of his target.

He was about to kill a cop. Nobody knew better than he did how serious that was, but it didn't disturb him. He was a professional.

The prisons were full of people who had killed but who weren't really killers. They were ordinary men and women who never saw it coming. They controlled themselves, buried themselves, until suddenly they snapped.

Nor did he have any time for people who enjoyed killing. He'd met plenty of those in the force and the army and the underworld. That was why he always worked alone. He didn't like to be around psychopaths – they took too many risks. They needed to take risks, because they needed the rush. Such people didn't understand killing in the way he did. He suspected they were no clearer on the subject than those who were afraid to kill. Both had bought the lie, as far as he was concerned. Killing could be right, and killing could be wrong, but it should never feel bad or good.

He felt neither one way nor the other. He felt nothing at all, and that was the dark secret that only he and a few others held. Those who knew didn't tell anyone. It was a magical secret, because it made you stronger to know it and weaker not to know it.

His method was always the same. No cruelty, no delay, no risks. Most of them never knew what had hit them. One second they were alive, the next they were dead.

And then he would walk away.

Detective Inspector Donald Casey was listed to appear on day two of the royal commission. He was, as Partridge had been informed by Wallace, the first witness who'd served directly alongside Superintendent Swann.

Swann was already seated when Casey's name was called. The DI strode to the stand with an expression of mild amusement, buttoning his suit jacket as he went. His shoes squeaked on the parquet floor.

He took the oath without taking his eyes off Swann, who returned the stare with a look of cold indifference. The DI shot the cuffs of his sleeves and leant towards the microphone. He spoke with authority, identifying his position and history of service, the expression of amusement returning to his mouth as he stared past Wallace at Swann.

The journalists were alert now, unlike during the testimonies given by Swann's superiors.

The precise nature of Superintendent Swann and DI Casey's relationship was something that Wallace should have briefed him on, Partridge reflected, especially the possibility of any bad blood between them. That the two had served together was barely the surface of it, even Partridge could see that.

He tapped his microphone to attract Wallace's attention, called the QC over to his bench. 'Mr Wallace, before you continue I would like to hear more about Detective Inspector Casey's history with Superintendent Swann.'

'Of course, your Honour.'

Wallace returned to face the DI in the witness box, pretended to read off his page of notes. 'Detective Inspector, I would like you to outline the history of your service alongside Superintendent Swann, specifically —'

'Our years together in the CIB, in Kalgoorlie? Certainly. And the reason I've been called here.'

It was just a glance in Partridge's direction, but enough to make clear Casey's resentment at being asked the question. A couple of journalists in the gallery noticed this too, and scribbled notes. Obviously DI Casey was not a man used to being put on the spot.

'Superintendent Swann and I served for two years alongside one another in Kalgoorlie, as detectives. This period ended when Superintendent Swann, then a detective sergeant, transferred back to the city for some time.'

Between the lines, Mr Wallace, Partridge urged silently. Requested a transfer, or was forcibly transferred?

But Wallace surprised him by proceeding directly to the heart of the matter. 'And what was the reason for this transfer, Detective Inspector? As it relates to the reason you are here today?'

'It's no secret that Superintendent Swann and myself are no longer friends, if that's what you're referring to.'

'Can you please be more specific?'

But there was no heat in Wallace's question. Instead, Partridge was left with the feeling that Swann and Casey weren't the only ones on familiar terms.

'Let me get this over and done with, Mr Wallace. The reason Superintendent Swann and I ceased working together was because I no longer trusted him. Partners need to trust one another, and during our partnership in Kalgoorlie it was made known to me that Swann was putting about rumours. Rumours that cast me in a very negative light. Just like he's been doing over the past few months. And I've had a gutful of it. The man's a hypocrite.'

Wallace did not even pretend to be taken aback, Partridge noticed, even though the journalists were scribbling madly and the detective inspector's face was flushed with anger. 'Why is Superintendent Swann a hypocrite, if you please?'

Detective Inspector Casey sat forward in his seat and spoke even more loudly. 'Because while the man has been spreading rumours about me, never having the guts to say things on the record, what *is* on the record is that he had a sexual relationship with one of his junior officers. A 24-year-old uniformed constable, someone for whom he should have been setting a good example, rather than taking advantage of.'

Wallace nodded with a new gravitas, his voice gently reproving. 'That may well be the case, Detective Inspector; however, as it relates to our purposes here, are you suggesting that Superintendent Swann's liaison might have had some influence on his allegations with regards to the murder of Ruby Devine? And if so, what evidence do you have to back up this assertion?'

Casey's anger was gone, just as quickly as it had come, and in its place was a new, sly expression. He lowered his voice, weighted it with a reluctance that was clearly an act. 'There are regulations in place about this kind of relationship – for a reason. It's bad for team morale. Bad for our image as professionals. Bad for reputations.'

So this is how it's to be, Partridge thought. Resentment at the recruitment of an outsider he had expected, a subtle testing of his authority he had expected, even the methodical dismantling of Swann's reputation, but this charade – no, pantomime – was beyond anything he had seen before.

'But as it relates to the reason we are here, Detective Inspector?'

'I think Superintendent Swann is full of shame. I think it's no coincidence that he hasn't returned to service since the truth came out about his relationship with a subordinate female constable. And I think that all this,' he cast his hands about him, 'is an elaborate diversion.'

Wallace frowned deeply, waited a beat before resuming his questioning. Ample time, thought Partridge, for DI Casey's words to hit home.

'Are you seriously suggesting, Detective Inspector, that Superintendent Swann has manufactured "all this", as you termed it, simply because he is ashamed about a sexual relationship with a junior female in his ranks? I'm sorry, but your choice of words . . .'

Casey nodded, withdrew into himself, looked down at his large hands. 'I'm suggesting that Superintendent Swann is not in his right mind. That he's suffering from a mental illness that has affected his thinking – something which is also on the record, I believe.'

Partridge had come out of retirement to take this commission, the highest honour in a long and successful career, and the only garland to have eluded his father. By rubbing Swann's nose in it they were also rubbing Partridge's nose in it, and that was something he would not stand for.

Wallace was still letting the silence build, showing no sign that he was prepared to intervene. When Partridge spoke over him, the QC looked startled.

'Detective Inspector Casey,' he said sternly. 'Character assassination is not something I will tolerate in my court. Nor am I pleased to see it abided by counsel.'

A blush of shame spread across Wallace's face but the DI did not appear chastened, although his jaw tightened. His eyes held again that curious expression of barely concealed humour. The judge had seen that look many times throughout the years, a strange marriage of menace and self-satisfaction, although never before from a policeman.

'Your Honour,' Casey said, 'I apologise for my tone. You see, despite some twenty years of loyal service, I still find that I'm a man of action and not of words, if I might put it like that, unused to these kinds of proceedings.'

Partridge leaned forward on his elbows. 'There's no need for you to address me directly, Detective Inspector. However, you are required to return to the question put to you. The Queen's Counsel asked you specifically whether you have any evidence to back up your assertion that Superintendent Swann's relationship with the junior female, as you have described her, is in any way relevant to the purposes of this royal commission.'

Wallace was looking down at his notes like a schoolboy caught cheating, but Casey had noticed the gavel in Partridge's hand. His eyes narrowed and he turned instead to the gallery.

'The junior female of whom I'm speaking has placed herself in my care because of concerns that are directly linked to her relationship with —'

Partridge interrupted in a steely voice. 'While it's admirable that you've taken such an interest in the guidance of this female officer, Detective Inspector, the matter is insufficient to our purposes here.'

He brought his gavel down before Casey had time to reply.

She was dressed for work. Miniskirt, a low-cut blouse showing her firm young breasts. Heavy eye makeup, with glam blue liner. A cluster of freckles across the bridge of her nose – she was obviously just of age.

Michelle, she called herself; Swann had no interest in her real name, or where she was from. But there was a coldness about her that meant she'd probably been sexually active before she was a teen – nothing left in that department she hadn't known, or been forced to know, since she was a kid.

They sat in silence waiting for Jacky to return, Michelle's eyes avoiding his. Behind them he could smell stale beer in the bar mats, and vulcanised pies in a warmer. A middle-aged woman at a table nearby was pencilling in the scratchings for the evening trots; she was all sprayed hair, Cardinals tracksuit, menthols smoked down to the butts. She stared at Michelle with a look of unconcealed hatred.

'There's a good girl, Shelly, mouth shut.' Jacky sat down next to her and placed three drinks before them. 'What they don't know can't hurt you.'

Swann took up his beer and inhaled the sulphurous flavour of unwashed pipes. 'Vote of confidence, Jacky.'

She laughed, but underneath her heroin drawl Swann recognised the nervous strain. Her grief was there on the surface like oil on water. The rumour that Jacky too had been murdered was one Swann had heard time and again in His Maj and the Paddington and the Shaftbury, and in other queer clubs on William Street – either that or she'd returned to St Kilda or moved to the Cross or fled overseas.

Swann had left the courtroom as soon as word came she wanted to meet. 'Where've you been, Jacky? I've been looking for you.'

'I bet you have.'

She lit a Winfield red and coughed, almost barked. She still wore her hair short, as Ruby had. Both of them had been prostitutes since they were kids, had long records for streetwalking and soliciting, and in Jacky's case, stealing and possession. At twenty-one she was twelve years younger than Ruby, but unlike Ruby, who'd had a family and a social circle that extended to sitting members and minor celebrities, Jacky had the hardness of the street about her.

A hardness made apparent every time she opened her mouth. 'Swann, we're here because Reggie set this up. Ruby trusted you coppers, but look where that got her.'

It was awkward with the girl there. While he'd never met Jacky before, he knew he could trust her. For the most part, Ruby Devine had been a pretty good judge of character.

But he knew nothing about Michelle. And Jacky seemed to be putting on an act, making it clear how things must be with a cop. Because it had been like that from the beginning. The first colonial building was a jail, and when the free men hadn't been able to make a go of it, the whole colony was turned into an open prison, populated by screws and cons, johns and janes, and nothing in between.

You still felt it as a cop on the beat through Perth or Fremantle on a Saturday night – that beery leer and barefaced hatred, and that just from the whites.

'So what have you got for me?' he asked.

'Tell him, Shell, before he busts a gasket.'

For the first time, the girl looked him in the eyes. She didn't appear to like what she saw. 'I was working in Kalgoorlie, for Ruby's shop. But after she got murdered Annie DuBois hired me. Now I'm working for Pat Chesson on William Street.'

A country girl, from somewhere around the Gascoyne. Her voice nasal and vicious. But he didn't get the significance of her CV, and it didn't look like she was going to enlighten him. It was rare for girls to shift from madam to madam, especially from someone like Annie DuBois to Pat Chesson. Ruby and Annie had been in alliance against Pat, who came from over east but like them soon had brothels in Perth and the goldfields. Now that Ruby was dead, Annie and Pat were the last two protected madams, both of them demanding loyalty from their girls, both of them fierce.

'Go on,' he said. She looked at Jacky.

'Tell him what you heard, Shell. And when. He's okay.'

Michelle's eyes darted as she tried to remember. 'It was the sixteenth of August – about a week after I started working for Pat. I remember because it was my first birthday party.'

And you were the cake, Swann was thinking. Still not sure where this was going.

'There were some businessmen, out-of-towners, one Chinese. But mostly coppers, far as I could see.'

'Do you know any of their names?'

'They wasn't hiding themselves, if that's what you mean.'

'Casey and Webb and Hogan were there, Swann. Your old mates.'

'Let her say it, Jacky, otherwise —'

'That was them. They wasn't hiding themselves.'

Jacky couldn't help herself. 'Those bastards had something to do with it, them and Pat Chesson. It's bloody obvious.'

Swann stared at the girl but she wouldn't meet his eye. 'You hear or see something at that party, Michelle?'

'Yeah,' she said. 'About a bloke called Cooper. One of them called him some funny name. I think . . .'

'Gin Blossom,' Swann said. Ruby's lawyer.

'Yeah, that's it. Gin Blossom. They said he —'

'Who said?'

'I didn't know them. They were the out-of-towners. Dings, or Maltese.'

'What did they say?'

'Said that Gin Blossom had been cooking the books, skimming off Ruby, but that he had to pay it back when she copped it. They both had a laugh about it.'

That made sense to Swann. Cooper had always run with the hares and the hounds. He was a bad gambler and constantly in debt. More important, he was executor of Ruby's will and estate.

'What else did they say?'

'That was it. Except one said, loud, like he didn't mind people overhearing, "If he does that to *me* I'll feed him to my dogs. I've still got my first dollar, and I'll know."'

'That's it?'

Michelle exhaled, puffed out her cheeks, sat back and nodded again.

More rumours. Things overheard. Nothing he could prove in court. He didn't bother hiding his disappointment. Turning to Jacky he said, 'What are you going to do with yourself?'

The grimace on her face said it all – she wasn't going to give him the satisfaction. Instead she put a cigarette into her mouth. 'Pass your lighter.'

He slid it across the table. Michelle had lapsed back into brooding silence.

'You didn't come here to tell me that,' he said. 'What's really going on?'

Jacky couldn't hide the fear in her eyes. He gave her a look that made clear what he wanted.

'Shell, go and sit in the car,' she said. 'I'll be there soon.'

Michelle rose obediently, moving through the tight shadows and hard eyes that followed her to the door.

Swann stared at Jacky until she broke her silence.

'You seen Ruby's kids?' she asked finally.

Swann shook his head. 'They're with the father.'

'They were good kids. I wanted to stay in touch with 'em but I've been in the Cross. Getting my head right. But lately —'

'I'm not interested in the state of your head. What do you know about *my* daughter? Those stories I keep hearing of her going shopping with Ruby?'

Jacky twirled her empty glass on the coaster, rubbed the condensation with her thumb. 'A week before Ruby was murdered she came home and said she'd bumped into your daughter, who told her she'd run away, so Ruby took her shopping, fed her.'

'And?'

'I was watching telly, didn't mean much to me. She said she gave Louise some money for a hotel, the Park Lane. That's about it. And I only remember that because Ruby seemed to be expecting me to say something, but I didn't.'

'What did she expect you to say?'

'Dunno. Probably ask why she'd help the daughter of a cop. Especially when Ruby was under the pump money-wise.'

'Did she say anything else? Where Louise was headed? What she was going to do for money?'

'Nope. I didn't ask. But Ruby wasn't lining her up for a job with us, if that's what you're thinking. She'd already told me you and her go right back to the Kal days.'

'Then why didn't she call me after she saw Louise?'

Jacky looked hard at Swann. 'You know why.'

He could guess. Louise had asked Ruby not to tell, had made her promise. The only reason Ruby would let him down like that. But she'd helped Louise out, set her up, hoped she'd come to her senses by herself.

'I kept an eye out for your Louise over east. Saw one of your posters on The Wall, another at Darlo station. Lots of new kids every day, and I asked around a bit. Know plenty of touts. But nothing.'

Swann nodded his thanks. Pushed away his empty glass.

'I did learn one thing in Sydney,' Jacky said. 'Word in the Cross is that most of the good smack these days is coming through Perth. Even a rumour there's a bit of green-lighting.'

This was news to Swann. Back when he was a rookie, there had been rumours of detectives dealing out of the evidence locker, and lately he'd heard of a protected marijuana trade – plantations grown in the market gardens and orchards around Perth by small gangs of Sicilians and Calabrians. But heroin was the new drug in town. According to Donovan Andrews, a kilo could be bought in Malaysia for ten thousand dollars and turned into a clear hundred thou overnight.

'If what you've heard is true,' he said, 'it won't have sprung up in the last six months. You have anything to do with the Drug Ds, any time?'

'We dealt only with Casey, occasionally Webb, Sherving. Other Ds had no reason to bother us.'

'Why did you bolt?' Swann asked. 'I could have used your help.'

Jacky laughed grimly. 'They got me. Verballed, pure and simple.

Two statements with my signature on them. One for if I'm good. The other if I'm bad. Casey typed them up right in front of me, made me sign 'em. I couldn't take the risk.'

'Did you ever see Ruby threaten Casey, or any other detective? She ever mention putting the word on them?'

Jacky stared down at her cigarette, burnt right to the butt. 'Ruby never told me much about that. She was worried about money towards the end, but she always reckoned she'd be looked after.'

'She say who by?'

'I assumed it was the Ds – Casey and the others she was paying off. She told me she kept a record of every payment she made.'

'Where did she keep the records?'

'Home.'

'You ever see them?'

'Sure, that was part of my job for a while. Every week I put five hundred bucks in an envelope, wrote "DC" on it and left it at the front desk for Don Casey or Webb, sometimes Sherving, to pick up. Made a note of it in the books, which I passed back to Ruby, who kept it in her safe at home.'

'Let me guess – cleaned out by Casey and Cooper the morning after she was killed?'

'They took everything. I was there.'

'What about somebody higher up? She supplied girls to politicians, lawyers' parties – she have anything over any of them, try to blackmail one of them? Help me with my debt or I'll tell your wives? She pass the hat around at any point?'

'Might have. But she wouldn't have told me that, especially if she had the wood on someone. Men and their bullshit needs was one subject we didn't talk about.'

'What about Sullivan? You ever see Ruby with our Minister for

Police? She ever mention doing business with him, investing in his name? Did he try and help her with her debt?'

'Not that I'm aware of. I knew they had some history, but she never mentioned any business.'

Swann sat back in his chair and picked up his cigarettes and lighter, stowed them away.

'You know, I stayed in touch with Annie DuBois when I left,' Jacky said suddenly. 'Called her every now and then. After what happened to Ruby she's kept herself to a few places in the 'burbs, does some strippers for the bikies. She's still got the green light, pays Casey regular, but reckons Pat Chesson's the new queen bee, making it hand over fist. Annie never liked Pat, but now they hate each other. Apparently, when a special little thing of hers didn't come home one night, she tracked her down to a place of Pat's, went round there herself. There was a bit of a blue.'

'That special little thing out in the carpark?'

'Yeah, her. What's the look?'

'You trust her?'

'No, I don't *trust* her, but Annie reckons she's all right. Michelle liked Ruby and she wants to stay on good terms with Annie. The kid's a kid. As soon as she heard that thing about Cooper, she got back to Annie with it.'

'It's not much. I can't use it.'

'I was just getting to that. After Michelle ran off to Pat's, and Annie went round there looking for her, Pat told Annie to fuck off or else she'd get what Ruby got – her exact words.'

'She said that?'

Jacky nodded. 'You know Annie. She's no slouch. But even she was worried. Then a few days after she told me, when I was in the Cross, I bumped into a working girl I remembered from over here, though I hardly recognised her, she was that fucked up on the gear.

And she was scared of me, anything that reminded her of Perth, since she'd done a runner. But we shared a blast or two and she loosened up, told me she'd done the big thing, twice.'

'Done what?'

'Carried. Been a mule. From Asia to here. Twice.'

Swann retrieved his cigarettes from his jacket pocket and lit one up. At last, something new. 'Who for?'

'Well, she was working for Pat Chesson. Though it was a bloke in a suit who talked her through it. Came into Pat's dog kennels and dressed her right. Packed her suitcase for her. Fixed her up with cash. Gave her tickets, told her where she'd be staying, who'd be meeting her. How to go through customs, everything.'

'She know who it was?'

'She'd seen him before – one of the Ds who came in for regular freebies. Undercover-looking bloke. Tall, with longish blond hair. Who does that sound like?'

'Did Pat know what was going on?'

'Not sure. You'd reckon so.'

Swann shook his head. He didn't buy it. 'You telling me they're getting working girls to carry? Very unlikely.'

'They aren't stupid, you know. Anyway, this girl said she got showed a photo of what would happen to her if she lost the suitcase or bolted. Not a pretty picture. Girl sitting on a loo, face all slashed up. Blood all over the place.'

'But you're a user – why didn't you know about this? And what about Ruby? She know girls were being worked like that?'

'Ruby was the one got me *off* the gear – the whole time I was with her. She might have known about the smack runs, but not that Ds were involved. I mean, coppers actually going out and getting into the biz themselves?' It was Jacky's turn to shake her head. 'Ruby would have told me. But that's not all. This girl in the

Cross reckoned the reason she bolted was two of her mates were murdered over it. Girls who'd been on a run but never came back to work.'

He frowned. 'I haven't heard about any missing girls turning up dead. And I've been looking, believe me.'

'She knew both of them. Reckons they probably blabbed about it or saw something they weren't meant to.'

'When was this supposed to have happened?'

'Late last year.'

'Were they locals?'

'Both Sydney girls, from what I heard. Pat's been bringing in plenty. She's still got a direct line to Abe Saffron in Sydney. Word is he's wholesaling smack now too.'

Swann considered. 'This Michelle, has she been asked to do a run?'

'No, but we're thinking the same thing.'

'That runaway in Sydney, would she talk to me?'

'Not a chance. And as for Michelle, I don't *like* the girl but I'm going to keep her talking. See what else she hears.'

It was getting close to knock-off time and soon the pub would be full. Jacky stood with Swann and pulled her truckie's cap low over her eyes, lifted her collar and set her shoulders square. Not much of a disguise.

'Don't say a fucken word,' she said, but managed a smile.

The afternoon glare was still hot through the windscreen of the Valiant as he cruised along the clanging dockyards into downtown Fremantle. He slowed to park behind a smallgoods van on High Street and had to pump the brakes a few times – low on fluid. The car was old but otherwise fast and reliable. He knew how to pick them, could tell by how they were tricked out whether they'd run all right.

This one was a '62 S series with a faded blue paintjob. He'd always loved Valiants, had owned every model from the S series on. Now he had a '72 E49 Charger. When he bought it he knew he would keep it for life. There was nothing to beat it for a tear in the country. The Charger was the last of the supercars, in his opinion, the best car ever built in Australia.

Out on the footpath the Fremantle doctor was gusting hard from the south, blowing rubbish along the gutters. There were pubs on every corner but he was headed up off the street. He turned down a laneway and skirted a derro with swollen bare feet sitting on the pavement rolling a cigarette. Through a double doorway he climbed a flight of stairs up to the working men's club on the second floor.

Dartboards, pool tables, a radio tuned to the jijis. The kind of place an SP bookie could work in peace, where police weren't welcome. A place where people could be trusted.

There were a few dockworkers leaning on the horseshoe, and a pair of old-timers in cocked trilbies seated beneath the dartboard. Unlike the pubs on the street, which smelt of stale beer and mildewed plaster, the club was spotless and airy, with the doctor cutting through the windows. The barmaid lifted her head from a chopping board where she'd been gouging pips out of a lemon. She didn't look him in the face as he ordered an orange squash and a bag of peanuts.

The two old men began arguing in Portuguese, but then just as suddenly were laughing. He felt someone behind him and when he turned he saw Marko Babich with his hands in the air.

'Know better than to tap you on the shoulder, mate,' Marko said.

He shook Marko's hand and patted his back. Marko had put on weight and grown a goatee since he'd seen him but he looked better for it.

'Last time I saw you,' said Marko, 'you had a knife in your hand.'

'That's not what you told the coppers. Everything set?'

'What mates are for, mate. But yeah, everything's set, pretty much. Getting the inboard tuned up, extra diesel in case we want to go out to the continental shelf. Looking to get scuba tanks too, case we want to dive some of those old wrecks. Still got to get some good maps. Those Abrolhos reefs are bastards with the wrong tides.'

Marko had been a drummer in the '50s, and had played on tour for a while with the Satin Satan, Johnny Devlin, before his amphetamine habit ruined his work and his health. He returned to Perth and when the shooter had known him was working as a slaughterman by day and a session drummer by night. Now he was a Coffin Cheater who went by the name of Kickstand. He lived in their Beaconsfield clubhouse and was carded up with the Maritime Union.

Marko grinned and the shooter saw that his front teeth were missing. 'You buyin'?'

The barmaid had already poured Marko's pony of draught. As soon as he took it she started pouring his second.

'Here's to Ringo, eh?'

He raised his glass and tapped with Marko's. The last time they'd gone fishing together, off the Quobba cliffs north of Carnarvon, a king wave had swept Marko's staffy terrier over the edge into the deep blue water. Ringo had paddled bravely while they tried to gaff him but a tiger shark had cruised up and taken him away.

'How's it working out on the docks?'

'Yeah, on the docks,' Marko said. 'Today I had to get off my arse *three* times to lift a boom gate. Getting some time on the tugs, though, gonna get my skipper's ticket, I reckon. Yer lookin' fit, you fucker. Army grub?'

He waved away the question. He'd told Marko he just quit the army. There would be time to talk later, out on the ocean. Marko pulled out a packet of Winstons from his shirt pocket, flicked the cap and lit one. Drained his beer, then reached for the second pony on the drip tray.

Outside, the doctor was making a racket in the tin signs nailed to the colonnades downstairs.

Marko scratched his gut beneath the blue singlet, looked at him speculatively.

'So Marko,' he said, 'what's on?'

Another toothless grin, and the two shared a knowing look.

'Who's who in the zoo, eh? That depends, mate. Whaddya wanna know?'

Reggie sat on the vinyl couch in Swann's hotel room, smoking a cigarillo and watching the blue smoke coil around his hand. He'd spent the day at the Land Corporation, collecting the final titles that Swann would tender as evidence. He placed the file on the coffee table, beside a stack of flyers on which the word MISSING was prominent, above a photograph of Louise taken at the beach earlier that year, her dark eyes smiling behind a curtain of hair.

Thumbtacked onto the plasterboard wall behind the couch was a map of Australia, blue pins designating the cities and towns where Swann had sent the flyers – to police stations, service stations, pubs, council offices – red pins the ones he was yet to contact. The blue pins punched the towns along the nation's coastline. There were hundreds of them, each cross-referenced to an exercise book containing names, addresses and phone numbers of contacts. The majority of the red pins were in the vast interior and the Northern Territory, small settlements and mining towns and truck stops in the main, but Swann would get to them eventually.

He'd received countless letters of support over the past months, from all over the state, and more correspondence from people in the towns to which he'd sent the flyers – managers of pubs and roadhouses, tourists, Rotary Club members, secretaries of footy clubs, country cops who felt for him. And mothers, so many of them mothers, but all of them people who'd been touched in some way by the photo of Louise, a self-portrait she'd taken with the ocean at her back. She looked happy, untroubled, her dark hair wild in the wind.

But none of them had seen her, none of them could help beyond promising to keep an eye out, buoying him up, offering a place to stay if he was ever in the area.

Swann brought Reggie up to date on his meeting with Jacky. On hearing the story of Pat's runaway in Sydney, Reggie grunted. 'Hard to credit, but then again . . .'

'Ten grand to buy, a hundred to sell. Say it enough times, it's going to start sounding good.'

'Especially if you're above the law.'

'Casey wouldn't think twice. All those years of grafting, and now finally the big time. He knows all the players in distribution. Knows all the dirt around town, in case he slips up and needs to call in favours.'

Reggie stood and began pacing the carpet. 'The Mancuso brothers would want to be part of it. Dom Franchino too, probably. Definitely Leo Ajello. All got links to the Mob in the east.'

'So does Casey. I heard he personally picks up Abe Saffron from the airport when he's in town. He's good mates with all the bent Sydney Ds too. He was always going over there on swim-throughs when I worked with him, still pissed when he got back here.'

'If we could get some evidence, the Commonwealth police might —'

'Bad idea. The blokes I know who went federal were sent there to get rid of them. Like a posting to the Land of Nod. They'll only take something if it's sliced and diced and put on a plate, and even then they're likely to sniff at it. Best they'll do with what we've got is make a few calls, which we don't want.'

Smoke from Reggie's cigarillo had filled the room. Swann got up to open a window and let in the sea breeze. 'What do you make of the story about Cooper cooking the books?' he asked.

'It fits with what we're looking at. It would account for why he's been so chary of us.'

Swann put his .38 revolver on the coffee table. He lit a cigarette and clapped his zippo shut, took a thoughtful draw, feeling no need to speak on the matter of Cooper just yet. Reggie and Swann always worked like this, circling around an idea before falling in, bringing the pieces together.

It was Reggie who broke the silence. 'But would Gin Blossom be channelling money into a fund managed by Ruby? You'd think there'd be offshore tax havens, Swiss bank accounts and whatnot. And why would he be holding money for the Northbridge dons? They can easily turn bad money into good at their gaming tables.'

'And everybody knows Cooper's got a gambling problem. Stands to reason he'd be dipping into any trust accounts he's set up.'

Reggie sucked on his teeth, rubbed his gout-swollen wrists and eyed the bottle of Jameson on the kitchenette bench. Medicine, but definitely not the cure.

'Let's just say the rumour about Cooper filching off Ruby is correct,' Swann said. 'Robbing Peter to pay Paulo.'

'Wouldn't that leave a paper trail, the kind of thing the taxman might follow?' Reggie asked. 'And if he's done it to Ruby, maybe he's done it to some of the heavier types he holds accounts for?'

Swann broke into a wide grin. Right there was what he'd been looking for, the cold chisel in his diminished box of tools. It would probably come to nothing, like so many of the other angles they'd tried, and yet for someone like Cooper the only thing more terrifying than doing time was being taken for the long drive, and if it was true he'd been dipping into some big man's money . . .

Swann shunted the door closed, yanking the handle to settle the lock. He led Reggie downstairs and into the street of blaring light and traffic. An acrid cloud of dust and exhaust sat high in the treetops of the deserted park.

Reggie hobbled on his sore ankles, balancing on his pain. Swann knew he'd be feeling nervous about the distance between them and the bank of lights ahead, behind which were the pubs and clubs and restaurants of Little Italy, but it was quicker to walk across the park than drive.

'Got a call from a staffer friend this morning,' Reggie said. 'Fuck me, feels like I've got broken glass in my legs.' But he didn't slow down, just kept stepping like he was walking the highwire. 'In the Melville office. His boss is the Minister for Housing and Public Works, bit of a blabbermouth when he's stressed. Reckons there's some more shit going on between Sullivan and the premier. Appears Premier Barth is going against the deal they made before the last election.'

Reggie had learnt from a Liberal insider that when it looked like Sullivan had the numbers for a leadership spill prior to the election, Barth had coerced him into holding off with some dirt relating to Sullivan's friendship and business dealings with Ruby Devine. But Sullivan had allegedly counter-blackmailed, forcing the premier to promise he'd serve only one term then hand over power. Reggie wasn't able to discover exactly what the Minister for Police had over the premier, but Sullivan was the party bagman, and he knew a thing or two about his colleagues' financial arrangements.

'Could be a putsch on, my man reckons,' Reggie added. 'Even though the next election's years away.'

'Sullivan doesn't have the numbers. Barth's still polling through the roof. What's Sullivan's real game?'

'Apparently he's demanding the mining portfolio.'

'That'd make sense, in the short term. Good source of income for him and the party until he takes the reins himself.'

'Kickback Sullivan in a hard hat, eh? Feel sorry for the miners if he does get it.'

'He'll get it. Whatever he's got on the premier, Barth won't risk it seeing the light of day.'

They were off the grass now and on the narrow cobblestone rise of London Court. On St Georges Terrace they stopped, the echoes of their boots catching them up.

'That look like Cooper's ride to you?' Swann asked.

'New England-green de Ville. Right where you said it'd be. The Grosvenor. Good work, detective.'

The two men shook hands. Reggie was headed out on a trawl through the better clubs to try to find some of his old lawyer mates who still had an ear to the ground.

'I look the part? Not too gone to seed?' He ran his fingers over his untameable red hair, wiped the corners of his mouth for spit, straightened his dicky bow and patted down his starched shirt, all in the one movement.

Swann nodded. He didn't have the heart. He watched Reggie negotiate the breaks in the traffic, limping towards the watering hole by the courthouse where the silks wet their beaks.

Cooper's de Ville was parked between a Nissan Cedric and a Morris sedan. It was a year old and fastidiously maintained, all nutmeg wood and maroon leather, glistening with wax, the floorpans spotless. Cooper had added a personal touch – a small black statue of a woman with a golden crown mounted on the dashboard. Our Lady of Loreto: Cooper's father had served as a bomber pilot over Germany.

There weren't any files or papers visible on the seats. Cooper spent a lot of time away from the office, Swann knew, and had the kind of clients who didn't like making appointments or putting things on the record, so there was no point fantasising about what might be slid under a seat, hidden in the trunk.

The Grosvenor was one of the last old colonial hotels on St Georges Terrace; it still had the jarrah duckboard laid out from when the street was mud, still had the pressed-tin ceiling beneath the balcony, and the black iron cupola, now sprouting weeds. Wedged between the concrete Friendly Building Society and the five-storey Bridal House Salon, the Grosvenor looked like a shaky drunk under escort.

Despite the pub's shabby external appearance, its interior had retained its grandeur, and its clientele was up-market. Swann had little trouble finding the flamboyant Cooper among the crush of dark suits and clouds of smoke. The lawyer stood giddy and flush-faced, one hand on the bar, the other gesticulating with his glass. He wore a cream silk shirt and maroon trousers, gold rings on his fingers and a single gold earring in his right ear. His spray-canned hair had been built around his balding scalp like a traffic cone. His green eyes were bright with a vicious humour that sharpened when he saw Swann.

The young man he was talking to had sideburns the same strawberry blond as his topiaried moustache. The kid wore a ruffled white shirt under a double-breasted purple suit, cowboy boots beneath his tight trousers. He had the same educated accent as Cooper, Australian but English, all rounded vowels and open-mouthed enunciation. The same class as Cooper too, no doubt, western suburbs all the way.

A consideration in the speaking; a pleasure in the hearing of your own voice, the impression it made. The younger man had the look of a stockbroker, or what they were calling these days an entrepreneur.

Cooper himself came from an old settler family, whose generations had increased their wealth and power despite bouts of bankruptcy and madness and the occasional imprisonment for fraud. He was only the latest in a line of sons schooled in exactly what could be got away with in the web of institutions and allegiances the family had created.

'Superintendent Swann,' he said without enthusiasm as Swann reached the bar. 'We're drinking cocktails, working through the book, A to Z. I'm on a brandy alexander. You?'

Swann shook his head but accepted Cooper's small moist hand. 'Celebrating, eh?'

'Every day's a celebration, Swann. This is Derek.'

The young man blinked at Swann and pushed his hair back over his ears. He smelled like cream and brandy frosted with an airy cologne. He knew Cooper well enough to squeeze his arm and leave them alone, having read the look in his eye.

Swann edged into Derek's place at the crowded bar, got an elbow up but shook his head at the barman. Cooper only came up to his chest, and Swann had to peer down at him.

'Not drinking with me?' Cooper asked, the derision in his voice responding to Swann's unspoken insult.

A surge further along the bar caused the line of drinkers to move and flex like a snake. The suit behind Cooper buckled at the knees, then pulled himself up by grabbing the lawyer's arm. With startling speed Cooper turned and shin-kicked him.

The drunk reared up out of instinct but just as quickly backed down. Nothing was said, but the apology was accepted. Cooper brushed cigarette ash off his sleeve.

Swann lit one of his own. 'Got to be advantages to hanging out with gangsters, I suppose.'

Cooper tried to smile. Sharp little teeth. White tongue.

'You have something on me, use it. Otherwise —'

'Not something on you, Cooper. Something *for* you.'

Cooper was looking at him hard, trying to read him. 'Subtle distinction, in my experience.'

'With friends like yours . . .'

'No need to trade insults. We're on opposite sides of this one, but we were both friends of Ruby. You know, she wanted to call you at one point, just before it happened. She said you were the one bastard left who could be trusted.'

'So why didn't she?'

'Don't know. Might have been better if she had,' he said ruefully. 'Things might be different.'

'Not sure what I could have told her. World's changed since I was last in town. But what about you? What sage advice did you pass on?'

'I told her I'd handle it, I'd deal with her tax problem. Genuinely thought I had it covered.' Cooper sucked down the ice in his glass, tried to catch the barman's eye. 'Ruby never talked about getting out of the game but she did say that you and Marion had done the right thing – taken your family and got away from all the palaver.'

It was true Cooper had always been a friend to Ruby, but only because there was something in it for him. And while he represented Ruby Devine and her girls, he also took care of the Italian gambling barons in Northbridge, men he was always in debt to, men who owed favours to the Liquor and Gaming bagmen who turned a blind eye. Despite all the money involved, information was the real currency of the black market, and nobody had been closer to Ruby Devine than Cooper. If she'd had information that might have harmed his associates and had threatened to use it, he'd have dropped her like a hot coal.

'So what is it, then,' Cooper said. 'This something for me?'

'Quid pro quo, Cooper. Where are you on the settlement of Ruby's estate? I'm interested to know what's happening to her investments.'

The lawyer put up a tired hand. 'That's some ways off, I'm afraid. Problems with the probate. Her affairs were a mess, as you can imagine.'

'I'm an impatient man, Cooper.'

'In any case, as I've told you before, only family members are privy to the conveyancing arrangements. Her children are under legal age and you're not family.'

The set mouth, the fierce green eyes, the sharpness in his voice – Cooper had been working himself into a state, which told Swann he had him.

'You're an arsehole, Swann, coming after me in this place.'

Swann nodded with satisfaction. 'Settle down,' he said, 'it's too noisy for eavesdroppers. I know it was a local who dobbed Ruby in to the tax office – got a friend in Canberra. I want to know who you think it might have been.'

Cooper shrugged, glad to be let off with such an easy one. 'Could have been anyone, you know that. A pissed-off girl. Some john. Moral crusader. Brought down Al Capone, didn't it?'

'In your opinion.'

Cooper's eyes darted left, then set on Swann's collar and rose to his neck. 'What do I get out of it? Especially when you're liable to quote me in court.'

Swann had to laugh at that. 'This is something I intend to settle out of court. My word doesn't mean a bloody thing on the record.'

Cooper's expression became less wary. 'You've only got yourself to blame there. If you'd listened to your mates, let this thing go.

I don't have kids myself, but I can imagine. What I'm saying is you've cut yourself off from a lot of help.'

Swann ignored him. 'What you get out of it is that my friend in Canberra is a *good* friend. So answer the question.'

Cooper considered, then leaned in confidingly. 'Well, I'd be looking at one of the other women. The competition.'

'What'd you hear? I want to know exactly.'

'Just that. Nothing specific.'

'Nothing specific's not going to stop the tax office getting ideas about your bookkeeping.'

'Okay, okay,' Cooper said quickly. 'I just heard that either Pat or Annie or both, I don't know, has hooked up with Mick Isaacs, brought him in as a silent partner.'

Mick Isaacs bought and trained racehorses. It was known around town that he and Cooper had fallen out over a gelding that Isaacs had trained for the lawyer and then refused to hand back.

'Come on, why would the women bring a thug like Isaacs into it? Why would Casey allow it?'

'I don't know.' Cooper's voice was tinny as he tried to make himself small, insignificant. 'He'd still get his cut, wouldn't he? Maybe Isaacs was the one Ruby was going to hand to the tax people. Maybe she'd heard that he dobbed her in. Like I said, if you hadn't burned your bridges with Casey, he'd be the one to ask.'

Swann tried to pass off a satisfied look. 'Well, you hear anything else about it, you let me know.' And having solicited the bullshit from Cooper, it was time to return the favour. 'This friend in Canberra – reckons the audit into Ruby's finances went further. Says you're being looked at too. Some of her money seems to have gone missing – this is where it gets confusing. They're following up on your trust funds, some of your other clients, transactions done in their names.'

Swann was reluctant to push it further. He slid a trusting tone into his voice, warmed his eyes to match. 'Some wider taxation thing. The guy couldn't be specific. But it was something big.'

Cooper waited a beat before lifting his face, outrage there in his small, lemon-sucking mouth.

'That's it? Did I hear you right?'

'Like I said, quid pro quo. I learn any more, I'll —'

'I've got nothing to hide – what the hell are they looking at me for?'

Swann shrugged. 'Look, I've gotta go, but you hear anything . . .' He broke out of the line of drinkers and turned to the door, suppressing his smile. Michelle's story about Cooper had legs, was the first promising sign in a long while. He nodded to Derek, waiting there with a brandy sidecar in each hand, then pushed through the double doors and out into the street.

Henry Barth, Liberal Premier of Western Australia for the past year, was, Partridge noted, a Master Mason like himself. He was a large man, and handsome, with the softened features of a matinee idol. The two had been introduced in the anteroom of the lodge shortly before the meeting, and in the premier's eyes and handshake and carefully arranged smile, Partridge saw the marks of a seasoned politician.

It was a small lodge in one of Perth's better suburbs, a suburb which had been largely bush during the premier's childhood and which his father, he claimed, had helped clear with an axe and a saw. Partridge was seated beside Barth as the guest of honour. He wore a borrowed apron of white silk and blue trim with a single emblem of a compass and square. It bore the traditional seven chained tassels, three rosettes and a gold-stitched, all-seeing eye.

The business part of the evening had been blessedly short; the secretary and treasurer read the minutes of the previous meeting, and this was followed by the confirmation of a candidate to the second stage of Fellow Craft. The Master of the Lodge held aloft each of the stonemason's tools – the gavel, the rule, the compass, the level and square – and solemnly described the moral lessons attributed to them, exhorting the young man to make manifest in every area of his life the Masonic tenets of brotherly love, charity and truth-seeking.

The candidate knelt with bowed head to accept his confirmation. He was in his mid-twenties, about the age Partridge was when he achieved his second degree. Partridge's father, watching from the pews, was already a Grand Master despite his relative youth, his own father a Master Mason before him, and one of the founding members of the Grand Lodge of Victoria. Partridge remembered the glow of warmth he'd felt as the Master intoned these same words he listened to now, and the look from his father – devout and proud – but also the strange regret peculiar to a young man of Partridge's background, with his future laid out there before him, his privilege such that he would never know defiance or struggle or hardship, merely the rituals of initiation.

As soon as the Master of the Lodge resumed his seat, the festive meal was announced, bottles of beer and wine were produced, and the formal atmosphere was replaced with the sound of conversation and laughter. Partridge allowed his glass to be filled with beer, hoping it might lessen his headache and accompanying sense of unease. He hadn't attended a lodge meeting for decades, but it befitted him to behave in a manner appropriate to the occasion.

The Master of the Lodge rose again and tapped his wineglass with a teaspoon. A hush fell over the tables. 'Brothers, before I open the floor to your toasts and songs, I have here a special personage, a distinguished visitor to our beautiful city. As you are no doubt aware . . .'

Partridge took a deep breath and another sip of beer, surprised to find himself anxious in the company of brothers. He even felt the old urge for a cigarette, something he had given away seventeen years ago, on the death of his father. He rose to respond to the toast, smoothed down his apron and raised his glass.

'Master, I thank you for your kind words of welcome to this inviting lodge. My father, who as you have just heard was a Grand Master, always preferred his humble suburban lodge, the same lodge attended by his lifelong friend Sir Robert Menzies, to the greater splendour of the Grand Lodge, which some of you may have visited in East Melbourne.'

He looked across the tables at the respectful smiles, and for the first time saw Wallace, seated in a far corner by the door to the kitchens. The QC's smile was rather less genuine.

'Like Sir Robert's family, the Partridges hail from Scotland, and I hope I'm able to do justice to the accent of the great Robert Burns.' He took a sip of beer to lubricate his throat and prepared to recite. ' "Ther's mony a badge that's unco braw;/Wi' ribbon, lace and tape on;/Let Kings an' Princes wear them a' –/Gie me the master's apron!" '

A cheer went around the tables as he finished the first stanza, his Scots accent finding its measure as the volume and tempo increased. ' "The honest craftsman's apron,/The jolly Freemason's apron,/Be he at hame or roam afar,/Before his touch fa's bolt and bar,/The gates of fortune fly ajar,/'Gin he but wears the apron!" '

Partridge held his glass higher, the sound of happy laughter egging him on through the rest of the poem. Amid the cries of approval when he was done, the brothers accepted his toast and drank deeply from their glasses. He bowed, then slumped in his seat, exhausted but buoyant.

Even the dour Master of the Lodge was smiling with pleasure, leaning across the premier towards him. 'Wi' a Scotsman's lilt and delivered like a poet.'

The premier nodded in agreement, dabbing wine from his

mouth with a napkin and taking up his spoon for the bowl of oxtail soup that had just been placed before him. He seemed about to say something when a burst of song rose from one of the tables. When he finally spoke it was from the side of his mouth in a firm whisper. 'You really broke the ice there.'

'The lasting influence of the Melbourne Grammar revue, I suspect.'

The premier's charming smile didn't waver for a moment but his voice became hard and blunt. 'We're among men here. Speak your mind.'

Partridge had been anticipating this. He leaned closer. 'The terms of reference appeared sufficient from a distance; however —'

'They are more than sufficient.'

'They are narrow, to say the least.'

The premier laid down his soup spoon, gently pushed his bowl away. 'Only if the superintendent in question is reliable. And believe me, he is not.'

'His accusations may yet hold water. Mrs Devine's murder was —'

'Regrettable, but in no way linked —'

'Without an investigative arm, it is very hard for me to determine that.'

Premier Barth smiled as though Partridge had made a joke. He clapped his hands together and sat back in his seat. 'There is no need to bring investigators into this matter. Superintendent Swann has made his claims; it's up to him to prove them. It is our – your – job to determine the credibility of his claims.'

'For a royal commission to dispense with investigative powers is unprecedented. It verges on the —'

'Now look here.' The premier's voice was quietly acidic but he was still smiling. 'Before we announced this royal commission we had investigators interview *all* of the people who had come forward.'

'But that was before I was appointed. And where are their statements? Why aren't they listed to appear in person?'

'Well, that's my point. Having been interviewed, all these self-proclaimed witnesses decided against appearing. They withdrew their allegations. Every one of them.'

'That is significant in itself, wouldn't you say?'

'Indeed it is. And it should tell you something about Superintendent Swann's credibility – that there's not a man or dog in Perth willing to stand beside him in court under oath. It's one thing to spread rumours, quite another to substantiate them.'

Partridge felt the pressure of blood in his neck, and in his temples, which ached. The premier returned to his soup.

'Who were these investigators, exactly? In what capacity were they employed?'

Barth's eyes narrowed. 'They were trained investigators. Professionals.'

'You don't mean they were detectives, surely? Policemen interviewing potential witnesses about the administration of the law that they themselves are charged with carrying out? That would amount to a clear conflict of interest.'

The premier placed his spoon on the surface of his soup, where it collected liquid and sank. His eyes never left Partridge's but there was a new, considered tone in his voice. 'Admittedly, we don't always do things here as you might over your way. However, it can be said beyond a doubt that every one of the witnesses appearing at your commission is doing so because they feel they have something important to say.'

Aware they might be interrupted at any moment, Partridge pressed on. 'None of this was made known to me before I accepted the commission. So I will say it again: without an investigative arm, this commission is toothless.'

The measured look in the premier's eyes evaporated. His response was abrupt, changing the subject. 'You took a very hard line today.'

'I felt that QC Wallace's questions were inciting and improper.'

The premier shook his head. 'Wallace's reputation, his experience and knowledge, cannot be faulted. Not to mention that he's lately a brother. You can trust him.'

'It is not a matter of my trusting Wallace, Premier. It is a matter of public trust.'

Barth scoffed. 'The public? As far as the public goes, need I spell it out? It's something I learned in the army, and which has held me in good stead ever since.'

'You don't set an inquiry unless you know the result,' Partridge finished for him.

'Quite so. Officially, our resources are limited. That is the end of it.'

'We shall see. There's always the governor.'

'Given what has just happened to Prime Minister Whitlam, I would advise against it. My opinion is that the governor would be very unlikely to intervene, in the circumstances. He is, however, an honourable man and I'm sure he will hear your complaints. I know this because we served together in the Intelligence Corp.'

The premier continued to stare evenly at Partridge. 'Alternatively, I understand that you are unwell. That is unfortunate. If you prefer to retire hurt, as it were, I will be happy to accept your resignation.'

A great roar went around the room as the Master of the Lodge began to lead one table in song against the other. It was an old school song that Partridge had heard on the rugby field as a boy. 'Scotch, Scotch, who are we? Scotch, Scotch, we, we, we . . .'

The premier nodded in amusement as the opposing table began their rejoinder amid hoots of laughter. 'Deus Dux, Doctrina Lux. We are Christchurch, Dux Dux Dux . . .'

Swann followed the Stirling Highway away from the city and down to the coast, crossed the traffic bridge south over the river into Fremantle and parked the EK by the hamburger bar near the docks. He walked along the wharf, where shark fishermen were unloading their catch, humping gutted bronze whalers on their shoulders up the ramp. A customs launch berthed with a thud against the stays, and masts whined and flags cracked in the southerly breeze. A V8 Valiant chugged past in the direction of the junkyards.

He called Marion to let her know he was coming by, then dropped another coin to dial Terry. It wasn't the agreed time to call but on the third attempt Terry picked up, back from a patrol. Swann asked him to check on Jacky's story about the two murdered prostitutes then hung up. Working girls were notorious rumour-mongers, and while Jacky mightn't have started this one, that she was shit-scared and on smack didn't exactly fill him with confidence.

He returned to his car and drove through familiar streets, and within minutes pulled up outside his home. It was in a quiet suburb not a hundred yards from South Beach, only a block from the house where he'd grown up.

Back then the area had been mostly factories and stables and fellmongers, knocked up on the sand dunes, and Swann could still smell the salt on the wind, and biscuits baking in the Arnott's factory nearby. Across the road was the small park that he and the neighbours had planted with tea-tree and peppermint.

He turned off the radio news – a hike in the price of OPEC oil – and listened to the gargling motor. The timing was out. The EK was the first and only car he'd owned and he'd always serviced it himself, although like everything else, that had fallen away of late. He switched off the ignition and heard the whispering of the wattle trees on the verge. Dogs barked, the lights in houses were extinguished. He peered across the passenger side to see if Marion was smoking on the front porch, then slumped back in his seat to wait.

Like most of the houses on the street, his was an ordinary fibro built from a kit. He and his father-in-law had knocked it up in five weeks over summer in '54. It was too small for their family of five but nobody ever complained. It had a good yard and a long driveway shaded by gum trees. The place was still home to Marion and Sarah and Blonny. The two youngest daughters shared a room; Louise's sleepout at the rear was waiting for her return.

At the sight of the family cat perched on top of a driveway pillar, Swann pushed open the driver's door. Charley came to him, sniffing cautiously around his feet before climbing onto his lap, padding and kissing his thighs with his claws, purring with his best captive expression, pushing a wet chin under Swann's shirt.

Louise had named Charley when he appeared one night, a stray from the local quarry. They found him sitting on the wing mirror of the Holden, a kitten with big yellow eyes and ribs showing through his chest. Now he was a fat old boy with a dribbling mouth and legs that shivered when he walked.

Swann lit a cigarette and rolled the window down further for Charley's benefit. He looked across at the park, now dark and quiet. By day it was full of children and dogs. The first time Louise ran away she had hidden there, so deeply in the lantana that he and Marion didn't see her, even though it was the first place they looked. He could still taste the panic he'd felt that day, as afternoon faded to dusk and Louise still hadn't been found. The whole neighbourhood was out searching for her; his colleagues from the station turned up in patrol cars and on bicycles. Marion's father set up a base of operations from his kitchen table. At his word, drinkers walked out of the local pubs and were put to the task.

By the time the sun went down, it had felt to Swann like he was losing his mind. Marion's face was so pale and her eyes so wide that he was frightened to look at her. Swann had been involved with missing children before but this was different. He had carried a drowned boy off the Point Walter sandspit to his waiting parents, but that was what it meant to be a policeman. This was what it meant to be a father. To feel a love so ferocious that he would follow her wherever she'd gone.

Louise had crawled out of her hideout just after sunset and wandered into the yard, rubbing her eyes. He could see that she was angry with him. She stood there with her hands on her hips and her mouth set and her dark eyes swollen with tiredness. She was four years old. Swann swept her up and burst into tears. He shouted at her and held her tight against his chest.

His love for her, his firstborn, had been pure from the moment she was handed to him, swaddled in a hospital towel. From that day, everything he did was for her, for his family. Everything, that is, until he met Helen.

Parked in front of his family home, he saw again the look on Louise's face when she discovered that he and Helen were lovers.

Her eyes flaring and her mouth opening – but too angry to speak. It was only later that Helen had told him about Louise's feelings for her; she had got to know Louise as her Police and Citizens volleyball coach. She showed him the letters Louise had written, although they too had stopped the day she ran away, the day Swann broke it off with Helen, and none of them had heard anything since.

He gave the letters to Marion before setting out to find Louise. He had no idea what had happened to them. Marion had never mentioned them again and neither had he.

All that mattered was finding Louise.

The front door opened and Marion came out onto the porch, holding two glasses and an ashtray. Swann picked Charley off his lap and carried him up the drive. He put him down on the porch and embraced his wife, all the awkwardness and embarrassment still there. It was dark but the moonlight was strong. Marion usually kept her hair short but hadn't cut it since Louise had left; now she wore it in a ponytail like Sarah and Blonny. She wore a long-sleeved cotton work shirt with cut-off denim shorts and bare feet. Her normally tanned legs were pale.

She sat down on the old wicker chair, which creaked when she leaned across to pass him his glass of rum. He lit a cigarette and passed it to her, lit another for himself.

'Kids?' he asked quietly.

'Blonny's been going out a lot with friends, Sarah's spending most of her time reading in bed. You?'

Swann shrugged. In the grey darkness Marion looked much like she had when he met her twenty-two years ago. He remembered how good she'd looked dressed up to go dancing, and she still had that way about her. He felt a stab of desire that didn't go anywhere. They were talking again, but whatever intimacy they'd had was gone for now. Louise's disappearance had made his affair seem even more pointless and stupid than it already was. Her prolonged absence had taken the joy out of everything.

'Here's my pay, minus what I need.'

He handed over an envelope and she took it and placed it on the bench beside her rum. Charley rolled onto his back and offered his stomach for scratching. Swann leant down and rubbed his fingers through the ragged fur and the cat began to purr loudly, in competition with the croaking of the motorbike frogs in the neighbour's pond.

'He misses you,' Marion said, as she did whenever he visited.

Out of habit she began to tell him about her day, the way she had every night since he started work as a policeman. Missing from her story was the fact that those of her friends who were also married to policemen had stopped talking to her, because her husband had turned on his own. That was the code; her father had been a detective and she had been brought up with it.

Some of those policemen's wives got told little by their husbands, either because they couldn't be trusted not to pass things on or because they couldn't handle the truth. It had never been like that with Marion – Swann had always been able to talk to her about his job, and her advice was always good. She knew how much he loved being a policeman, and what was likely to happen once the royal commission was over. She had never complained about the difficulty of her life, or her fears for him, and Swann was reminded again that the only good parts of himself had come from her, and from her father.

It was because Detective Sergeant George Monroe was a policeman that Swann and Marion had grown up in the same suburb without meeting. From an early age Swann worked his way around the bars in the West End. During the Second World War, Fremantle was the largest naval base in the Southern Hemisphere, and a good source of pocket money. As a child of seven and eight, Swann had conned drunk Yanks and run errands for merchant sailors. He worked as a go-between for his stepfather, delivering money and liquor and taking messages to ships. Years later he took over a newspaper concession by beating a kid in a fight, put up to it by Brian. He would stand beside his mound of papers until late at night and for a fee direct sailors and visitors to prostitutes who worked nearby. He told them where after-hours drinks and French letters could be bought.

One day, Detective Sergeant Monroe stopped to buy a newspaper. Swann knew who he was because it was necessary for him to know all the jacks, but he had never seen his daughter before. He hadn't been brought up to be friendly to coppers but he was sixteen and cocky and good-looking, and so was Marion. He could see from the way she looked at him that she liked him, despite his black eye and bodgie style, and he'd asked around and got the name of her secretarial school; had waited for her one day in his best jeans and drape coat and bootlace tie, and asked her out. Before long they were going dancing regularly, the rock'n'roll scene in full swing at that time. Marion was even wilder than he was.

At first he avoided her father, assuming he wouldn't be accepted, with his teenage history of fighting for small stakes, and his stepfather an occasional crim and a bad drunk with a reputation for hating police. But to his surprise, George Monroe saw something in him that nobody else had, even encouraged him to join the force. In contrast with his stepfather, Monroe was a man Swann could admire. He was tough but not mean, fair but not weak – everything Brian wasn't.

Swann would sit at George Monroe's kitchen table sharing a beer, despite being under-age, and from that vantage point, being a cop looked pretty good. It would sure draw a line under his old life, rub Brian's nose in it. He was sick of being angry. Perhaps it was time to put what he had to some good use. He knew he could do the job, handle the knocks and still deal with people straight. He was in love with Marion and wanted to be like her father. Being around them made him want to do better. Becoming a copper wasn't going to earn him any friends, but at the same time he would never be on the outside.

On the day Swann was made a detective, his father-in-law told him that now would begin his test of character. The purple circle would be watching, and if he wanted to advance quickly he'd have to earn their trust, but if he wanted to come up straight then he needed to keep out of their way. And if he was told to do something he really didn't want to, he was to come and tell George.

But it had never been necessary. Swann was never asked to do anything beyond act as driver and bagman on a few occasions, and he'd always assumed that this was due to his father-in-law's influence. He'd never been ordered to go the bash on a civilian witness, or remove evidence from the lock-up safe, or warn a crim of an upcoming raid, or salt the mine and plant evidence, or coerce a guilty plea out of an innocent man. He had taken George's advice and kept his nose clean, and the purple circle left him pretty much alone. The same couldn't be said for Donald Casey, and plenty of the others he'd known in the academy. Even when the two of them had been partners, and long before they'd fallen out, Casey had been protected when he slipped up.

Marion knew Casey well from their days in Kalgoorlie, and while Swann brought her up to date on the royal commission he could see the concern surface in her eyes. From a young age she'd known about the ruthlessness of cops like Casey, and that nothing could be done about it.

'Dad?'

Sarah was standing behind the screen door, looking out. He

waved her onto the porch and she came and sat beside him on the bench. She was in her pyjama shorts and smelt of Nivea. He put his arm around her and kissed her ear and she laid her head on his shoulder. He wanted more than anything to be at home with his daughters, but if the bastards were going to come at him, he wanted it to be well away from his family.

On the floor beneath them the cat sat to attention and listened to something scratch in the darkness. Marion sat back in her chair and tucked her feet up under her buttocks, staring down at Charley as she sipped her rum. Sarah put her toe gently into the cat's soft belly and rubbed the tanned skin on Swann's forearm. He gazed at the grey moonlit boards and the cat playing mouse with his daughter's foot, and despite all his numbness felt the love of those who remained.

Back at the phone box on the docks, Swann put in a call to Reggie. Across the carpark a diesel tanker was berthed, rusty flank looming and generator thudding in its cavernous belly. Swann glanced at his watch as Reggie picked up. Just gone midnight.

'Learn anything around town?' he asked.

'Plenty of money being splashed about but it's all nudge nudge when I walk up. Wasn't even allowed into the Perth Club, can you believe that? My father and grandfather were secretary and president. Whatever the definition of a gentleman is, apparently I'm no longer it. What about you?'

'Cooper knows something. Pretty sure he believed me. We'll know for certain if he gets back to us. Thought I might go over and check on Jacky at her motel.'

'Good idea. Stay in touch, I won't be sleeping.'

Swann hung up and wandered over to his car. Ignition on, he put both hands on the wheel and closed his stinging eyes. Tipped his head back and opened them again. Got sick of staring at the roof lining and poured himself a cap of whiskey to get him back on the road.

Jacky's motel wasn't a smart choice: Vic Park was too close to town. She'd registered under a false name but it wouldn't take half an hour to track her down if word got out. Swann parked next to a bricked bin enclosure under a spray of purple bougainvillea. From here he had a clear view of her ground-floor room. After a scout around to make sure there were no footprints in the garden bed outside her window, no lights taken out in the access corridors, no doors ajar or windows open in the rooms opposite hers, he settled back on the Holden's bench seat. He tilted the rear-vision mirror to cover his vulnerable side and lit a cigarette.

Once again he had to watch and wait. Shallow sleep if he could manage it, sitting upright. It didn't pay to get too comfortable. He'd trained himself to wake at the slightest noise, to feel the darkness like a child feels it, as a thing alive. When they came at him they'd want to make it look like suicide. No comeback on that one. No great surprise to anyone either, considering that he was supposed to be mad.

But they wouldn't get him without a fight.

Swann had seen how fear could eat at a man until he was grateful to be captured, thankful not to have to endure himself any longer. It was what Casey would be counting on. Casey and his surrogate sons. The games they played with him, the petty humiliations.

He took another sip of whiskey, pacing himself. The moon cast a silver light over the motel walls. These were the worst hours, between now and dawn. There was whiskey enough to see him through, if he took it slowly, but he knew that wasn't going to work this time. Without thinking he went out into the pale glow.

Jacky's voice behind her door was assertive but bitten with fear. He followed her inside, where the small television was tuned to the test pattern – a close-up of Humphrey B. Bear and two blond children smiling.

'You must be lonely too, Jacky?'

She looked at the TV and grinned. 'Nah, fell asleep during the late show, a rerun of *Division 4*. Still can't believe they axed that show.'

'Always preferred *Homicide* myself. But I never got that guy Humphrey. Fella lacks pants, for a start.'

'You want a cuppa?'

Swann held up the whiskey bottle. 'No thanks. Join me?'

She pointed with her chin to the coffee table, where her works were all laid out – needle, saucer, cotton balls. 'You trying to kill me, detective?'

'Not something my generation knows a lot about, is it?'

'Fair enough.'

Seating herself cross-legged before the table, she waved him towards the couch. 'You mind?' she asked, without looking up or hesitating.

'None of my business.'

'Couldn't handle it out there in the car, eh? Can't say I blame you. Moonlight always freaks me, for some reason. City girl, I guess.'

She tipped the powder into the saucer, followed it with a splash of water from the syringe. Swann fought to keep his mouth shut as he watched. Jacky was hardly older than Louise but she looked all worn out.

'Aren't you supposed to heat that on a spoon, make sure it dissolves?'

Her fixed stare of concentration didn't alter as she rubbed the mix with the black end of the plunger. Only when she'd finished did she answer. 'Nah, that shit's just for the movies.'

She slipped a dampened piece of cotton onto the saucer and moved it around, put the plunger back into the syringe and drew the liquid up through the cotton. Tilted it and flicked it and gave it a little spray.

Swann looked away while she worked the needle into a vein on the back of her wrist, turned to see her draw a plume of blood and send it back in.

'How many times a day you do that?'

She ignored him, chin on her chest, inhaling deeply, trying to keep some oxygen in her blood. Her eyes were closed and her head was bowed; she looked like she was praying.

Then she jerked upright. 'Depends,' she answered finally, her voice a slow drawl. 'It's medicine to me, nothin' else. Got any kind of pain, Lady Hammer's gonna take it away.'

'Lady Hammer, eh? She any relation to the Grim Reaper?'

'Nah, Swann. Not like that. What I've got right here and now, it's not pleasure, just no pain.'

With her close-cropped hair like a boy's, her rounded shoulders and muscled arms, no fat on her at all, Jacky could look harsh, but she was softened now, slumped over like a melting candle. Suddenly her eyes opened, and stayed open, brought to life by something that had cut through. She looked him right in the eye and he saw tears welling. 'Who am I kidding, though? About no pain . . .'

He couldn't hold her gaze, stared instead into his drink. 'Yeah, it never goes. Nights like this I can't sleep, can't think, can't even get drunk.'

He felt like a fool for doing it but he toasted her with his whiskey bottle. Took another long draw.

'Must be even harder for you.' Her eyes were still on him, searching for insincerity, signs of betrayal. Suspicious like a vulnerable kid.

'Hard for both of us.'

'I ran away from my father when I was even younger than your daughter. Thirteen I was. Didn't think anything of it at the time. Looking back, I can't believe I did that to him. Can't believe I felt nothing about doing it, either. Now it's too fucken late.'

Swann saw the misery there, some of the childhood pain she was trying to step on, and it caught in his throat. He tried to think of something to say to her, something a father might say. The expression on her face changed and he realised he'd been staring at her, seeing Louise.

'Don't worry,' she said. 'Your daughter won't end up like me. It wasn't my dad's fault, what happened to me at home. His fucken *brother* . . .'

Swann couldn't help himself. He knew it was bad timing after what she'd just said, but the question came out anyway. 'Did she say anything else to Ruby? When she was coming home?'

Jacky lit another cigarette, ignoring the one going in the ashtray. 'Even if I'd seen her I wouldn't have asked that shit, the whys and the wherefores. You don't ask that stuff to runaways, unless you want to hurt 'em more.'

They sat there in silence. Jacky nodded off but Swann kept drinking, waiting for the images of Louise to return, as they did every night. Every night the look on her face the last time he'd seen her, him trying to see it there in her eyes, her broken heart. But all he saw was the same kid who'd run away so many times, the anger and frustration that could only be released through escape.

There was one memory that kept coming back to him; it was one of his strongest memories of her, he didn't know why. They were living in Kalgoorlie at the time and Louise was nearly eight, a buck-toothed tomboy with brown legs and a permanently sunburned nose. He could have caught her as she was leaving; Marion had called him to let him know. 'Louise's running away again.'

Except that by the time he got home from the station, rounding the unmarked Holden into their street, he'd decided to let her go. He parked and watched her set off from their suburban home, pedalling away from its yard of red desert sand that stretched off into the wandoo and jam-wattle scrub. The truth was that Swann was curious.

Louise rode in little tumbleweed bursts. After a couple of minutes he started the car again and followed her slowly from a distance. When she reached the dirt track and her wheels began to slide in the gravel, she got off and walked down the baking hillside before ditching the bike under a saltbush. She looked along the track towards the empty blacks' camp, but thought better of it. They had all heard strange sounds coming from there at night, and the neighbourhood kids thought it was haunted. Instead she marched up past her abandoned bicycle to a vacant lot and sat beneath a casuarina tree, on a carpet of thin brown needles.

It was getting even hotter as the morning wind off the desert picked up strength. From the distance of a couple of hundred metres, Louise was a tiny figure slumped against the trunk of the casuarina, drawing pictures in the dirt. Swann watched through his service binoculars as she attempted to climb the tree, gave up, then set about throwing stones at a cannibalised station wagon. She built a little wall with bricks and a sheet of galvanised iron across them. She cut her finger on the browned steel and cried and bandaged her hand with the plastic wrap from her already eaten sandwiches. She held the empty cordial bottle above her mouth and waited for the last drops to fall. Then she packed her bag and retraced her steps along the street and down to her bicycle.

She pushed the bicycle along the track with one hand, waving flies away with the other, then tentatively rounded the corner of their street. It was so hot now that Swann was worried. He knew that the tar on the road would be soft underfoot. The pavement would be hot enough to fry an egg on. The air would be burning his daughter inside and out. She walked with her skirt tucked up into her underpants; her sandals were covered with gritty red dust.

He drove down the street after her and parked in front of their home. She threw down her bike in the front garden and her eyes were black and angry as he came towards her.

'I'm not running away today, Daddy,' she whispered hoarsely. 'It's too hot!' She hugged him quickly before pushing her way back into the cool dark house.

Marion had already run her a cold bath and set a glass of water on the tiles beside it. Louise sat in the tub and drank the water in one long draw through cracked lips, her sunburnt nose poking over the top of the glass. Swann refilled it and Louise drank it straight down again. And another. Then she started to cry, just like all the other times, before confessing the reason for her escape – some trouble with kids at her new school. She wailed for her father to make it better, to take notice.

One of the reasons Swann had subsequently taken the position as superintendent of Albany regional was so he could spend more time with Marion and his daughters. In the city, he worked a city detective's hours, long days and late nights. In Albany he could live within walking distance of the station, and the kids could go to the local school. But when Louise became a teenager she spent most of her time with friends, or reading, and not from the books on the shelf by the telephone, the Zane Greys and Alistair MacLeans and Nevil Shutes, but books she borrowed from the library. Swann was proud of her, seeing it as an expanding outwards rather than a withdrawing inwards, which was how Marion couldn't help but see it. Louise was civil and clever and dry, but she was also secretive. Her secrecy worried her mother, but Swann put it down to teenage growing pains.

Looking back on it now, there were many things about Louise's behaviour that Swann hadn't understood. Things he would have liked to have spoken with Ruby about. Perhaps he could talk about them with Jacky, when he got to know her better.

He heard the kettle boiling and saw that Jacky was gone from the floor. He shook himself awake.

'We've got to get you another place, Jacky. Somewhere more discreet.'

'Like a safe house?'

'Like a safe house. Out in the suburbs.'

'Annie DuBois offered me somewhere but I'm paid up here for one more night.'

Swann thought about that, didn't like it. 'You spoke to her after our meet?'

She brought two coffees and placed them on the table. 'Yeah, we spoke. Nobody else, though.'

'She's not going to tell anyone?'

'Nah. Only her boyfriend, maybe. But don't worry, Sol's hip.'

'You know how it works. He tells one person . . .'

'He's not like that.'

'I don't even know this bloke. Who is he?'

Jacky laughed at him. 'You don't have to worry about Sol, I told you. He's a businessman, a real suit, and he's been seeing Annie for more than a year – a bloody madam, for Chrissakes. Hardly anybody knows. That's one guy knows how to keep a secret.'

'Maybe, but Sol who?'

'Solomon Sands. Come over from Melbourne. Big hairy fella, like a bear. Dresses expensive to hide it.'

'What kind of businessman?'

'Something to do with tax. Tax agent? Something like that.'

'He ever do any work for Ruby?'

'Jesus. Once a cop, always a cop.'

'I'm still a cop.'

'There was one job. Only a small thing. Some john wrote Ruby a dud cheque, and you know what she was like with principles. The cheque had a company name on it that she didn't know – she assumed this bloke was in town for a convention and she wanted to find out where he was from. So she asked me to run it by Sol, who knows all about company stuff. I dropped it off at his place. I'll never forget it, either – joker was dressed in gold Speedos, drinking a martini poolside. Hairiest bastard I've ever seen.'

'Did he come through?'

'Right away. Ruby got the money next day. Sol said he checked out the company directors, made a few calls. That was that.'

Jacky had that look in her eyes again, trying to avoid her works on the table, sipping on her coffee.

He stood. 'You got a phone I can use before I go?'

'Do you have to leave? You're welcome to the couch.'

He shook his head. 'But if you move today or you need anything, you let me know, okay?'

She nodded, staring at her works. It didn't look like she'd be going anywhere soon.

It was barely an hour until dawn. Partridge sat on the edge of his bed inspecting his hands. He had no idea how long he'd been sitting there staring. He lay down again and closed his eyes, but there were still coronas around the edge of the darkness.

He tried to clear his mind but his headache and the events of the evening at the lodge wouldn't let him. He was out of painkillers again, had tried his breathing exercises, but the throbbing flooded into his limbs with every weak exhalation. He couldn't concentrate anyway because of his anger. It was outrageous that the premier should suggest he quit the commission. Not to mention the smug look on his face for the duration of the evening, chatting amiably through the second and third courses with the supplicants who joined them at the head table.

Partridge had waited in vain for another opportunity to speak with Premier Barth alone. He'd been forced to field polite questions amid the smoke and laughter, while Barth sat there smiling and listening and sipping his single-malt.

What had most annoyed the judge, the thing that made it impossible for him to find peace during the long night, was the premier's bald admission that the royal commission was one great lie. Barth was far too confident that Superintendent Swann would find it impossible to substantiate his claims of police corruption, as was usually the case with allegations against secretive institutions. Where such proof did not exist, of course, the benefit of doubt had to be given to the government, something Barth had doubtless been counting on when he set the terms of reference.

All evening, Partridge observed the premier sitting among his fellow Masons like a prophet come to take them to the promised land, a land already their own but not yet fully realised. In Western Australia the harsh realities of the frontier had only recently been subsumed beneath suburban lawns and macadamised byways. What had most surprised Partridge was the almost nationalistic fervour with which the men regarded their state. They seemed uninterested in the recent events in Canberra, had made little mention of the sacking of the federal government by the Queen's representative, something Partridge took as evidence of their fierce antipathy towards the eastern states. It was a sentiment that showed through under the gentility of their private-school accents, which had become broader the longer the evening continued.

There was plenty of work still to be done, the men's discussions had made apparent. There was wealth and opportunity in abundance, but it would take the stewardship and guidance of a man like Premier Barth to ensure the dream, not only for them but for their children and their children's children, to keep it safe from the meddling of the federal government and the wrongheaded Catholic contrarians of the other team.

At one point Wallace had joined their table and seated himself beside the premier, filling his whiskey glass from a crystal decanter and chatting with ease. Talk turned to the movement among civil libertarians to remove the death penalty from the statute books, as had been done in every other state in the nation. Partridge wasn't surprised to hear Wallace's opinions on the matter – the judge already knew the well-publicised opinions of the premier – but he was intrigued to learn soon after, the discussion having turned to Cyclone Tracy, that Wallace's father owned and ran a working cattle station in the Kimberley, and that Wallace had grown up riding horses and shooting crocodiles. It was a background at odds with the man's affected dress and manner, but not, Partridge supposed, with his accent, which like the others had broadened with the quantity of drink.

Perhaps he shouldn't have been surprised. He was aware that in Western Australia there still existed strong links between the city and the country. There didn't seem to be any notion of the urban parasitism so familiar to him at home, especially now that he'd moved to the country himself, where his neighbour had charmingly described the relationship of the city of Melbourne to the state of Victoria as a tick burrowing into its own backside.

His assistant Carol had in-laws who were farmers. The receptionist at his hotel had only recently moved down to Perth from a cattle station. The woman who cleaned his room was married to a miner who was away for months at a time. There was a sense of the state working as a kind of simple machinery, with clear lanes of mobility and interchangeable parts. There was a degree of opportunity and choice that had been lacking in his own upbringing.

Partridge got up and made himself a cup of tea, the whistling of the kettle bringing him around. He spooned in two sugars and opened the sliding doors to the balcony and the cool night air. In the smudgy darkness the city resembled the crayon drawing of a child. Even the great brown river that sloped past seemed to move on rollers. During the day the river was covered by a flotilla of pleasure craft that wouldn't look out of place on a suburban pond. And yet there, across the river, was the golf course where the body of Ruby Devine had been found.

It was nearly a year since Partridge had stepped down from the bench, but his retirement hadn't turned out as he'd expected. Indeed, he felt as though he'd aged more than in his last decade of work. He didn't know why this was the case. He couldn't have hoped for a better companion than Margaret, and his life was comfortable. Perhaps too comfortable. He had kept up his subscriptions to legal journals as a way of staying in touch, and had returned to the classics in order to keep his mind sharp, rereading Gibbon and Shakespeare in their entirety.

But even the literature and the time spent with his wife and the weekend visits of his children and grandchildren couldn't keep the creeping numbness at bay. Life did not owe him anything – something that had been drummed into him as a child – and yet he'd expected his retirement would bring at least contentment, at least satisfaction with what he had achieved.

From his balcony at Lorne, with its view over the ocean, he often stood as he did now, cup of tea in hand, watching the icy squalls roll across the grey waves, the cold on his skin, his eyes watering in the wind, feeling the discomfort as pure sensation.

He was reminded of something his father had told him when he was a child of six, in his first year of school. His father, then a district court judge and a staunch defender of the death penalty, said that to sentence a man to life behind bars with the possibility of parole was the cruellest kind of punishment. If released, his father claimed, most lifers died within months of walking out the jail gates.

This was presented to Partridge as a riddle, a paradox to be deciphered, not then and there but after some reflection. He was expected to enter the den where his father worked and smoked his pipe at night, and sit on the stool by the glowing hearth and explain this latest conundrum. Like all the others, it required an imaginative involvement in the fate of another, but this was one that Partridge had never been able to answer as a child.

For the sake of Margaret's feelings, he had feigned reluctance when offered the royal commission. The truth was, however, that he needed a challenge, something to focus his attention and energies. It was also his hope that an absence from home would help him regain his bearings, achieve some perspective on the years left to him.

He looked once more across the river to the golf course, then went back inside to resume his work.

Half the streetlights were out on the Great Eastern Highway. Mist drifting across from the riverine swamps painted the Holden silver. Swann tipped his beams but didn't slow down, veering into the oncoming lane as he sped past the neon signs of the cheap motels that lined the way to the airport.

He ducked his head to look through the steering wheel at the dashboard clock. The plane was due in at five but he could already hear it in the darkness overhead, groaning above 'Bohemian Rhapsody', the song on high rotation on every station.

Swann had got the news from Reggie when he called from Jacky's motel room.

'Good stuff. The Cootes are on the red-eye from Singapore. Last leg from London.' Reggie, buoyed on coffee and cigarettes, had been waiting for his call.

One of Reggie's contacts at Qantas had been checking the flight manifests for months now, in the hope that when the Cootes returned to Perth, Swann could get to them first. Timothy Coote had taken a job as a schoolteacher in rural England right after the murder of Ruby Devine, and his wife Jennifer had subsequently written a letter to the CIB regarding the case.

Suddenly there was a truck coming the other way. Swann cut back into his lane, slowed and took the airport turnoff, then accelerated down the final stretch of blacktop, lined with spindly gums and wax bush and bleached grass. The red and green runway lights were eerie in the mist.

The Boeing was screaming on the tarmac when he pulled into a loading bay by the arrivals terminal. He'd made it. He surveyed the carpark and concrete apron by the entrance: taxis, a TAA minibus. A few people smoking and waiting in a huddle across the road. No sign of police, no unmarkeds.

Perhaps he was in luck, and Casey didn't know about the Cootes. Either that or he was getting lazy.

Swann ran a hand through his hair and wiped his face. A secretary on the front desk at Central had mentioned Jennifer Coote's letter to Terry before it could be sent on to the CIB. Mrs Coote had written from England that the family were on their way to the Perth airport at two a.m. when they noticed a '60s Dodge and a police wagon parked on a fairway of the South Perth golf club. They hadn't thought anything of it at the time, assuming the Dodge had been stolen, but friends had since written to them about Swann's allegations and the royal commission, giving the details of Ruby's death.

In her letter Jennifer described everything she'd seen, 'hoping to assist'. She wasn't to know that two a.m. was a full five hours before the first officially documented police presence on the scene. Here was proof that uniformed had found Ruby Devine by accident and been warned off, and it had to have been by someone in the CIB.

Inside the terminal Swann stationed himself beside a Coke machine with a view of the arrivals hall. He drank a ginger beer and smoked a cigarette, tapping ash into a potted palm. Passengers began to clear customs and emerge through smoked-glass doors, juggling laden trolleys, weary children and duty-free. The kids snivelled and dragged at their parents' legs, dazed and confused.

All Swann knew about Timothy Coote, apart from his being a schoolteacher, was that he'd rucked for Swan Districts in the late '60s and had worn glasses in his Bassendean High School photographs. Swann wasn't confident he'd recognise him when he saw him. Every now and then a squeal of joy went up as someone broke from the crowd to embrace a family member, but mostly the new arrivals were silent and exhausted.

But Timothy Coote, when he appeared, was immediately recognisable. He looked exactly like an ex-ruckman who was now a family man and English-county schoolteacher; he was tall and bald and thick-waisted, limping as he carried a sleeping child under one arm.

Jennifer Coote was towing another child, who dragged a cuddly lion by its tail across the floor. Swann chose Jennifer, rather than her husband. Not only was she the one who'd written the letter, she looked more rested, sharper, more in control.

He took a last look around the hall before stepping forward and opening his badge. 'Jennifer Coote? Wonder if I could have a word?'

'What? No, sorry.'

Snappy. Scared. A mother's voice. Swann smiled to reassure her and pressed on. 'Homicide. It's about the letter you wrote concerning Ruby Devine.'

No trace of relief in her eyes, or even recognition. She turned to her husband, who was right there at her shoulder, staring down at Swann's badge. Timothy Coote's eyes were small and bloodshot, his glasses smudged where his daughter had groped them off his face.

'Just a few minutes,' Swann insisted. 'It's urgent.'

Jennifer Coote looked wistfully at the taxi stand and the growing queue. Her assured attitude had been a façade; she was just as exhausted as her husband. The older child began to whimper and kick at her ankle.

Swann let their frustration build before offering them a ride. He would drop them off at their door, he said. They could talk in the car on the way. He was parked right by the entrance.

Timothy Coote puffed out his cheeks and exhaled. His wife closed her eyes and took a deep breath.

They lived in Bayswater, fifteen minutes away if he took the shortest route to Bassendean and the nearest bridge across the river. A purple light was breaking over the ranges and plains. Swann left the radio off so as not to disturb the children, who lay with their heads in their father's lap in the back seat. Jennifer Coote had shunted the passenger seat forward to accommodate the reach of her husband's legs, and with both kids asleep she began to revive.

Unlike her husband, she was clearly excited to be home. The largesse she had brought with her took up the entire boot – Swann had to fix their suitcases onto the roof rack. Neither of the Cootes seemed to find it strange that Swann was driving a family wagon while on duty. Perhaps they were too tired for it to register. Jennifer was a middle-class girl from Swanbourne, he discovered, and private-school educated by the sound of it, but she didn't so much as blink when Swann's bottle of whiskey rolled onto the floor-pan at her feet.

He was going to have to work backwards. Neither of the Cootes knew that the royal commission had already begun. Jennifer appeared surprised that her evidence might be crucial. She didn't seem worried by Swann's suggestion that she present a statement to the commissioner, but her husband was more circumspect.

'Of course we don't mind helping, but we *are* on holiday. We only have two weeks.'

What he really meant, Swann could tell, was that pointing the finger at the police didn't sound real smart. He was trying to make eye contact in the rear-vision mirror. Swann looked at him evenly. He wasn't about to lie.

'That's exactly why your written evidence is so important. It's new evidence. You make a statement to me, sign on the dotted line, then go back overseas, no harm done.'

But Jennifer had sniffed her husband's fear. 'Others must have seen the same thing as us,' she said. 'There was plenty of traffic for that time of night. Cars parked on the fairway, one of them police, right next to the highway – you couldn't miss it. Why is what we saw so important?'

'Because those other witnesses changed their minds soon after being interviewed. Funny that, if it was as clear as you said.'

'It was as clear as day. But . . .' She fell into silence while she worked it through, watching the wreaths of mist lift above the narrowing river and burn away in the sharpening light.

Swann was searching for a hook. He was suspended from duty, he couldn't offer them protection. Or a reward. He couldn't play on their egos, the need for notoriety – they were too level-headed. Nor could he plead social responsibility – they were parents. Eventually Timothy Coote sat forward, leaning over his sleeping children, a hand on each head. 'What did you say your name was again? Superintendent Swann? Aren't you the guy . . . ?'

Swann met his eyes in the mirror again and held them for a long moment before turning back to the road. 'I'm due in court in about three hours. Look, I understand your position. But you can say your piece and leave, go back to England. It may not make any difference to the commission, but then again yours could be the first story that puts the official one in doubt. After you, others might agree to follow.'

'But we already wrote a letter. Can't that be tended as evidence?'

'That letter no longer exists. Like lots of other evidence in this case. If you could give a formal statement . . .'

The excitement had gone out of Jennifer Coote. She seemed to have shrunk and had shifted away from him. They crossed the bridge over the river, tyres drumming on the jarrah beams, ducks squawking in the wattle scrub, magpies calling across the park, but Jennifer didn't look down, didn't look at the awakening suburbs, curtains parting, inviting the sun. She stared instead at her hands.

'Just tell me off the record then,' he said. 'Everything you saw.'

His own exhaustion sounded in his voice now, and Jennifer responded to that, watching his profile as he drove.

'Like I said in my letter,' she began, 'we were running late for our plane. We're not stickybeaks or anything, but as soon as I saw the Dodge and the police car, well, I had a second look.'

'It was a white police panel van,' Timothy corrected. 'An HQ panel van. Turned side on.'

'That's good,' said Swann. 'What next?'

Jennifer adjusted her position on the seat. 'Well, let's see, the policeman we saw was tall, really tall, like Tim.'

Uniform, Swann was thinking. Then again, every CIB detective had a uniform in his cupboard.

'And?' he prompted.

'And he was leaning on the roof of the panel van. And then we'd gone past. Both of us mentioned it. You don't see that many Dodges. Thought it must have been stolen.'

Swann nodded his thanks. 'I'll tell you something,' he said. 'That police panel van you saw, there's no record of it. The official report has the first police on the scene at dawn. And you're right – there were other witnesses who saw the same thing as you, but they've all been convinced they were mistaken. I checked the incident reports for that night myself, and they show nothing at all coming in between midnight and dawn, which in my experience is unprecedented.'

'Did you check the roster for that night?' Timothy asked. 'What my wife said is quite correct. The policeman we saw was unusually tall.'

'Nobody tall was rostered on that night. I followed that up as well.' Swann felt the anger rise in his voice. He'd failed to rouse them. They were good people, but he could see from their body language that they wouldn't be coming through for him. He'd seen that look too often. Resentment and fear in equal measure. Shame in there as well. The idea you'd had of yourself being quickly reassessed: you weren't who you thought you were.

'We're sorry about Ruby Devine,' Timothy Coote said by way of apology, sitting back again. 'We'll speak to some friends. Have a think. Get back to you either way.'

'Sure,' said Swann. 'You do that. Here's my number.'

He handed Reggie's details to Jennifer. He turned into the Cootes' street, tracking the houses. Californian bungalows with peppermint trees and yard swings. Workers' cottages with rose gardens and mint lawns. An assortment of weatherboard and fibro and brick-veneer. Galvanised-iron and red-tile roofing. A man was tying his bootlaces on his front porch, a thermos and a cut lunch in a paper bag beside him. An old woman watered her garden while her husband washed the car, a cigarette dangling on his lips. Not unlike Swann's own neighbourhood, and it hurt to look.

The Cootes' home was salmon brick and blue tile, a Canary Island date palm on the dewy lawn. The louvres were open, airing the bedrooms, the front door was ajar.

'Nanna!'

The youngest child, suddenly wide awake, squirmed to get

across her father, yanking on the window handle. Nanna was on the porch now, squinting into the sunshine, then breaking into a smile. Timothy Coote got out of the car and walked up the drive carrying boxes, hiding his limp, grinning at his mother, shooing the kids inside. Jennifer had gone down the side gate, calling out for a pet.

None of them looked across the road to the white unmarked parked under a bottlebrush. Engine still ticking. Fresh oil on the dusty macadam beneath.

Swann climbed out and began to unstrap the suitcases. He couldn't see the driver behind the tinted windows but it didn't matter. He dumped the cases in the driveway and got back into the station wagon. It was a pity about the Cootes, but he'd done them one favour at least – Casey's thug wouldn't need to enter their family home now. Most likely he'd just wait there for them to notice him. When they came out for the paper. To check the mail. Walk the dog. They'd see him there smoking and staring, smiling at the kids even, but his eyes not smiling at all.

On the third morning of the commission, QC Wallace stood before Superintendent Swann with his typed page of notes shaking in his hand. It hadn't occurred to Partridge that the lawyer might have a drinking problem on top of everything else, but he certainly looked the worse for wear after his night at the lodge. To his credit Wallace had shown more restraint in his dealings with Swann this morning, and so far Partridge hadn't found it necessary to speak over him.

The QC strolled to and fro before Partridge's bench while he waited for Swann to formulate his response.

'Yes, you might say I was instrumental in setting up the policy. Although policy is too strong a word. Nothing was ever written down. But that's the kind of flexibility a mining town like Kalgoorlie demands. Like it or not, since the first discovery of gold, prostitutes have been part of the local community.'

Swann paused and wiped his hands across his lips, a gesture that Partridge had come to recognise as a precursor to a risky statement, an intellectual gamble. Learning to read the mannerisms of his witnesses was always as important to Partridge as listening to what they had to say, especially when they were under pressure.

'From my years in Kalgoorlie,' Swann continued, 'I learnt that many ordinary women work in this industry. Having made some money or met a suitable companion, they go on to other things. Very few stay for long in the work, with the exception of those who become proprietors of establishments themselves, Ruby Devine being a case in point.'

Wallace ceased his restless patrol and faced Swann directly. 'We will come to Mrs Devine later, Superintendent Swann. Could you please outline for us the situation in Kalgoorlie vis-a-vis prostitution on your arrival there, and the manner in which you were able to alter the policing during the term of your employment?'

'Certainly, for his Honour's benefit. Everyone else in this room would be aware of the kind of town Kalgoorlie was, and is —'

'Thank you, Superintendent Swann.' Wallace smiled and plumped out his chest, trying his hardest to be polite. 'Now, if you could answer the question.'

'The situation as I found it had existed for close to a century. As I said, Kalgoorlie has always been famous for its prostitutes, many of whom came to the goldfields from France, later from China. Prostitution therefore has been long tolerated, while remaining a crime. Officially, of course, it was the job of the police to charge and arrest those who broke the law. An unnecessarily large amount of time was spent rousting prostitutes from public houses and motels, and arresting those who were foolhardy enough to solicit on the streets. The penalties were such that it was only a matter of time before these women were at it again, and so the cycle continued. As a newly appointed detective —'

'You took it upon yourself to ignore the law?'

'Not as such, and I didn't act by myself.'

'You mean you consulted with your superiors, with the town council, with the local member of parliament? With the metropolitan legislature?'

'Even if I had, Mr Wallace, I have already stated that nothing was written down, and so nothing I say here can be proven or otherwise. What I mean is that I worked with my partner, Donald Casey, then also a detective constable.'

'It all sounds like an ambitious challenge for a young detective constable,' Wallace continued. 'You were in your twenties at the time?'

'Yes. And I *was* ambitious. In the sense that I wanted to improve the situation. I thought we could make a difference.'

There it was again, Partridge thought, that tone in Swann's voice that set him apart from the others. For a reputedly unstable man, he remained optimistic in his body language, continuing to engage with the hostile forces around him, but it was more than that. For all his well-groomed confidence and capability, Superintendent Swann's courtroom manner displayed none of the performative flair of the others, and suggested nothing of crusading madness.

Swann was looking up at Wallace now, waiting for the next question. He was red-eyed and sat with his palms down on his knees, his shoulders rounded, his expression patient and sceptical, precisely as it should be. Partridge had lived the examined life, but that didn't make him interesting to himself. Swann, on the other hand . . .

'Did it occur to you, Superintendent, that by attempting to control an illegal industry you might be placing yourself in a position of temptation? That as a young detective you might be vulnerable to manipulation by outside influences?'

Swann didn't take the bait. 'The way I saw it, Mr Wallace, I was merely returning the situation to an earlier state of toleration. And I can assure you there was no danger of *outside* manipulation.'

The words he didn't say were conspicuous. Minister for Police Desmond Sullivan was in court today, himself an ex-policeman. A hulking, many-chinned man with heavy shoulders, he sat with the other notable guests of the commission in the seats usually taken by the jury. He wore a navy-blue suit and tie, as though he were still in uniform, and with his pale neck and plump face, he resembled a great white grub.

Partridge knew something of Sullivan by way of a good friend in Melbourne, an engineer who not long ago had decided to expand his company's operations to the north-west. But the price to set up a business in Western Australia was twenty thousand dollars in cash, payable to the Minister for Police himself, otherwise there was no possibility of a permit. Partridge's friend had been informed of this by Sullivan himself, at a cocktail party in a revolving restaurant overlooking Perth. The engineer had laughed at first, but Sullivan wasn't joking.

The operation never went ahead. The engineer flew home the next day, well aware that he would be paying continual bribes to a host of different players at every stage of the project. He had told Partridge the story in humorous terms, because with the boom on he regretted not paying the twenty thousand, and the rest. Some of his competitors had adapted to the situation, as they liked to put it, and were thriving in the new can-do environment of the Liberal government.

Sullivan leant across to whisper something in the ear of his secretary, seated beside him, and as he did he caught Partridge's eye. He returned the judge's stare with an accent of interest.

'Please describe for us, Superintendent Swann,' Wallace was saying, 'the manner in which you and Donald Casey were able to "control" prostitution in the Kalgoorlie area, as you put it, and the subsequent effect this had on the way in which matters were managed in our capital city.'

'We instigated small changes which we felt were in the best interests not only of the prostitutes, but also the wider community. These consisted of placing limits on the physical area used for prostitution and on the number of establishments, and the women who ran them were known to us. In this way the involvement of opportunistic men was averted. It was the women's responsibility to ensure regular check-ups for their girls with a certain doctor, also known to us, and to make sure that no one with drug or alcohol problems worked in their establishments. And no under-age runaways. These arrangements proved successful, and lasted for the duration of my posting in Kalgoorlie. Upon my transfer to the metropolitan area I encouraged the practice here.'

'Thank you, Superintendent,' said Wallace. 'And how would you characterise your relationships with the . . . madams during this time?'

'It was in everyone's best interests to comply with our terms.'

'Meaning?'

'Meaning our relationships, if you want to call them that, could be characterised if not always by mutual respect, then at least mutual understanding.'

'But not friendship?'

Swann accepted the direction Wallace was taking him in with a single nod. 'Yes, in some cases.'

'Would you describe your relationship with Ruby Devine as friendship? Were you ever a guest at her place of residence, for example?'

'Yes, I would – and yes, I was.'

'Given your *friendship* with Ruby Devine, would it be fair to say that she received at your hands what might be called preferential treatment?'

'No, that was not the case. She was treated just like the others.'

'And did this friendship involve the soliciting of monetary or sexual favours, Superintendent?'

Partridge found himself leaning forwards on his bench, much like the crowd in the gallery.

'No, it was not *my* practice to solicit monetary or sexual favours from Ruby Devine, or from anyone else.'

'Meaning that, as you have claimed, it was the practice of other detectives to solicit such favours?'

Swann nodded. 'As you know, I am already on the record as saying that there has never been a time in the history of this state when prostitution and some of the policemen who controlled it haven't come to a financial understanding. I can only assume this is still the case today.'

Well put, thought Partridge.

'But do you offer us any proof of this nefariousness, Superintendent Swann? Given the alleged extent and duration of this illegal activity.'

Swann couldn't stop a smile at the ridiculousness of the question. 'Mr Wallace, the detectives of the Criminal Investigation Bureau are well versed in the art of evidence, in what constitutes it and how to avoid it. However, there is one aspect of this matter that cannot be explained away. I have here . . .' And he raised a sheath of documents in the air.

The room buzzed with anticipation. At last, something tangible. Wallace looked pale. Partridge glanced across to the Minister for Police, whose eyes flashed. The QC stepped forward and took the papers, rifled quickly through them.

'Superintendent Swann, this is a royal commission. All evidence must be tended prior to the commission's commencement, to establish whether or not the evidence falls within the terms of reference. I'm afraid, in this case . . .'

Wallace walked the papers over to Partridge, passed them up to the bench, a satisfied smile on his face. Swann was shaking his head. Partridge flicked over the first page; the noise from the gallery was rising fast.

'Silence in the court!' he bellowed, and when it had become quiet resumed his examination. Land titles, dozens of them, in the names of a Juliet Casey, a Rosemary Webb, a Deborah Sherving. He returned the top sheet and leant towards the microphone. 'Mr Wallace, you are quite correct that all documentary evidence needs to be examined prior to the commencement of the royal commission. However, in this case I will allow it. You asked Superintendent Swann whether or not he had evidence to support his assertions. Given your specific request, his tendering of the evidence is appropriate. Superintendent Swann, you may resume your statement.'

QC Wallace's face dropped as he recognised his blunder. He blurted, 'No further questions, your Honour,' and made for his seat, face averted.

Partridge stopped him in his tracks. 'No further questions, perhaps, Mr Wallace. But Superintendent Swann has not finished answering your current question. And I, for one, would like to hear his answer.'

Wallace returned reluctantly to his place by the witness. He nodded his head for the clearly surprised Swann to continue.

'As I was saying, I'm sure you might imagine a situation whereby a harm-minimisation system of the kind I just described could end up serving the interests of those who administer it.'

Wallace had recovered his composure enough to inject a steely tone into his voice. 'You're talking about graft. That is a very *serious* allegation. I would take this opportunity to remind you that just because you are a witness in a royal commission doesn't mean you are immune from the laws that govern defamation.'

Swann ignored the threat. 'I'm talking about tithing, as we call it, a sort of levy. Specifically with regard to Ruby Devine and the financial arrangements that existed between her and some of the detectives now investigating her death. I resigned my position in the

CIB, transferred to a lesser position in the uniformed branch and took a posting to the country. I will leave people to draw their own conclusions about my motivations for doing that. What I've just given you are the accumulated assets of just three CIB officers, who between them own sixty-five properties in the metropolitan area. In their wives' names, I might add, who are all unemployed as far as I can tell.

'Now, before you tell me that it's not within the terms of reference of this commission to pursue this matter, for reasons that many people find mysterious, let me just say that there's plenty more to know – about investment companies, trust funds, rural properties, mining leases owned by officers inferior in rank to my own, as well as by those higher up the chain. Much higher. What I've given you is just the beginning.'

Swann turned very deliberately to stare at Sullivan. A silence had descended on the courtroom and the stunned Wallace let it sit there, until it was broken by Swann.

'A brothel owner is viciously murdered in a public place, CIB detectives on minimal salaries own riches beyond the dreams of any ordinary man, and yet this royal commission is unwilling to draw the obvious conclusions. Instead —'

Uproar from the gallery now, which Partridge felt hit the cork wall behind him. He beat his gavel and called for order.

Police Minister Sullivan sat staring impassively.

The briny smell of the river was carried by the sea breeze right into the heart of the city. Partridge paused at an intersection to retrieve the scrawled address from his shirt pocket: 37 William Street. The dramatic day in court had rejuvenated him, prompting him to take Carol's advice and walk to the GP's, rather than make use of the driver and car allocated to him.

There were no street signs, but above his head a building name was legible enough to make out the Chung Wah Association Hall, 25 Francis Street. The lights changed and the traffic broke past him, raising a faint veil of dust that he could taste but not see. He tugged down the edge of his fedora and raised a hand to protect his eyes from the glare shearing off the rooftops across the street.

He became aware of somebody next to him, and turned to find an elderly man and a dog waiting for the lights. The man appeared to be a darker version of himself, similarly taut and compact, his white terrier barely the size of a loaf of bread. Partridge held up the scribbled address and the man squinted at it, then broke into a smile and jerked his thumb back over his shoulder in the direction he had come.

Carol had assured him he couldn't possibly get lost in Little Italy, repeating this twice in the expectation that he probably would. The GP was her husband's cousin, and while his surgery was on William Street, a seedy part of town after dark, during the day it was perfectly safe. Partridge had been prescribed Dispirin by his own GP in Melbourne, as a way of keeping the fever down and easing his headaches, but the pills were no longer effective. His doctor had told him that his blood pressure was high, possibly as a result of the influenza, and that he should consider having it checked in Perth if the symptoms did not improve.

Partridge nodded his thanks to the old man, who stepped off the kerb with the cambered walk familiar to those with bad hips. The sight of him limping in pain reinforced Partridge's second reason for walking to the doctor's. Ever since his retirement he had taken long daily walks with Margaret, regardless of the weather, and he suspected that his recent lack of exercise was contributing to his sleeplessness. He turned and began to walk back down into the valley of stalled traffic and Italian restaurants and nightclubs and travel agents, green, white and red flags fluttering in the breeze.

Number 37 was an avocado-green, double-storey weatherboard with a corrugated-dirt lane running down one side. Fronting the lane was a placard declaring 'Private yard no Parking', which had been crudely crossed out and replaced with 'Casual Parking 20 cents per Day'.

On the other side of the lane was the Zanzibar Nightclub, a concrete affair painted in black-and-white zebra stripes, the footpath by the front door littered with cigarette butts and broken glass. This was the fifth or sixth nightclub Partridge had passed in as many minutes, all of them behind darkened windows and garishly named in neon signs – the Glamarama, the Klondike, the Glass Slipper, the Love Seat – and all of them smelling of yeasty carpet, even from the street. Between the nightclubs and the adult bookshops and the Italian restaurants and greasy spoons were massage parlours, whose purpose was betrayed by the naked red globes lighting the doorsteps and by the hard-faced men in miner's dungarees smoking as they waited outside.

It occurred to Partridge that he didn't feel in the least bit self-conscious, which wouldn't be the case were he to find himself in such a location in Melbourne. He wondered whether this was a feature of being out and about in the cooling amber dusk, but on looking around at the men of varying ages drifting along the street, their eyes trawling, unafraid and cheerful, he realised that his cocktail-hour mood was more likely the result of his anonymity, his distance from the awkwardness that would define his presence in a red-light district on his home turf.

He paused at the foot of the gloomy wooden stairs of number 37, with their threadbare carpet, loose nails and ancient musty reek, and he smiled, pleased at having embarked on this curious adventure. He took his wrist and felt for his pulse – it was insistent, invigorated by the walk.

The stairs creaked under his step, the noise startling in the narrow space within the floral-wallpapered stairwell. But more surprising was the weightlessness he felt as he continued to climb, as if something heavy had seeped out of him while walking, like a trail of sand from his pockets, the lightness bearing him up the stairs a clear dizziness now, a rising above himself and a floating there, trying not to topple back. And then the sudden pain, burning in his chest, as he clambered up the final steps towards the door.

Swann waded until the backwash carried him under towards the reef. He held his breath and kept his eyes closed. The current quickened as the channel deepened but he didn't lunge for the surface. He let himself be dragged across the bottom, sand scraping on his belly.

It was only when red lights appeared out of the darkness and the current finally let him go that he opened his eyes. He sat on his haunches, feet ready to spring, until he couldn't take the thudding in his head any longer and drove himself up to the surface.

The light was soft and clear over the ocean, the land alive under its tender glow. A gull sitting nearby regarded him suspiciously. The distant sound of traffic was a measure of how far he had been carried from the shore. Before him the sun was sinking into the waterline, and an orange blush spilled across the sea. Now came the best part – the stabbing light of the day having gone, the water and sky and reef, and the succulents on the dunes behind were all startling and new, like after a rain.

He rolled onto his stomach and crawled across the water, peering down at the weedy ocean bed. He felt refreshed but not clean. A residual anxiety he had hoped to purge with breathlessness remained deep in his lungs.

He had won his morning in court, no doubt about it, but releasing the land titles of Casey, Webb and Sherving was going to cost him. The countless hours he'd spent in court observing lawyers had taught him well, and he'd been ready for Wallace. He knew the QC would assume he didn't have any evidence – had wanted him to assume just that, which was why Swann hadn't given the titles to the media. And Wallace had walked right into it.

But the repercussions were going to be harsh. Swann had broken the code all over again – he had named names.

His satisfaction had indeed proved to be short-lived. The morning in court might have gone his way but the afternoon seemed an eternity of disgrace. The trick cyclist Wiener was called to document Swann's alleged breakdown. Swann hadn't seen the shrink for months, by choice rather than mutual agreement, and this appeared to have angered the man. Professor Wiener, Head of Psychiatry at the University of Western Australia, reminded Swann of the old man in *Twelve Angry Men*, but he was nowhere near as polite. He was a Jewish refugee from Budapest, a ferocious lover of his new country but for the matter of his children, one of whom was in jail for fraud and the other dead by her own hand.

In their three sessions, Wiener had probed Swann with questions he tried not to resent. He was on extended special leave and eager to get back to work. The one obstacle in his way was Wiener and his questions.

Now Swann regretted telling him anything at all. Wiener had sat in court with his hands on his walking stick, speaking directly to the gallery. Some witnesses were like that. The majority looked to the judge when they talked, others stared up at the ceiling, but Wiener made sure the gallery didn't miss a word, the journalists in particular. He repeated himself on occasions, like a patient lecturer, making sure they got it all down. His mild accent gave his words added authority, as though Freud himself were in the room.

The psychiatrist's discretion extended only as far as the rules of his employment. He did not relate Swann's actual stories, as told in his consultations, but described Swann's 'illness'. He spoke in strong terms and lurid tones, as if he were an inspector gazing over the rotten wares of a fishmonger, pointing out the grey flesh, the rouged gills, the oily scales.

His discussion of Swann's symptoms had led to a diagnosis: a clear case of clinical depression with evidence of paranoid episodes. It was the paranoia that was troubling to Wiener, because depression wasn't unusual in men of Swann's age and occupation. Wiener testified that the human nervous system inevitably deteriorated with years of strain and hard drinking: he presented this opinion with an air of tolerance and objectivity. But paranoia, stated Wiener, amounted to nothing less than a plot against oneself, a self-destructive projection of one's guilt onto those that most resembled oneself, a projection of all the worst characteristics found in oneself which one was too cowardly to acknowledge.

Having said as much, Wiener made eye contact with Swann for the first time that afternoon, just before delivering the final nail in Swann's credibility. Such persons, claimed the doctor, not only made unreliable witnesses, they could also be highly dangerous. As the psyche continued its struggle to reveal the truth to itself, it sought also to destroy itself in order to bring the conflict to an end.

Without raising his eyes, Swann sensed that the swell had increased as he neared the beach. Any moment now a wave would break over him. If he was in the wrong place it would spear him down into the sand and hold him under until it passed; if he was in the right place he would ride it until his weight dissolved and he found himself delivered gently onto the shore.

Brushing the sand from his legs he felt strangely earthbound. The exercise had done him good. But when he'd towelled off he glanced up to see Marion further down the beach. She was looking for him among the sunbathers on the slope facing the departed sun, where he usually was. The only person who knew Swann was at the beach right now was Reggie, and Marion wasn't dressed to swim. When she spotted him she didn't wave, and he felt something lurch in his chest.

On reaching each other she removed her sunglasses and he saw the tears on her face, her red eyes. Her mouth an open maw. He couldn't bring himself to ask, because he already knew.

'They've found someone,' she got out finally.

'Oh.' It was all he could manage. 'Not . . .' He couldn't say his daughter's name, even though they'd both rehearsed this moment a thousand times, waiting for the call they knew would come.

'Come with me,' was all she said, and set off in the direction of the clubhouse.

There was no question of his following in the Holden. He went instead to her Datsun and stood waiting by the passenger door while she got in. He couldn't rid his head of the image of Louise laid out dead. Or worse, those moments before her death, waiting for him to find her, her eyes pleading.

'Light me a cigarette,' she said as the engine fired.

He lit one for himself as well and didn't ask where they were headed. Didn't want to hear the name spoken.

There was violence in the way Marion worked the gears, even

though she wasn't driving quickly. She waited patiently at stop signs and lights and allowed traffic to cut in before her. She wasn't normally such a courteous driver.

'I've left the girls alone,' she said. Then broke. 'I don't want to see this.' Her tears started again, spreading across the stains left by the earlier ones, dropping down onto her shirt.

Swann could put a name to every corpse he'd ever seen. He had never become jaded about murder, like some of his colleagues. He had been to victims' funerals and held the hands of their loved ones and had thought he understood.

He'd understood nothing. The pain that he felt now – there were no words for it.

She pulled into the forecourt of the Park Lane Motel.

'Oh no,' he whispered. He'd assumed they were driving to the Gnangara pine plantation, where the bodies of the murdered were routinely dumped. He had been called there countless times, through the eerie spaciousness between the rows of trees, symbols of a violent order that drew murderers to it.

But the Park Lane Motel was right in the heart of the city, not far from Swann's own hotel. It was also the last place Louise had been seen alive.

There was a terrible familiarity about the way they climbed the stairs, moving soundlessly towards the room that Louise had stayed in, and had disappeared from, leaving nothing behind but an unpaid bill and her name in the ledger.

Swann knew they were headed for her room. And he knew his wife knew it. The hotel manager who greeted them knew it. And perhaps her murderer was even now watching as Swann approached the semicircle of uniformed police and detectives and forensic staff gathered around the door.

They didn't see him until he was right behind them, then they turned as one, taking in his swimming trunks and thongs, and Swann saw in their faces that the dead girl in room 83 wasn't his daughter.

They let him through and Marion followed. The window was open to the traffic below and all the lights in the room were on. The girl was in a kneeling position on the bed, propped against the window, the sea breeze blowing her hair. As he stepped forward a gust slammed the door shut behind them.

Her face and breasts were pressed down onto the sheets. Her arms were stretched out in front of her, palms up. She looked to be in prayer, except that she was naked. A needle remained in her left arm, beneath a cord tied round her lower bicep. Her hand was purple with trapped blood.

Michelle.

He took Marion by the arm and led her out, downstairs into the wind and dusk.

He opened the afternoon paper and reread the unremarkable article on page thirteen relating that morning's events at the royal commission, through which he had sat for a few hours. The single column was wedged between a piece on a new land release at a place called Koondoola and a larger article about another arrival of boatpeople from Vietnam.

On the opposite page, right above an item about the premier's proposed tour of the north-west, was a large advert for a local car yard featuring expensive imports, American models mostly. It carried a photo of the owner, one friendly, honest, smiling Leo Ajello. His moustached face was plastered above every new-model Corvette and Cadillac and Mustang crowded into the ad. It made the shooter laugh out loud. Marko had told him Ajello was Perth's biggest green-lit drug dealer.

He took a sip of wine to check himself. It was a burgundy, very young, tasting of plum and berries and tannin. Here he was, in one of Perth's finest restaurants, and he was surprised to find that the wine wasn't at all bad. Things seemed to have changed since he'd gone east.

The menu, however, was no surprise. For entrée a choice of avocado prawns, lemon salmon crêpes or crab quiche, and for mains Hawaiian chicken, langouste mornay, steak diane, beef wellington, steak veronique, crown roast of pork.

As a vegetarian who ate seafood, he was limited. He didn't rate crayfish, even when it was called langouste, and not only because his grandfather had used it for garden fertiliser, acquired for nothing and buried whole beneath his citrus trees. He decided on two entrées, the avocado prawns and the crêpes, and hoped the salmon was fresh. Experience had taught him that if it wasn't, the belly fat tasted rancid. There was no salmon fishery within four thousand kilometres of Perth that he was aware of, and that it was even on the menu seemed odd. But it was a favourite of his and he ordered it anyway.

He spoke to a young waiter whose hair reeked of the medicinal scent of pine needles – Norsca shampoo – and whose armpits gave off an aroma of damp Johnson's baby powder. The restaurant had begun to fill up. Mostly older couples in evening wear, no doubt headed after dinner to the philharmonic concert a ferry ride across the river. A large group of men took their seats at a reserved table nearby. It had a good view of the city lights shining over the water, although none of them seemed interested in the view.

There'd been a few Ajellos living in the foothills when he was growing up there, tough Sicilian kids who'd outgrown their peasant parents by the time they reached their teens. He watched the old couple at the table across from him and wondered what they would make of Leo Ajello and his secret life. They were both eating the crown roast of pork, and he wondered too if they'd ever seen the slaughter of a pig, the cutting of its throat, the bleeding out onto the dirt.

Growing up with Italians meant that he'd seen this often as a kid.

He had even learnt to pity the animal as it was fattened in the yard before being led up to the shed. The couple eating their pork had the same dim look as those pigs. You held an animal down and slit its throat, and you held a human down and slit its throat, and there was no difference at all. Neither wanted to die.

His avocado prawns arrived. He tasted one with his eyes closed. Room-temperature, firm texture, a good citrus dressing with strong flavours. It occurred to him that he killed with his eyes open.

The large table of men had warmed up over a few drinks and were now laughing like boys at a birthday party. Their waiter was passing out plates of steak tartare, the raw egg wobbling on top of the raw mince. It wasn't on the menu but that was the whole point. A champagne cork popped, and another.

He wasn't like these men, who had come together to celebrate but who were all rivals. He wasn't like them and yet he was in the life. He considered the lairy suits they wore, the fashionably longish hair. The alcoholic flush on their faces was accompanied on some by cocaine grins. They sweated, despite the air conditioning. One of them looked to be politician material, or maybe a journalist. Like the others, he had a strong voice and a charming smile. Like the others, his smile slipped when he thought no one was looking. What was left on the man's face when he stopped smiling wasn't pretty.

In the shooter's line of work there weren't more than one or two jobs a year, and he had plenty of time on his hands. He read psychology texts and sat in on lectures at the university. He'd always assumed he was different because his father had been a detective, because he himself had been a policeman, but there were other differences too. Ever since he was a child he'd wanted to understand what he was capable of. What his limits were. What he couldn't, or wouldn't, do. He wanted to see behind the stage. Behind the masks.

Who held the real power? He wanted to know these things because without knowing them he was just another mug. Another pig in the paddock.

One of the men was talking loudly now about hiring a private jet. He was shouted down by another who claimed he was in the process of buying one second-hand from President Suharto. Their flash suits and the silver service didn't hide the fact that there was something numb and stupid in their eyes. They were no smarter than the average criminal, just better actors.

It was his father who'd lamented there were no real criminals left. He lamented it because he believed that real criminals made for real cops. Whatever these men were celebrating, it wasn't to be discussed. They would all be in legitimate business as well, but it was black money they were flashing about. Drug money, no doubt. The drug trade was a business. It took managers to run it, not everyday criminals. His father had seen this coming but he still wouldn't believe it if he were alive today. He belonged to a generation in which working-class men didn't get to be this rich this easy.

His crêpes arrived. He lifted the edge of one and, as he feared, the flaked salmon smelt fatty and rancid. He pushed the plate aside.

The waiter attending the large table returned with a trolley. Laid out on a silver platter was a whole suckling pig. Instead of a carving knife, the waiter took up a dessert plate. So tender was the flesh that he pared it away from the spine with the plate, before placing it with a spoon on a silver serving dish. The men toasted themselves and drank and ate and laughed. The remaining pig sat there on the trolley, and the man closest to it wrenched off its head and held it up next to his face. He stood up and addressed the table with it, as if with a ventriloquist's dummy.

'Oink oink. I'm watching you, Moncrieff. I'm watching you, Bartlett. I'm watching you, Dodd.'

The men hooted and jeered. One laughed so hard he had to spit out his food.

'I'm watching you, Dyson. Watching you, Strachan. I'm watching you . . .'

Partridge adjusted his position on the bed, curled into the crisp white sheet. On the bedside table was the bottle of nitroglycerine tablets prescribed for him by the GP, to be taken every two hours or at the first sign of pain. Next to them was the luminous face of an alarm clock turned towards him, although he didn't remember setting it there. The clock told him it was a mere three hours since he'd entered the doctor's surgery complaining of chest pain.

Lying on the trolley bed in the doctor's rooms, he had been short of breath, the pain spreading to his jaw. The doctor squirted something bitter onto Partridge's tongue, then held an oxygen mask over his mouth and nostrils and took his pulse with a stethoscope, giving gentle commands to his receptionist to bring a blanket, increase the oxygen, adjust the pillows.

All the while, Partridge stared up at the doctor's eyes, listened to his calm voice, tried not to be afraid, although the pain made him wince. Then he saw Margaret and the house they had built in Lorne. He saw her face in the doorway, the dog scampering at her feet, the sound of the grandchildren behind her, the smells of the kitchen, and then the word *ambulance* had pulled him out of his reverie, the pain abating now.

They had fed him oxygen through the mask until the nitroglycerine spray dilated the blood vessels around his heart, he learnt. With his pulse stabilised and the pain gone completely, the doctor asked him a series of yes or no questions. Had he suffered from influenza recently? Had the pain built steadily or erupted suddenly? Had it come in moments of quiet or of stress, or both? Did he have a family history of heart disease?

By the time the two medics arrived, Partridge was sitting upright, drinking a glass of water, the blood-pressure balloon still affixed to his arm, the oxygen cylinder beside him no longer necessary. He had suffered what appeared to be the onset of angina pectoris, according to the doctor. One of the medics shone a light in his eyes, took his blood pressure again, and was apparently satisfied with the diagnosis. The fact that Partridge had responded so well to the nitroglycerine suggested it was unlikely to have been a more serious cardiac event.

Angina indicated possible coronary disease, but it was manageable with the right medication, changes to diet and improved fitness. Indeed, the doctor confessed, he had suffered from angina himself for close to a decade, and it was all too common.

At that point Partridge made it clear that he did not wish to accompany the medics to hospital, despite the doctor's advice that it would be best for him to spend the night there under observation.

But Partridge was insistent. He felt fine. All the pain had gone. He would call the hospital during the night at the first sign of trouble, he assured the GP, who conceded there was no immediate danger as long as Partridge continued to take the nitroglycerine. But until tests were done there could be no guarantees, the doctor cautioned, and he advised visiting a specialist at the first opportunity.

The tests would be taken care of on his return to Melbourne, if not before, Partridge promised. A specialist friend of his was a big name in heart surgery, and the mention of his name convinced the GP. Partridge gave his word that he would get plenty of rest and have his blood pressure monitored daily by the hotel doctor. The ambulance medics were dismissed and Partridge accepted the GP's offer of a lift, desiring nothing more at that point than to take to his bed and sleep.

But he was unable to sleep. The doctor had warned him against taking his regular sleeping pills, or anything else that might act as a depressant, including alcohol, at least until an X-ray was taken.

So Partridge had got up, showered, and now stood barefoot in the breakfast nook, dressed in blue silk pyjamas, stirring sugar into a mug of black tea. His fingers were still cold but he felt no concern now. His father had suffered angina from early middle age, before his final heart attack at the age of eighty. But his father had also smoked forty cigarettes a day, on top of his pipe smoking, and dealt with his chest pain by ignoring it. Partridge, on the other hand, had always looked after himself physically, and Margaret made sure that he ate well.

He could see how his father had been able to dismiss the symptoms for so long. For Partridge, it was almost as though the afternoon's events had happened to someone else. The only residue of the episode at the doctor's was the peculiar fascination with which he now found himself regarding things, the heightened intensity of his senses. The teaspoon caught the light in a band of diamonds, the steam from the mug seemed to curl onto his fingers as though it were animate, and the smell of the tea struck his nostrils like an elixir, almost making him swoon. Every little thing seemed alive and significant.

To break the spell he placed the hot spoon on the back of his hand, a trick his wife used to startle him back into her presence. From outside came the distant sound of traffic on the Narrows Bridge, the chop of gear changes and whining decelerations. He heard the padding of footsteps in the room above.

He was carrying his tea out onto the balcony when he was surprised by the phone ringing. He had asked the receptionist to hold his calls so he could rest, and to forward any that were urgent on to Carol. He hoisted the receiver.

'I'm sorry to disturb you, your Honour,' said Carol. 'I know it's late but I've just received a call from the premier's office. A staffer. Wallace is already aware.'

'Aware of what?'

'We're being moved out. I'm calling from your office in the supreme court. There are men here packing boxes now.'

He blinked, closed his eyes, but he could already feel his temples start to pound again. What on earth?

'And has the reason for this been explained to you?' he asked, forcing himself to stay in control.

'I was told that a very serious trial needs the courtroom, starting tomorrow.'

'But this is *ridiculous*. And moved where? We're in the middle of a royal commission, for God's sake. What could be more serious than that?'

'Please don't come down here, your Honour. Please just rest. Leave it to me. I'll pick you up in the morning. Then you can decide.'

'Decide what?'

She didn't want to say it, didn't need to say it.

'You can tell Wallace, or anyone else who asks,' he said, 'that I will not be retiring from this commission.'

'Very well,' she finished, and hung up.

He found himself unable to do likewise. One hand was clenched around the receiver, the other was formed in a fist in front of him. His chest was beginning to hurt again as his blood pressure rose.

Swann retrieved his car from the beach and headed south across the river. To the east the rising moon was so bright it looked like an arc welder at work against the seam of sky and land. There were bushfires down near Pinjarra, the smoke blown along the coast by the southerly.

He pulled up at Jacky's motel and parked next to the office. There were kids in the pool spear-diving through a truck's inner tube. He could smell seared chops and fried onions, hear a speedway race call on the radio in one of the rooms above. He slid his hand into his jacket and cocked the revolver's hammer, slowing as he neared Jacky's room, aiming into the open doorway.

As in Michelle's room, all the lights were on – desk lamp, galley light in the kitchenette, the light in the open fridge, the main light overhead.

Then a toilet flushed and he took his eyes off the blood-spattered walls to crouch. The short corridor to the bathroom was even worse, blood-sprayed, and looked like a crazed painting. Swann trained his gun on the bathroom door, stepping around a puddle of blood that contained scraps of hair.

As he moved to the door he heard a sigh. A woman's sigh. And then the sloshing of a mop. The clang of a bucket.

He peered through the doorway and saw her bent over the bathtub wearing a plastic raincoat and rubber gloves. Thongs. A hibiscus-patterned shower cap. He eased down the hammer on his gun, holstered it as she straightened up. She turned and saw Swann and sighed again.

'You the husband or the lover? Or the father? Either way, yer a bit fucken late.'

Pink froth all over her ankles. Her mop heavy with blood. 'My fucken cleaner took one look an' quit,' she complained. 'Interviewed all right, said she'd seen a thing or two. Didn't believe me when I said you ain't seen nothing yet, sweetheart. Full moon in the animals bar at the Roebourne pub's nothin' to what people do every night in motel rooms. Anyway, the ambulance took her away. She was still breathin'. Got the full send-off.'

The woman turned back to her bucket. 'Listen to those kids, eh? You'd think it was Christmas.'

'Anybody see who did this?'

She shrugged and squeezed her mop. 'No. And none of the usual effin' an' ceein' either. Them kids was right there too. I saw one of the ambos pull panties out of her mouth. Whoever did it took a shower after,' she added. 'Wet towel on the floor. Mirror still steamed up. But the girl was all dressed.'

'Anybody tell you to leave this alone? Not touch a thing?'

'Them Ds? Nope.'

'You call them in?'

'Dunno who called them. They was just here when I got here. But it was them who called the ambos.'

'Any uniformed turn up?'

'Nope.'

'The Ds, one of them have wet hair?'

The woman thought about it, blinked when she understood. 'The blond bloke did. Ah . . . okay, I get it. Time to shut me mouth. You won't have to tell me again.'

'No, it's not like that.' Something in his voice made the woman stare at him strangely.

'Oh gawd. You're that copper in the papers. Who was she? Not yer daughter? Oh gawd . . .'

Swann shook his head but the woman's sudsy hand was on his arm already, tears in her eyes.

'The fucken bastards. Oh son, you shouldn't see this. You shouldn't —'

But he wasn't listening. First Michelle murdered in Louise's old room, and now Jacky had copped a brutal bashing. Both were messages for him.

In the corridor the blood on the light bulb was starting to dry. It smelled sweet, like toasted marshmallow. By morning it would smell like pig iron.

Swann parked on Beaufort Street in Mount Lawley and walked back to the boarding house. The house that Pat Chesson had paid for with cash, according to Donovan Andrews, to house her girls. The gutters and footpath in the street were still covered with dried leaves but the branches of the Chinese tallow were green and alive with the racket of cicadas.

Most of the houses were dark and silent. Many were derelict and boarded up. On the porch of the terrace next door, an old couple sat drinking wine and peeling apples. They stared at him as he stepped over the rusting gate.

The front of the boarding house was an enclosed balcony tacked onto a gold-rush weatherboard, its painted flanks long since peeled away. A broken weathervane hung off the chimney, replaced by a cheap television antenna. From the gutters dangled Christmas lights that had fallen into the dense branches of a climbing rose.

The last time Swann had come here he was looking for Louise. The front rooms were loud with laughter and music then, the air rich with the smells of Irish stew and apple sponge. A cloud of steam hung in the air beneath the stairs, where the single shower was never empty. The house had twenty rooms, which Pat had filled with bunk beds to multiply the number she could accommodate. The boards creaked and the walls vibrated with a water hammer that beat through the pipes from the shower. Most of the girls had been getting ready for the night shift, towels around their heads, cigarettes in their mouths, while those who'd just returned were playing cards at the kitchen table, sharing bottles of moselle, waiting for their turn in the shower.

But there was nobody in the kitchen tonight. A fluoro light buzzed over the table, its laminate surface wet with a slurry of cigarette ash, tissues and beer. The sink was full of dirty dishes and the bin by the fridge was crammed with beer bottles. The shower was silent. The television was off. The only sound came from floorboards that creaked above his head.

There was a time when Swann had known every working girl in the city by their first name, but that time was gone. He didn't recognise the girl in the room at the top of the landing. She sat alone on her bunk in jeans and a pink sloppy-joe, staring at the smoke rising from her cigarette. She looked at Swann with wary grey eyes and exhaled through her nostrils, tapping ash into the mug in her lap. Her long blond hair looked newly permed.

He showed his badge and she looked unsurprised, just angled her head.

'Michelle's room's at the end of the hall, number 1. The one with the Bon Scott posters.'

'You already heard?'

'Mitch told us about twenty minutes ago. Got us all together downstairs.'

'Mitchell Davey? Pat's husband?'

'He's here somewhere. You should speak to him.'

'I will. Did Michelle have her own room or share?'

'Share.'

'The girl who bunked with her, where is she?'

'Trace? She's gone.'

'Gone where? When?'

Now the girl looked uncomfortable. She uncrossed her legs, put her hands on her knees. 'Look, I'm new here. I don't even know her second name. She just didn't show for work this morning, just like Shell. Mitch said she's gone home.' The girl sniffled, wiped her nose on her sleeve. On the top bunk was a bare mattress with her belongings sprawled across it. The whole lot would have fitted into a shopping basket. Beside her was a sleeping bag that had been opened out to make a blanket, the cover stuffed with enough clothes to make a pillow.

She noticed his gaze. 'Glamorous, eh?'

'You got a driver's licence?'

She didn't complain, as he might have expected. He held the licence up to the light. 'Marcia, from Dubbo. How long have you been away from home?'

She nodded as if it were a reasonable question. 'Eight and a half months. Something like that.'

'Your parents know where you are?'

She sighed, took a deep breath. Gave him a Shirley Temple smile. 'Yes. No. They think I'm up the coast, cooking on a prawn trawler.'

Naïve, but an act. Probably well aware she'd be putting out on a trawler too, whether she consented or not.

'Policeman, you should really speak to Mitch now. I've got a headache.'

'Sure, Marcia. I'll do that. Where are the other girls?'

'There's a party on, down there in Katy's room, number seventeen.'

He listened. Couldn't hear anything.

'Not invited?'

'Headache. Could you turn the light out when you go, please?'

Nice kid. Not a good liar. Definitely not a player. Swann turned out the light and closed the door.

Katy's room was across the hall, three locked doors down. Her party wasn't like any Swann had seen. Total silence, two girls on each bunk, three more on a mattress pushed against the wall. A home-made bong on the floor that didn't smell like it had been used. Only one of the girls lifted her head off her chest.

'Fuck,' she whispered, then blinked and rubbed her jaw. She peered down at the steel fit in her hand – it looked more like a shank, was clearly not made for IV. Still, it had done the job, on her and the others.

'Mitch said youse Ds weren't comin'. Where is he?'

'You Katy?'

She shook her head, then changed her mind and nodded. 'Yair. I know what you are, but *who* the fuck are you?'

'My name's Swann. Katy, where's Tracey? I'm looking for Tracey.'

One or two other girls opened their eyes, had a little scratch then went back down. Swann crouched on the floor next to the end of Katy's bed. She was older than the rest, probably mid-twenties, but she smelt of baby powder. In her lap she cradled the head of her sleeping neighbour, whose face was concealed by long black hair and who was breathing slowly, too slowly.

'You should ask Mitch that, Mr Swann.'

'He's not around.'

Katy shrugged, closed her eyes but pulled back from the nod. 'She went to something better paying, Mitch reckons. He always says, You look after Mitch, he'll look after you. Mitch an' the dobbin bitch, eh? Whatever she told him about Michelle, though . . . Well, lucky for her she's gone. Mitch, he can try and make up with us all he likes, free gear for a party, sure, but . . .'

Then she was down again, this time into a nodding embrace. He found her handbag under the bed. Condoms. A lighter, knife. Makeup kit. Lipstick. Wallet. In the wallet was more money than Swann earned in a month, a tiny foil packet and a photograph – of Michelle and herself, Kate Hilsdon, formerly of Newtown, Sydney. Her licence had expired in '74, but Swann wrote down the details on the back of the photo and slipped it into his pocket.

Michelle's room was locked, which gave him some hope that it hadn't been cleaned out yet. It was an old lock and the jamb was loose. He lifted the handle and pressed, then slammed his hip into the door.

It splintered on the first try, broke right open on the next. He put the light on. Bon Scott everywhere: newspaper cut-outs; posters of the hometown hero shirtless and reclining on a purple Monaro; shirtless and kneeling onstage, gilded with neon sweat, leering into the camera. Against one wall was a small dresser with a mirror covered in lipstick kisses. A toiletries bag, hand cream, makeup. Vaseline and condoms in the drawer. A building-society passbook with weekly deposits of four hundred dollars. A photograph of an old woman on a farmyard porch, stroking a border collie.

The top bunk was stripped down but the bottom bed was unmade – pillows and a doona – and a sports bag underneath it. He pulled it out and put it on the bed. It was packed with neatly folded washing, a brand-new Barbara Cartland novel, and a leather diary with a pencil on a string and a small brass lock.

Swann pocketed the diary and turned, just as the softball bat arced past his head and smashed onto the top bunk, sending a metallic shiver through the thin walls.

He snapped a reflex punch into the ribcage of his assailant and barely had time to recognise Mitch Davey, whose head was pulled in as he came again at Swann. There wasn't much room up against the bunk but Swann got inside the next swing and bumped him off, grabbed him by the shoulders and slipped on a chokehold. He tried to throw Davey onto the mattress, got a hand on the back of his head and yanked the chokehold tighter.

But Davey had other ideas. He brought out a shiv from the front of his belt and stabbed backwards over his shoulder, just missing Swann's throat. Swann let him go and sank an elbow into his spine. Davey was short but fast, and fighting on instinct. He flipped around and sliced the air with his knife before Swann got a rabbit punch into his throat, then another smack into the side of the head. It sent Davey to his knees, although he was still cutting the air with a broken left wrist that he hadn't noticed yet, his eyes black and empty like a shark's.

Then he was up and coming at Swann again, who fended off the knife feints and waited for the big lunge. He caught it on the follow-through and this time got behind Davey and brought up the knife arm, shoving him forward, one hand in Davey's hair. He knew he had him now, and he smashed his face into the doorframe, bringing Davey's arm up all the way and forcing him back to the floor. He could feel the sinew rip and then the collarbone pop and the shoulder dislocate like a rotten stump pulled out of the earth.

Mitch Davey screamed but didn't let go of his knife. Swann stamped on his broken wrist, jumped back and started kicking his neck, his back, his head, slamming the door on him with his free hand as Davey's eyes rolled and the air went out of him.

Swann knew he had gone too far, but no voice was calling him back. The walls closed in like grey waves and then the revolver was in his hand and he too was on his knees, in the blood, pushing home the stubnose barrel and shouting at the top of his voice, daring Davey to show him the colour of his eyes.

Donovan Andrews didn't appear to notice the blood on Swann's boots, or on his knuckles. It was congealing now, making the skin on his fists feel like bad-fitting gloves. He had changed out of his blood-spattered jacket into an old windcheater he had in the car – there was no need to alarm Andrews further – and it was dark enough on Kings Park Bluff for Andrews not to notice the state of his trousers either, or the .38 tucked into his waistband.

On the path circling the bluff, angled lamps shed an emerald light on the trunks of the lemon-scented gums that stood like sentinels over the city. The bench where Swann and Andrews were to meet – an arrangement made via Reggie, at Andrews' request – was surrounded by wax bush and stands of fennel gone to seed. There was nobody there when Swann arrived but the air around was thick with cigarette smoke. Swann took a seat and lit a cigarette of his own, and waited.

'Detective?'

'Come on out, stud. It's all right.'

Swann's hands had stopped shaking but it took a conscious effort to keep his voice steady. He knew he'd left Mitchell Davey for dead. It was a relief when Andrews started right off complaining.

'Why'd you get me asking about Michelle? Why didn't you tell me she was Jacky's little pie? Now she's carked, I look like —'

'That's what they're saying, is it? Michelle and Jacky were an item? You taken some extra knocks on the head lately?'

'They're saying a lot of things.'

'How many people did you actually ask about Michelle?'

Andrews was clearly rattled. In the thin light cast by the moon, Swann saw the nervous tic beneath one eye, the ridge of muscle where his jaw was clenched. Andrews blinked a couple of times, as if he were staring into smoke, started saying that he'd come straight from work, having spent the day gutting and butterflying sardines, even longer cleaning squid and sticking the knife into live octopi, their big black eyes looking right at him while he stabbed them and turned them inside out. He was licking his lips and gulping air, desperate to keep talking. All the usual signs that Swann had got to know over the years.

'So what did you want to tell me?' Swann asked when he paused to draw breath.

'I mentioned it last time, right? How I'm going straight? Got a job down in Freo —'

'Yeah, you told me. I'm very pleased for you, Don.'

'Look, I'm working in a new restaurant, the Il Pomodoro Siciliano, down on South Street. It's owned by Nick Mancuso.'

'Mancuso? What's he got you doing? And don't tell me washing dishes and gutting fish.'

'It's true. He's not a bad bloke, Nick.'

'But?'

'He only has good words to say about you as well. Boasted

that you grew up together. Said that when you were a nipper you had a newspaper corner on High Street that you took off a Greek kid. Said his big brother tried to take it off you later but couldn't scare you off, even with backup.'

'That's the way it was then.'

'Nick also said your dad had you fighting sailors, that he ran a book on 'em, that one fight on the Esplanade went for near an hour. Big Samoan guy, but you stopped him. He was on his arse, you were on your knees. That made you the winner.'

Andrews clearly had something he wanted to get off his chest, but he was too nervous to go at it directly. Swann would have to be patient. After what had just happened, the talk of fighting made his guts churn. It had all seemed less real when he was a kid.

'Nick reckons he couldn't believe it when you became a cop.'

'What are you doing talking about me with a Mancuso? You know what they are. How they make their money.'

'You think I'm crazy? I wasn't talking to him, I was listening from the kitchen. They were boasting about knowing you.'

'Let me guess. The restaurant's always empty but the till's always full. You're working in a place that launders drug money, Don.'

'Jesus, that's true of lots of places in Freo.' Andrews shifted on the hard bench, rotated his head, cracked his neck. 'Look, these guys, it's not like the old days. There's five grand in cash, at least, behind a pecorino wheel out in the fridge – and that's just the stash I know about. And the restaurant *is* always empty but the till's full, like you say. They're pretty good fellas, the brothers, but for that much money it's not gonna take much for 'em to knock someone, to make it worth knocking someone. Know what I mean?'

'That how my name came up?'

'That's what I wanted to tell you.'

He stopped, and Swann had to nudge him over the line. 'Go on.'

'I was cleaning up the tables last night while Nick and his mates were drinking, getting ready to go out, when there's a bang on the door. It's not locked, though. In comes this fella I've never seen before, but I still spotted him for a D right off. He's followed by a bloke in a flash suit, never seen him before either. Both of 'em drunk as fish.'

'What'd the D look like?'

'Real tall. Walked like a soldier – turned out I was right, the guy's a Vietnam vet. He's Casey's new driver, name of Gilmartin.'

'I know him, worked in Traffic. He's a detective now? Bloke's a bash artist, dumb as a bag of hammers.'

'Well, get this. He's bent like all the others – the chef in the kitchen tells me he's worked with Nick for years, helps him rebirth cars and that. Anyway, he's walking over to the table, the fella in the flash suit behind him, and Nick stands up, gunslinger-style, y'know. Nick has a few wines, gets a bit silly, right?'

Andrews put his hands out full span, trembled them above his hips. 'Like that. He draws, fires a few pretend shots at the D, full sound effects, blows the smoke off the ends of his fingers. Then he starts shouting, "Killer! Killer Gilmartin! Come and have a beer, mate!" And the guy just freaks. Went for Nick with his bare hands. Got a few rabbit punches in before the other blokes pulled 'em apart and Nick calmed him down. Even apologised, somethin' I never thought I'd hear from a Mancuso.'

'He see you there – Gilmartin?'

'Yeah. I mean, I saw the whole thing. Mad fucken eyes the bloke's got too. Shouted out, "Who the fuck is that?" Kept goin' on and on about me; they had to calm him down all over again. I had to go and introduce myself like the new kid at school.'

'What did he want to know?'

Swann had heard Casey had a new driver, someone who got the

job in no time at all, privy now to all Casey's movements and meets. And it made sense that Casey would use someone like Gilmartin, a bloke who wasn't squeamish about violence.

'Nick did most of the talking for me,' Andrews said. 'Told them I was a good bloke who could be trusted, except around women. Said that's why he had me workin' with a poofter in the kitchen. Made Gilmartin laugh, and he did calm right down, even got friendly with me. Asked me where I lived.'

'What did you say?'

'You know me, I never have regular digs.'

'They stick around after that?'

'For a couple of drinks.'

'What was the other guy about?'

'Tax agent, according to Nick.' Andrews shrugged. 'Anyway, Nick's buying into some trucking business, picking up stuff from caterers, that's all I could make out. I was back in the kitchen by then. Guess the other guy's doin' the paperwork.'

'That's good, Don.' Swann gave Andrews a pat on the shoulder as he made to stand up.

'There's another thing. Ray Hergenhan, you know him?'

'I know him.'

'Well, he's banged up in Freo, hard time. I didn't hear this at work, just roundabout, that he had something to do with Ruby Devine. Least that's what he's putting out there. He always was a bullshitter, but.'

'Yeah, he is. Still. I already heard the rumour about him once tonight. And he's the kind of bloke always knows *some*thing. Might be his way of getting me down there.'

Andrews looked surprised. 'I only heard it today. No shit.'

Swann nodded. 'Mitchell Davey just told me.'

'Never took Mitch for a fizz.'

'There you go. Anything else?'

'Only that Michelle, she was Hergenhan's regular root. At least before he got banged up.'

'That's good too, Don.'

'No worries.'

Swann offered him a cigarette, tapped out a Craven A. 'You mentioned the other night you're thinking of bolting.'

'Yeah, we are. But gotta get a stake first. Then figure out where.'

'You should go and see your mother. Get away from those Mancusos, Don. They're into some serious shit.'

Andrews nodded but didn't look convinced, no doubt had his eyes on the five grand in the refrigerator. Swann stood up and put out a hand. He'd never done that before with Andrews, and it made the younger man nervous. He didn't want to let go of the hand.

Swann pulled it gently loose, patted him on the shoulder again, before turning away into the shadows.

There was little chance of sleeping now. Partridge sat on his bed and waited for the call. He was still furious, but the premier's actions, no doubt the result of Swann's revelations in court today, also had the effect of firming Partridge's resolve. What's more, they confirmed the decision he'd taken that morning before court, to hire his own investigator. The withholding of investigators from his commission was a deliberate and provocative act, and Partridge had been given no choice but to take the initiative. He would even pay for the PI out of his own pocket, if it came to that.

He had a contact in Sydney who'd helped in similar cases demanding discretion and tact, and Partridge had called him to ask for a counterpart in Perth. But all the Perth PIs this man knew were ex-detectives. Better that Partridge remain anonymous, and for the Sydney PI to make the inquiries himself.

At the agreed hour the phone rang. Partridge knew the PI wasn't one for small talk, and so he merely said, 'Go ahead.'

The PI had a voice all gravel and glass. He would probably never find out who'd actually pulled the trigger on Ruby Devine, he said. But it was the lead-up to the murder that was interesting. There was the matter of the seventy-odd thousand dollars in a Hong Kong trust fund that Ruby was responsible for as an alleged investor in property, although when pressed by the taxation department she had refused to state where the money had come from. Money laundering for others, in other words. Faced with a large tax bill for the money in the fund, Ruby had become anxious about the possibility of losing not only her savings, but also the marks of her status – her large home in a well-to-do suburb, her swimming pool with her initials inscribed in golden letters on the bottom. She had sought the help of politician friends, and friends in the media, but to no avail. Then, two days before she was due to have another interview with the taxation department, she told Jacky White she had a 'big business meeting' that would solve all her problems, and as a result had asked Jacky to leave the house.

All of this was on the public record, according to the PI, as was the fact that Ruby Devine had contacted her regular babysitting agency that afternoon but was unable to secure a sitter at late notice. Put together, the fact that she had asked her lover to leave the house while also trying to secure a babysitter for her daughter told the PI that Ruby was expecting to be collected from her home, by someone who didn't want to be seen. Someone who must have been dropped off at Ruby's and then later picked up at the golf course, given that she'd been murdered in her own car.

Also on the public record was the statement of the next-door neighbour, who had seen a girl at Ruby Devine's front door just as she was leaving. Since her daughter claimed to have been upstairs watching television, that meant there must have been a babysitter that night. According to the PI's source at the local newspaper, Ruby had occasionally used her working girls to babysit when she was unable to hire an agency sitter. And yet the statements of Ruby Devine's prostitutes, taken down by Detective Inspector Donald

Casey, were all identical, to the word; all denied ever having babysat for Mrs Devine, which suggested that either some of them were lying or their statements had been coerced or dictated.

Given that the girl was seen at the door close to the time of Mrs Devine's departure, it was possible she alone witnessed who visited that night, the presumably male person who lured Ruby to the golf course where she was murdered soon after.

When the man stopped talking, Partridge thanked him and said, 'Keep looking. But I want you to concentrate in the following area . . .' He explained what he wanted and hung up. He could stay upright no longer.

He set his alarm for six, although he doubted he'd need it. He lay back, closed his eyes and began his regimen of deep breathing, sifting through the memories of his afternoon, distracting himself by taking flight in the story of the murdered woman, a jigsaw of fact and detail that he must reassemble, organise, perhaps even understand.

Swann had slept little and woken early. He got up, bathed his knuckles in iced water before heading down to Fremantle prison. But now, as he approached the front gates, he felt the usual trepidation. He had been to the jail countless times over the years but it never got any easier. The limestone walls glowed in the morning heat as the guard over the watchtower paced his rat-run, .22 rifle in a sling. Swann pressed the buzzer on the gate and waved his ID to the guards in the booth. His insides were clenched and his palms were sweaty – guilty or innocent, inside jail all were the same.

The convict-built prison looked down over the port city as a reminder of the hard truths of crime and punishment. Wherever you went in Fremantle the jail was always there, its stone walls looming on the hillside. It was right beside Fremantle Oval, and watching the footy as a child Swann would imagine the men inside and wonder if they heard the shouts of the crowd and what they must think. On a clear night he could see the guards pace the rat-runs with their rifles and their backs to the town. The prison's inhabitants were mute and invisible, but their silence and invisibility had the power to enter Swann's dreams at night, when he saw men breaking rocks in the sun and going over the walls, just like in the stories his stepfather told him. Brian had spent a year in the prison as a young man, for stealing a car, and he was at his most eloquent when cursing the screws and railing against the walls that had once kept him inside and still kept his mates there. Brian always said it was a short walk from freedom to the iron gates, and Swann should never forget that.

The first time Swann entered the prison he was nineteen years old. He'd always expected to be inside one day, but never imagined it would be in a police uniform. His uniform was still new, his boots polished to a high shine. The day was hot and the sun pounded the walls; the light coming off the limestone bit his skin and filled his eyes with red marbles. He felt the strange dread that was also a kind of excitement.

Behind the big black gates the prison opened up into a large yard with flowerbeds and white rope skirting chalk paths. The cell blocks were low and flat like bricks laid out to bake. He had come to see the driver of a hold-up at a local savings branch who'd crashed and broken both legs while his mates escaped into the Coolbellup bushland. The driver was just a kid and had been put in with the perverts. Swann was there to offer him soft time in another division, if he was smart and gave up his accomplices.

What he remembered from that first visit wasn't the frightened kid or how easily he opened up, but the moment of stepping into the exercise yard of the block where he was being held. The yard was empty, but as soon as he entered he felt a crackling that stopped him, made the hairs on his neck stand up.

The guard with Swann laughed. 'You feel it, eh? This is New Div, where we keep the sex offenders. That's where your CIB mates asked us to keep your man. He's in with the knuckle-dragging boong who runs the place. He hasn't stopped shaking since he got here. Come on.'

Swann could barely move his feet. All his instincts told him to turn and run. It was only thirty metres across the yard but it was the longest walk of his life.

Ray Hergenhan was in Fourth Division, along with the other long-termers. The block rang with the sound of guards' boots on meshed-steel walkways and concrete floors. Naked globes hung on thin cords from the ceiling over the rapidly emptying hall. Prisoners in green tracksuits moved towards their twelve-by-eight-foot cells. The prison was so overcrowded that they were locked up in pairs for sixteen hours a day.

The stench of shit buckets and male sweat and rotten feet and cheap tobacco hung in the air. Baking hot in summer, freezing in winter, the prison was brutal – even the gallows remained in commission as a defiant gesture towards the civilisation evolving elsewhere in the country. Inside the walls nothing had changed in more than a hundred and twenty-five years of unbroken use.

Yet some men called the prison home, and Hergenhan was one of them. Swann knew him well from the days he worked standover for loan sharks and bookies. His specialty, however, was armed robbery, and as a result he'd spent a deal of his short life inside. At six-foot seven, with greasy blond hair and a skinful of bad tattoos, he was easily identified. He was a smart-arse too, disliked by his peers, and it was never long before someone gave him up for a carton of cigarettes or a private cell or a few more weeks of freedom. The skinny from Swann's friend in the prison administration was that Hergenhan was back working standover for some of the older crims in the better cells.

Despite his youth, Hergenhan was old-school and would never talk unless his survival was at stake. When Mitchell Davey had broken and told Swann that Hergenhan knew something about Ruby's murder, Swann racked his brain for an angle, and now, thanks to Donovan Andrews, he had one. Michelle had been Hergenhan's girl.

For a carton of beer at the main gate, Hergenhan's cellmate had been moved elsewhere for an hour. Swann wanted it publicly known that Hergenhan was talking to a cop, but he didn't want the details of their conversation getting out.

The cell door was open. Hergenhan was sitting on the bottom bunk, writing in a journal that he closed and put under his pillow when he saw he had a visitor. He reached for his tobacco as Swann sat on the stool opposite. The shit bucket by the door was empty but the room stank of farts and unwashed feet. Hergenhan's fists were freshly scabbed and his eyes were bloodshot. White scum had dried in the corners of his mouth and his greasy hair was peppered with dandruff.

Swann offered him a Craven A. Hergenhan took two and put one behind his ear. He tucked his packet of White Ox into the waistband of his shorts.

'Well, this is a fucken honour. Swann the dead man. Still walkin' and talkin' but dead dead dead. And look at your knuckles, boy. You been layin' down the law, eh? Snap!' He held out his own scabbed hands.

'There's something I thought you'd want to know,' Swann began.

'Dead dead *dead*.' Hergenhan's smile revealed a set of yellow teeth. 'You know there's a contract out on you, detective? You're lucky I'm banged up. Very tempted I'd be otherwise, number of times you've put me away, you bastard. Still, I shouldn't be gloating. Coupla days left and you wanna spend it in my little patch of paradise. It's a bloody honour.'

Swann felt the power return to his bruised hands. Hergenhan was a bloke he could take it out on and nobody would care. His fingers began to shake and he could feel the blood in his face. It would be nothing to reach across and snuff him, smash his head against the floor, push thumbs into his eyeballs, crush his throat.

But he needed to be calm for this to work.

'In a coupla days I'll be able to tell the world that jus' before he died Swann came to pay his old mate Raymond some final respect.'

Swann waited, holding the shin of his crossed leg with one hand, smoking with the other, looking out the door.

'How I love ya, how I love ya! My *dead* ol' Swanny!'

'Your girlfriend Michelle is dead.'

The shutters came down fast, but not fast enough. In that brief moment, Swann saw right into the place where Hergenhan had watched as his elder brother beat their father to death; into the borstal where he'd been gone through, had gone through other boys. Right into the place where the people Hergenhan had tortured until they gave him what he wanted waited for him, and would wait as long as he drew breath.

'Just last night,' Swann added.

Hergenhan tried to hide the panic in his eyes. 'Doesn't surprise me. She was a slut.'

'I suppose she was.'

Hergenhan busied himself lighting his other cigarette. 'I told her it was dangerous work. How'd she go?'

'Overdose. I was there.'

'Nah. Nup,' he said warily. 'Must be some mistake. Shelly was no user. I told her I'd kill her if—'

'You weren't there. How would you know what she was or wasn't? You've been locked up for five months.'

'Yep, yep,' Hergenhan agreed. 'And ten years to go, with hard fucken labour. But nah. She visits here regular. No way. I'd know.'

Swann flicked his butt into the shit bucket. He smoothed his hands along his trousers and waited. '*Visited* here,' he corrected. 'She won't be coming again.'

'No fucken way,' Hergenhan repeated, and farted absentmindedly.

'You're probably right. They're saying it was an OD but I was there, I saw it. It looked all wrong.'

'Whaddya mean?'

He described how Michelle had been found, right down to her hair being whipped by the breeze. Hergenhan was tense in every muscle. Swann could almost hear the whirring and clicking as Hergenhan projected the names and faces of those who might want Michelle dead.

'Your old mate Mitchell Davey just dogged you to me, Ray. Told me you know something about Ruby Devine's murder. That you've been saying things. Boasting about it. That true?'

Hergenhan tried to remember how to smile but his face didn't work. Swann decided to back off a little. He didn't want him doing something stupid.

'Is it possible someone murdered Michelle to get at you? Because you've been talking out of school?'

'That Mitch's blood on your knuckles, Swann? Thought you were better than that.'

'Just answer the question.'

'Sure, it's possible.'

'Then perhaps I can help.'

Hergenhan shook his head. 'That's very kind of you, dead man. But no thanks.'

'You sure about that?'

'Oh yeah, lemme see now, you help me if I help you. But then you get knocked off and where am I then, dead man? Eh?'

Swann shrugged. The bloke had a point, but his own point had been made. Whatever Hergenhan knew, and whatever he might decide to tell Swann, it wouldn't be done in the here and now. It would take time for Michelle's death to get past the smart mouth and the hard eyes and settle deeper. But late at night, in the dark and quiet, alone with his fears, his self-loathing, then maybe.

'I don't know what it's like out there, detective, but in here every man and his bumboy knows that when the royal commission is done, you're done as well. There's even a book going on how long you'll last. So what the fuck?'

'You talk on the record and I'll get you looked after. I'll get you a new life – new city, new state. New country if you want.'

'Bullshit. I talk and I'm as dead as you. You think your mates won't be able to find me? Gimme a break. Those boys know I'll never talk.'

'You've already been talking, Ray. Never could help yourself. And now Michelle's dead.'

'That's bullshit too. I haven't said anything. You reckon you can come in here, shake ol' Raymond down an' see what falls out of his pockets?'

'Michelle came to me.'

Hergenhan sneered. 'Then she deserved what she got.'

'Sure you didn't put her up to it, Ray? You've got me here, haven't you?'

He got no reply to that. 'Just like in the old days, Ray. We helped each other a lot, no?'

'Keep yer fucken voice down,' he growled. 'Less you wanna get me killed. That was out *there*.'

'We can come to the same arrangement.'

'Bullshit. I know every black hole and blind spot in this prison. I still got choices. I'm safer in here than you are out there.'

Swann grinned. 'That isn't true, Ray. You tell me or don't tell me, you're still talking to me. I'm *here*. They're all going to be interested in that, your so-called mates, inside and out.'

Swann stood and tossed his packet of cigarettes to Hergenhan, who let them fall to the floor.

'Dead man, I want for nothing in here.'

Swann strode out onto the iron walkway. The other cells were locked down but he could feel the eyes staring at him as he headed to the door.

From the public phone at his hotel he checked in with Reggie and then called Terry. He asked him to pull a file on Solomon Sands, should one exist. Jacky's description of him matched the tax agent Donovan Andrews had seen in Mancuso's restaurant, and the filing room at Central was a place that even Terry, a uniformed plod, could access. It might have been where all the confidential records of arrests and investigations and unsolved cases were kept, but even when Swann was a rookie the lore was that it was kept unlocked so that the purple circle could come down whenever they chose and disappear the files of mates, and others – put the blame on uniformed if it came to that.

After hanging up he went to shower and change his clothes, which stank of Hergenhan's cell. Before the bathroom mirror he buttoned his shirt, fixed his necktie. The interview with Hergenhan hadn't been a complete waste of time, even if the rumours of him being the killer were most likely crap.

It didn't make sense that the people behind the hit would use someone like Hergenhan, and would only mean there'd have to be two murders, the second to silence the first killer. Hergenhan was tough but he was no pro, and could be broken with fists and boots in a matter of hours and made to squeal.

But there was another reason why an outside hit was unlikely. The purple circle were lords of the town; they had dirt on judges and politicians and did whatever they wanted. Some of them had brains and some were just bash artists, but they all had one thing in common – they shot their own meat and framed their own pictures. One man to pull the trigger while another kept guard, the others in the circle of knowledge bonded to silence.

Swann slipped on his jacket, put a foot up on the sink and buffed his shoes. The pain in his hands was returning and he'd just decided to pour himself a shot when the phone rang. He checked his watch – ten o'clock – and went to answer it. At first he thought it was a woman on the line, but the sobs and the slurred voice belonged to Cooper, drunk and maudlin and raving.

'Swann, that you, mate? Mate?'

'What's up, Cooper?'

'I think I did something, mate. You're my mate, aren't you Swann? Jesus. What am I saying? You fucken hate me.'

'What are you on about? I can hardly —'

'It was Ruby. It was me.'

'You're pissed. Put the receiver next to your mouth.'

'I did a terrible thing. It was me. She told me, she told me. She was so *angry.* She was gonna get some people back if they didn't put money in the hat.'

Swann felt adrenalin flood his body. 'Shut up right now. I'll come —'

'I was playing the tables at Il Travatore. I'm in deep there, too deep. I mentioned what Ruby had said to Nicky Mancuso and his mates. I was drunk, Swann, I didn't mean to —'

'Cooper, *Christ*, not on this line. Meet me at that last place, in —'

He heard the sound of glass breaking, then Cooper cursing.

'Cooper? Cooper?'

But the line was dead.

Partridge's new desk was a trestle table overlaid with a black cloth. The commission had been relocated to the cafeteria of a nondescript public-service building awaiting renovation on the edge of the city. The table where Swann sat was undressed, and behind that were three rows of plastic chairs, then the long empty hall. Dust motes hovered in the light coming through the glass-brick windows near the ceiling. The change of venue had not been noted in the morning paper and the rows of plastic seats were empty but for Pat Chesson and two of her friends.

Partridge leant forward and tapped his microphone and the portable PA system hissed. 'Counsel, when you're ready.'

He was determined not to let the conditions get to him, at least until he'd managed to discuss the matter with the governor, whom he'd asked Carol to contact that morning. Wallace, on the other hand, was looking discouraged as he picked up his page of typed notes and walked across the checked linoleum floor.

It didn't bother Partridge to see Wallace knocked down a few pegs, just so long as it didn't affect his performance. In fact Wallace's fall from grace might work in the judge's favour. Not only had the humiliation visited on them caused Wallace to lose his arrogant manner, but a new atmosphere of co-operation had been apparent during their morning briefing.

That briefing had related mainly to the nature of Pat Chesson's business, and the news that one of her prostitutes had been found dead the previous afternoon. And yet she had not requested her appearance before the commission be deferred, which was something that even the QC found unusual.

Wallace cleared his voice and placed a hand at his spine as he stood under the fluoro lighting. 'Your Honour,' he began, then paused while a group of journalists entered.

Partridge wondered whether one of them was responsible for the article in the morning paper. While the police were on record as saying there were no suspicious circumstances regarding the death of Pat Chesson's girl, the newspaper also reported the savage bashing of another prostitute, Jacky White, the lover of the late Ruby Devine. White was in an induced coma in Fremantle hospital, with serious head injuries.

Superintendent Swann sat immobile at the table, surely aware that the violent events outside the courtroom had strengthened his allegations. An execution-style murder, an apparent overdose and a savage beating, all among prostitutes and all in a short period of time – events that bore the hallmarks of organised crime. And where organised crime existed, so inevitably did police corruption.

It would be most interesting to hear Pat Chesson's view of the matter.

'Your Honour, I call Mrs Patricia Chesson.'

She stood and walked to the microphone alongside Swann's table, so that she couldn't help but look down at him. Considering that one of her employees had died the previous evening, she appeared remarkably untroubled. She took her oath in a broad accent, with the air of one used to being in court.

Wallace's shoes scuffed on the lino. 'Mrs Chesson, you have admitted to being a brothel keeper in this state for some years. Would you please relate the changes you have witnessed over that period in terms of the enforcement of the laws that make prostitution illegal.'

Pat Chesson smiled unexpectedly, revealing a set of polished teeth. There was something shocking about their high shine, studded into bright-red gums.

'How long have you got, Mr Wallace? There's a lot can be said on the matter.'

'Take your time, Mrs Chesson. That's why we are here.'

She shrugged kittenishly, something that alarmed Partridge even more than her teeth. In her sleeveless floral dress and sandals she resembled the plain, thin-hipped suburban girls he remembered from his youth, except for the gutters that fanned away from her smoker's mouth.

'Mr Wallace, it's like this. When I first arrived to set up my business here, there was understandings between myself and the police. We kept our part of the bargain, they kept theirs. We made sure all our girls was clean and well behaved. We kept a quiet profile. You wouldn't know, walking past one of my businesses, what it was. And anyone who went outside the rules was run out of town.'

She paused to dowse her gums with a mouthful of water. 'Things were better in the old days, but that said, I'm a businesswoman and I have my family to feed. I'm a survivor, so I just go along with it. But I've been known to complain about it to whoever'll listen – I even had a meeting with the premier.'

'A meeting that he has no recollection of.'

'And the Minister for Police.'

'A meeting he also has no recollection of.'

She shrugged again. 'But then Ruby was done in and I've kept my trap shut ever since.'

'Did you see Mrs Devine as a rival? A business competitor?'

'No, me and Ruby was great friends. In the old days there was plenty of room for everyone. Ruby even helped me set up. She could tell I was a professional.'

'Do you have a personal opinion as to why Mrs Devine might have been murdered?'

'No, I don't, Mr Wallace. It was as much a shock to me as everyone else.'

'Did it make you worried that Mrs Devine was killed in so ruthless a fashion? I'll rephrase that question – What do you think of Superintendent Swann's conviction that payments made to certain detectives might be in some way related to Mrs Devine's murder?'

There was no reaction from Swann but Pat Chesson exhaled audibly into the microphone. 'Well, I used to have a lot of respect for Superintendent Swann and I understand that he's had some personal difficulties, which I sympathise with. But I don't really know what he's talking about.'

'You're saying he's making it up? Haven't you just finished telling us that, what were your words . . . there are understandings between you and the police?'

'No sir, it's just that – I wouldn't know about that. I'm old-school, sir, old-school in every way. I run a clean house and mind my own business.'

Wallace conceded the point with a single nod. He let the silence hang there, waiting for her to take it up.

'Me and Superintendent Swann were fine until after Ruby's murder. But then, what with his personal difficulties, you see, he started to act strange. You know all this, but he was in contact with me a lot. At first I understood it, what he was on about, but some of the things just didn't make sense. He wanted me to help find his daughter, you see. And he was kind of blaming me at the same time. He thought I owed him information, like in the old days, but I hadn't heard anything. And he started saying threatening things against me. He said I was the one to gain from Ruby's murder, that with the CIB's help I was trying to force her out of business, which is a lie, sir, a lie. And then he started saying things in public, and not just about me but about . . . But you know all this,' she repeated.

'Did Superintendent Swann ever threaten you physically, Mrs Chesson?'

'Yes, he did. He said he would get revenge for Ruby.'

'And what did you say to that?'

'I didn't say anything. I stopped talking to him after that. And I reported the matter to Detective Inspector Casey, who told me not to worry about it.'

'Thank you, Mrs Chesson, that will be all.'

'You're welcome. Thank you for the opportunity to have my say. I hope some of the important people have been listening and will take note of the problems facing a businesswoman in these difficult times.' She looked around at the largely empty room and unclenched the powerful little fist that had been punctuating her speech throughout, tapping rhythmically against the bone of her right hip.

Outside, a cloud passed across the sun, and in the diorama of the courtroom the light began to flicker and run away to the walls. Pat Chesson rejoined her companions and took her seat. The journalists began to whisper and compare notes. Annie DuBois was called to the witness stand, where she stared at Pat Chesson with an obvious distaste.

Partridge looked down at his brief and noted the names of those who would follow her: two former detectives and a former minister for police.

Tomorrow was Saturday, and his birthday, the first he'd spent away from his family. He had a lunch engagement with a politician, but Carol had managed to clear the rest of the weekend. He imagined what it would be like at home, his grandchildren tearing into his presents, his three children toasting him at the table laden with roast meat and salad, and felt his heart grow warm in the knowledge that this was what he would return to as soon as the commission was over.

When he looked up again he made eye contact with Swann for the first time that morning. Here was a father who had lost a daughter, and what the weekend held in store for him, Partridge hated to imagine.

The late-afternoon southerly was cool on his back as Swann walked briskly from his hotel across the park towards the bistro, pausing to light a cigarette beneath the giant arms of a Moreton Bay fig, out of the wind. He was sure he was being followed but it didn't worry him. He had been followed by an unmarked all the way from the prison to the hearing that morning, where he had sat the day out on a hard plastic seat.

The royal commission had adjourned for the weekend. Perhaps Hergenhan was right and they'd wait until it was finished before they tried to kill him, but in the meantime they'd made their tactics clear with Jacky's bashing and Michelle's murder. Michelle had been put down like a dog, and the fact that it happened in his daughter's old hotel room only made the message clearer.

A few hopeful gulls traced the edges of the streetlights, beaks open as they waited for the darkness to come. Swann stepped out into the wind and jogged the last twenty metres to Bistro Gregorio, pushed open the heavy door. As always, the chime rang to announce his entrance, Reggie waited in his dark corner, and Greg slid a drink ironically down the counter.

'You heard this before?' Greg asked him.

'Can't say I have.' A blues harmonica soaring over a noodling guitar.

Greg smiled and shook his head. 'This,' he said, 'is a bootleg of Norman Gunston on harp playing with Frank Zappa in Melbourne. Unfuckingbelievable.'

'Not bad,' conceded Swann. 'The little Aussie bleeder might have a career beyond television.'

Greg laughed. 'They always say that's a good idea, yeah.'

'Keep 'em coming.'

The barman nodded, lost again to the chugging rhythms of the guitar as he filled a cocktail shaker with vodka, ice and vermouth for some customers by the piano.

Reggie blinked, by way of saying hello. On one side of his head his orange hair was flat, while the other was bushy. His eyes were wild. 'I've just come from seeing Jacky,' he said. 'She's going to be all right, they say.'

'Isn't she in a coma?'

'Only when the coppers are there.' Reggie looked at Swann with renewed interest. 'I also saw what you did to Mitchell Davey. Fractured skull, broken jaw. Fifteen cracked ribs. Broken wrist.'

'He launched the boat. What's he saying?'

'He's not saying anything. His jaw's trussed up tighter than a virgin's daughter. But the nurse told me he got hit by a truck.'

'Not very original. Surely he would've been more believable if he'd said Pat was the one who bashed him. You hear what she did to him last year?'

Reggie laughed. 'Oh yes, the superglue.'

Sick of Davey sleeping with her girls, Pat Chesson had reportedly superglued his prick to the inside of his leg while he was passed out.

'Surgery was involved there too, as I heard the story.'

'No doubt.' Swann took his notepad from his pocket and flicked a page. 'This is what I asked Terry to pull. Two years ago a bloke name of Solomon Sands was declared bankrupt. He disappears to Sydney for a year and comes back a multimillionaire.'

'Why's he on file?'

'He was accused about twelve months back of swindling some investors in a gold-mining venture. They're still after him. Now he's rebadged himself as a tax agent. New house on the river. Vintage cars. Holidays in France. The full wanker's trifecta. But that's not all. His missus, according to Jacky, is Annie DuBois.'

'Jesus.'

'That's what I thought too,' Swann nodded. 'Ruby might have threatened to trade off more to the taxman than the identities of Casey and the others.'

'Some other tax scam. But what? What's Sands up to?'

'That I don't know yet. I don't even know what a tax agent does, exactly.'

'Can't be too straight if his form's anything to go by. Leave it to me. I'll ask around, see if I can get a list of his clients, find out how he makes a quid.'

'You get the rest of those land titles?' Reggie's insider at the Land Corporation had agreed to search out the titles for all the Ds who'd attended the false raid in Rawson Street.

Reggie nodded. 'Must be true what they say about Tupperware. So many wealthy housewives.'

Swann buried his nose in his tumbler, drank down the last finger of whiskey and tipped the ice into his newly delivered glass. The muscles in his arms felt like wood. His knuckles were tattered and swollen. 'I told you about the diary I found in Michelle's room,' he said.

'She say anything useful?'

Swann shook his head. 'Fantasy love letters to Bon Scott mostly. *Explicit* fantasy love letters to Bon Scott. Not a good advertisement for the state school system either.'

Reggie leant forward. 'It's even worse than that, I'm afraid. The reason I came straight here from seeing Jacky. She told me that Michelle phoned not long before they came for her. Said something that meant she had to die – Michelle was the babysitter.'

Swann felt a surge of anger. Ruby Devine's babysitter, who might have seen who went with her that night, delivered to her death. Now on ice at the morgue.

'Christ, why didn't they tell me earlier? I could have protected them, got them out of town.'

The biggest break so far. Yet he had sat with Michelle over a glass of beer and learnt nothing. He could barely contain his bitterness.

'Not even Jacky knew until Michelle called her. She wanted money, Jacky reckons, otherwise she wouldn't speak. Jacky told her she'd get her the money somehow, but of course . . .'

'I went to see Ray Hergenhan this morning – Mitch Davey put him in. He's not the trigger man but he knows something. He might have put Michelle up to it. Michelle must have told him something, who she'd seen.'

'You think he'll talk, after what happened to her?'

'Wouldn't count on it,' Swann said. 'Now that Michelle's dead it's his word against whoever she accused. And the word of a bloke locked up for a hard ten at that. But if I could get a name, take it to Partridge, I might be able to get Ray an offer, soft time, maybe even a new start.'

Reggie was looking at him and shaking his head. 'You've got that look in your eye.'

Swann stared down into his glass and saw an image of Michelle laid out on a steel slab, just like Ruby before her. He lit another cigarette and signalled for more drinks. When his Jameson came he nudged a mouthful between his teeth, tossed the rest down his throat to prepare himself for the morgue.

‘Are you all right, Harold? You sound tired.’

It was good to hear Margaret’s voice, but Partridge was conscious of keeping the events of the past few days out of his own.

‘It’s the heat, my dear,’ he lied. And then couldn’t help himself. ‘“Oh wind, rend open the heat,/cut apart the heat,/tear it to tatters . . .” ’

‘You philistine,’ she laughed. He had a history of reciting badly that had begun during their courtship, but Hilda Doolittle was her favourite poet and he knew she couldn’t let it stand.

‘*Rend* it to tatters,’ she corrected him. ‘“Fruit cannot drop/through this thick air –/fruit cannot fall into heat . . .” ’

He missed the sound of Margaret’s easy laughter. Fifty years and the ritual still thrilled him.

‘On the subject of grapes,’ he said.

‘Yes, they’re coming along. Dusty from the driveway, still waiting on the paving contractor, of course, but coming along, you might even say round. Are you really well, my love?’

‘Of course,’ he replied, alert to the concern in her voice. ‘I miss you,’ he added.

'And how will you be celebrating your birthday?' she asked. 'Hard to believe you'll be seventy-three.'

'Yes,' he agreed. 'And I still feel . . .' He was unable to finish the sentence, overtaken by the image of Margaret the day he'd met her. Playing tennis with her chestnut hair tied back, and those magnificent legs. Partridge sipping a gin and tonic beneath the jacarandas as he watched her through the dappled shade, a carpet of purple flowers at his feet.

'Yes?' she prompted. 'You still feel what?' The hint strong enough for Partridge to pick up, amazingly, the lines he'd spoken those fifty years ago and not once since. It had been the first time he flirted with her, beckoned her, and the old desire stirred in him again. *Gather ye rosebuds while ye may,/Old Time is still a-flying . . .* But he couldn't say the words.

'Complete. In answer to your question, I feel complete.'

But his voice must have given him away. 'Oh Harold, you're still unwell. Shall I join you? I can call TAA and get on the next flight. It's the weekend – perhaps we could go for a drive?'

'No,' he replied. 'As much as I miss you. Perhaps afterwards. Or perhaps in a day or two, when I've got a better idea how long I'll be here.'

'If you think that's best. Well, we all miss you too. We'll celebrate your birthday the day you return; that's a promise. Please look after yourself over there. And I'll call tomorrow, of course.'

When he'd put down the phone he drank a glass of water. He hadn't mentioned it to Margaret, hoping he was wrong, but it didn't look like the commission would last much longer. Just hours ago, in the office attached to the cafeteria that now served as his chamber, he'd been informed by Wallace that Swann was about to be accused of improper conduct by the young policewoman with whom he'd allegedly had an affair, the same woman that DI Casey had introduced in his testimony a few days earlier. This young woman had subsequently quit the police force, according to Wallace, who had been contacted by her legal representative, and she was demanding to speak at the commission.

There it was, the *fait accompli* Partridge had been waiting for, the final nail in the coffin of not only Swann's credibility but also his reliability as a witness, as a man of good character. And yet Wallace had relayed the news apologetically, not at all as Partridge might have expected.

'Why haven't the police pressed charges against Swann, if indeed it was a case of assault?' he asked the QC. 'Are they intending to?'

'Not to my knowledge, your Honour. At least, her barrister didn't mention any such thing.'

But Wallace wouldn't meet his eyes, and stared instead at the unpolished boards at his feet. One of his shoelaces was partially undone.

'Because,' Partridge pressed, 'you can imagine how it looks to me. The young lady prepared to make such an accusation in open court and yet the police force for whom she worked not pressing charges.'

'I can imagine how it looks, yes.'

'No doubt the official reason for not charging Superintendent Swann would be that there's no evidence to support the woman's claims. That it's a case of her word against his, and she understandably wishes to avoid the trauma of a public trial – and yet she's prepared to destroy Superintendent Swann's reputation, very publicly, in my courtroom.'

'That might well be the thinking – all of those things.'

'What else aren't you telling me?'

Wallace shuffled. 'It will be in the papers tomorrow.'

As good as an admission, thought Partridge. As good as an admission of guilt.

He dismissed Wallace with a peremptory flick of his wrist, not bothering to hide his disappointment and anger.

As he waited for the PI to call, Partridge rinsed his glass and placed it back in the minibar. The PI was punctual to the minute, but his voice was laden with fatigue and he sounded wheezy.

'It's been productive. More than I thought. I've been talking to both sides of the street. There're links even I didn't know about.'

Partridge waited for a coughing fit to cease. He heard the hiss of an asthma inhaler, a long draw and some throat clearing.

'That's better. God, I can breathe again. I asked around the business community, and your story about the Minister for Police checks out. Famous for extorting kickbacks. Had a couple of unlikely wins on the jiji's too, apparently. It's the wild bloody west out there, is what I keep hearing, and he's not the only one. Got a pen?'

'Go ahead.'

It took a while, and when it was done the PI said, 'And like you suggested, I contacted a friend in Canberra, a taxation guy – he's more than happy to conduct an audit into the assets of the detectives you mentioned.'

'We'll see.'

'He also told me that he's just been assigned an investigation into a tax agent in Perth, a suspected heroin trafficker by the name of Solomon Sands. Now, get this – Mr Sands has links to members of the Liberal cabinet. In fact, eight of the eleven MPs on the Liberal Party Finance Committee, along with the president of the party, have been dealing with this bloke – some new dodgy tax scam. But Crown Law over there, who are supposed to be collecting evidence as part of my mate's test case, well, they aren't. Been dragging their feet apparently. The whole Crown Law office is being – what did my mate say? – wilfully obstructive. So there's another thing you might want to look at.'

If only that were possible, thought Partridge. But his suspicions had been justified. 'How does it work, this scheme?' he asked.

'They're calling it the Bottom of the Harbour tax scheme. Sounds sinister, doesn't it? Reads like old-school asset stripping to me: you strip a company of its assets and profits before tax comes due, on-sell the shell to some dope who claims not to know the history, then make sure you lose all the books so the ATO gets nothing – send them to the bottom of the harbour. The tax agent pays tax only on his commission, which in turn is only a proportion of the price of sale. Meanwhile the assets are transferred to a new company and it's business as usual. For my mate to get so excited means there must be lots of brownie points in it for him, lots of garlanded heads to roll – pollies, bankers, businessmen. He reckons there are potentially tens of millions of dollars wrapped up in this scam, and it's something that started in Perth. Now it's taken off around the country. Maybe Ruby Devine got mixed up in it, or knew something about it, threatened to use it as leverage in her negotiations with the tax office.'

Partridge thanked the PI and hung up. His head was swimming. When he thought of the possible scale of the corruption, the farce that had been made of the royal commission – *his* royal commission – and what he might have done with it had he been given the chance, his old ambition turned into a terrible frustration, a bitterness of a kind he hadn't felt for many years.

The coroner's office, buried beneath five storeys of the Royal Perth Hospital, was nicknamed the bunker. The hospital windows cast a sepia light over the new macadam around the service entrance. Despite the reek of burnt tar, Swann could already smell the formaldehyde and ammonia.

Behind him in the waste-disposal site, a steel grate clanked and a blast of red from the hospital furnace threw his shadow across the brickwork. Body parts, garbage and infected linen joined the cremation flames, making the narrow black chimney rumble like a steam train building up a head.

Swann descended the stairwell to the coroner's office and knocked on the dented wooden door. It swung open to reveal a coronial assistant standing under dazzling fluoro and framed by white tiles and white walls. He was wearing white dungarees tucked into white gumboots, and rubber gloves. A face mask was pushed down his stubbled chin.

'Jesus, that was quick.' Darren Plant was barely out of his teens and hadn't yet learnt to conceal his enthusiasm. He seemed genuinely pleased to see Swann.

'Come again?'

'You're bloody quick. Spooky voodoo quick. Just hung up a minute ago, now here you are. Beam me up, Scotty!'

Perhaps it was the fumes, but Darren could never get a message across without the signal breaking up.

'What are you on about, Darren? You looking to get fired? Let me in, for Chrissake.'

'Not to worry, Superintendent. There's only old Abraham over there at the furnace. Biblical name, biblical job.' He laughed and stood back, ushering Swann past with a bow. 'The dungeons await your inspection, sire.'

'Cut the Addams Family shit. Where is she?'

Plant led him through the chilled steel doors of the autopsy room. 'Homicide dropped her off about thirty minutes ago. She's laid out till next week, when the Prof gets back from a conference in Montreal.'

It was Tracey, Michelle's roommate, Swann was sure of it, going by Donovan Andrews' description of her as a city black, pale-skinned, half Irish.

A month or so before, Plant had called Swann to tell him that the corpse of a young woman had been retrieved from the bush near Pinjarra. All he could say was that she was a brunette in black lingerie and that it was a definite homicide. Her face was so bashed she was unrecognisable. The photo Swann had given him of Louise was no use. But she was a brunette, like Louise, and Swann rushed to the morgue, heart pounding.

The murdered girl had been cut open. Her stomach was sprawled over a set of scales; her heart and liver sat in shining steel bowls. The top of her skull had been sawn off and her brain removed. A plaster-of-paris cast of her teeth was drying on the bench beside her organs. Swann had stared at the smears of black blood running across the grey skin of her chest and stomach, at her horrifically beaten face, and the sickening relief that it wasn't Louise made him weak at the knees.

'Media got this yet?' he asked Plant, nodding at Tracey.

'Nope. Probably won't either, they rarely do. Didn't seem to be much fuss. Another accidental drowning is what one of the homicide Ds said. Waste of bloody time, he reckoned. Amazing what some blokes'll pay for, he also said. You know her?'

'Why did you say *another* drowning?'

Plant looked surprised. 'She's the third in a year. I never told you because none of them was your daughter. Look, I've still got the photo of her.'

'Don't worry about that. Explain.'

'Like I said, first one about a year ago, another just after. Deaths by misadventure, the coroner ruled. Soon as the cops looked at them they walked away.'

Nothing suspicious about their deaths: the reason Terry hadn't been able to find a record of them at Central.

'Were they ever claimed? They have any ID?'

'Sadly, no. We cremated one of them a couple of weeks ago. The other one's due to be cremated tomorrow. It's been a year and nobody's claimed her.'

'Is it possible to hold off the cremation? I don't think their deaths were accidental.'

'Not unless the police open an investigation. And the coroner didn't find anything suspicious.'

'I want to get a tox done on her blood, for opiates.'

'Too late for that. She's been drained. Twelve months in the cold room won't help either. I do remember that the coroner found a high concentration of alcohol in both of them, which is why he figured they'd gone swimming drunk and drowned.'

Swann turned back to Tracey's body on the slab. 'She look roughed up to you?'

Darren Plant leaned over and lifted back some of her matted hair. There was beach sand in it, and in her scalp. Her eyes were closed, her mouth was open. She still smelt of the ocean.

'Some bruising – see there? Up the neck.'

'You mind?' Swann asked.

'Nope.'

Swann peeled back the canvas tarp and dropped it to the floor. Tracey was wearing a bikini; there was seaweed caught in her toes. 'Where'd they find her?'

'Off a northern beach. That's all I heard. Some blokes trolling for tailor saw her near a reef.'

'But she's covered in sand.'

'They couldn't get her into the boat. Didn't want to gaff her or leave her there, so they towed her to the beach.'

Gently Swann lifted her arms, peering close. Finally he found what he was looking for, on a vein over her ankle. The smudge of a bruise. A lifted red spot, like a mozzie bite, where the needle had gone in. He took a polaroid of it to show Reggie, and another of her face.

'Don't care how you do it but make sure the coroner tests for heroin on this one, and has a close look at the bruising. Let me know if she was already dead when she hit the water.'

'Roger that.'

'And I'll get you an ID by tonight. She'll be from over east, just like the other two. I want you to take that to the media.'

'But the police have said it's not suspicious. The autopsy hasn't been done.'

'Say what you like, but make it good. Point out that this is the third drowning in a year, in roughly the same area. And that a full-spectrum tox and autopsy will be carried out to determine whether or not she was dead before she went into the water.'

'The coroner will know it came from me. I'm the only one here.'

'Say one of the homicide Ds mentioned it. Asked specifically for the testing.'

'The bastards'll come back on me.'

'Look at her – she's your age. She was done in and dumped like garbage.'

'But —'

'If they come back on you, tell them I made you do it. They'll believe that. Tell them I threatened you. Because I'm about to, if you don't.'

Plant looked at Tracey and the still-wet sand in her sightless eyes. 'Okay,' he agreed.

The two of them placed the canvas shroud back over her corpse. It was icy-cold in the refrigerated room, three degrees Celsius according to a red dial by the gurney. Swann had goosebumps on his forearms but even so he was sweating – he could smell himself over the chemicals in the room.

'Now,' he said, 'where's Michelle?'

'Who?'

'The OD who came in yesterday. The one in the news.'

'This way.'

The autopsy hadn't been started on Michelle yet either, something to be thankful for. Plant guided Swann down the corridor, his gumboots squeaking on the tiled floor. He pulled a drawer out of the wall and unzipped the body bag. Michelle was naked inside it. There was bruising on one arm where the needle had been forced in. Her fists were clenched.

Swann took another photo, the flash burning her image into his eyes. When he opened them it was dark again. The polaroid popped from the camera and he shook it dry in the frozen air.

He passed Darren Plant the fifty he owed him for the information, for the access. 'I'll get that name to you. You give it to the media.'

'All right. But it won't stop the other cremation going ahead.'

The Fremantle doctor was still gusting but even the salt wind couldn't clear away the stench of the morgue. Swann could taste the formaldehyde in his mouth, feel it on his skin.

Ruby Devine's next-door neighbour lived in a Californian bungalow across the foreshore from the dark river, a humble house in comparison to those alongside it. He parked on the street and walked up the path to the front door. Merle Shannon was an old woman but despite the lateness of the hour she answered the door without asking first. She was dressed in a beige cardigan and a tartan skirt and tartan slippers. Swann could smell mutton fat and pipe tobacco in the lounge room, where classical music wafted from a transistor.

He'd already interviewed Merle twice but he needed to make sure. Merle had described to the case detectives and the media and then to Swann and Reggie how, on the evening Ruby was murdered, she had been weeding among her roses. It was mild then, but turned rainy later on. Concealed at first by the side fence, Merle had stood up to see Ruby, dressed in one of her glamorous numbers, pressing the front doorbell and peering into her handbag. Her Dodge Phoenix was parked in the driveway, partially obscured by shrubs. Merle wasn't able to see whether anyone was in it, but she did see a young girl open the door and then stare strangely across at the car. None of this being unusual, Merle had gone back inside.

Swann apologised to Merle for bothering her again, declined her offer of a cup of tea. He took out the polaroid of Michelle and passed it to Merle, who grimaced at the death mask blasted with white light. She peered down her bifocals at the black eyes and dark hair and red lips that together made a face. She nodded tentatively.

'Like I said last time, my eyes aren't so good. But this could be her. Yes, I think it could be her. My God, so young! Is this the one in the papers?'

Swann squeezed Merle's forearm and put the polaroid away. He felt her eyes follow him down the path through her roses, but when he reached the car and looked back she was gone.

Next door, Ruby's house was dark and silent.

Donovan Andrews didn't look as frightened tonight. In the grey light cast by the old cenotaph, Swann could even see a grin on his face, and he didn't drop it when he saw Swann. Instead he shifted over on the park bench and jerked an arm behind him. Parked near the closest of the trees was a motorbike, polished and gleaming.

'BSA Gold Flash,' Swann observed. 'That a '61? I used to have one of those.'

Andrews' grin widened. 'I know. That's why I bought it. You always talked it up.'

'Common as a buggered back in my day, the BSA. Don't see them much any more. A bloody good bike, that one. Mancuso lend it to you?'

'Nah. That mug rides a Moto Guzzi. I bought this myself, with my hard-earned. That's my touring bike right there.'

'Jesus, Don, you don't muck around.'

'Gotta good missus finally, like I said. This one's a stayer, I reckon. I like her more than anyone yet.'

Swann sat down and spread his long legs over the grass. The city lights were reflected in the low cloud, the still river, the white trunks of the lemon-scented gums around them.

'That blood on you, Don? You done something I should know about?'

Andrews chuckled and looked down at the black stain across the front of his jeans, along the arms of his jacket. 'Nah, that's squid ink, mate, bits that missed my apron. Beyond caring about all that guts and stuff, I am. Even getting used to the smell of sardines. Might be something I could do up north too. Nick Mancuso's always goin' on about how the north's opening up. Maybe I could work on the boats, or do some drilling.'

'Where'd you get the money? That what you wanted to talk about?'

Andrews lit a cigarette, and for a moment his smile was dented by worry.

'Come on, Don. I've got to get to jail before lockdown.'

'And I've got to get back to work. How about I race ya; see who gets to Freo first?'

'How about you get on with it? Just come out and tell me.'

'Well, I didn't steal it, but that lawyer bloke workin' for Nick I told you about the other night? The one with that crazy D? He came back this afternoon looking for me. Said he'd give me a thousand bucks just to sign my name on a piece of paper. Wait, don't look like that. Nick was there, said it was all right, nothing dodgy brothers about it. Said he'd put in a thou to match the lawyer's.'

'Everything about Nick Mancuso is dodgy, Don. He's a heroin dealer for a start. Before that he sold stolen cars. Before that marijuana, in weight. Before that —'

'So he can afford it, right? All it was, Nick's buying some gear off old Franchino, some trucks and restaurant stuff – ovens and ranges, like I told you. They just wanted me to sign on as one of the directors of the old company. Nothin' can come back on me. I'm like a silent partner, don't have to do anything.'

'This is a scam, Don. Knowing about it might even be what got Ruby Devine killed.'

Andrews thought about that, but not for long. 'Two thousand bucks, man. Right then and there. That lawyer guy said if ever anybody asks me about it I just have to say a bloke came up to me in the pub, offered me a hunj for my signature. And that I was drunk so I did.'

'That company's designed to go bankrupt, Don. They sign on directors who can't be found, or who can be trusted to keep their mouths shut. Meanwhile Mancuso keeps all the merchandise. Did you see any other names?'

'Just mine and some guy called Casper Murray, a Painters and Dockers bloke I remember from years back.'

'What was the name of the company?'

'Hannan Enterprises, something like that.'

'They've got a sense of humour, at least. Sands must have stumbled over this tax loophole the way Paddy Hannan stumbled over that lump of gold.'

'Well, I wouldn't know about that.' Andrews bent over and tucked his boots inside the cuffs of his jeans. 'I'm leaving here, anyway. All that doesn't matter to me, or my girl. But before I go I'm still keeping an eye on Mancuso and the biz. As soon as I see something, beyond piles of money, I'll let you know. You can count on that.'

The earnestness in his voice was genuine, his need to please something Swann had always taken advantage of. And yet all this talk of leaving town – for Don's sake Swann hoped he meant it.

Swann was running late for his next meet, with Cooper in Nedlands, and was relieved to see the de Ville parked in shadows alongside the jetty, across from Steve's Hotel. It was quiet on the foreshore except for some prawners wading out in the black water down near the breakwall, head torches jumping in the low swell.

The parking spaces next to the de Ville were empty and Swann pulled into one. Cooper was sitting on the bonnet of his car, legs folded beneath him, drinking from a bottle of champagne. Beside him was a punnet of strawberries and a styrofoam tray containing the empty shells of a dozen oysters on a bed of melting ice. The radio drifted out of the open windows of the de Ville, dash speakers heavy on the treble.

'You heard this? Elton John. Saturday night's *alright* for *fighting*.' Cooper shuffled his arse around to get comfortable. 'I met Elton once, at a party at Ruby's house. Great party too. Even Elton ended up in the pool. Have some champers, Swann?' He held out the bottle.

Swann took in the label and thought about it, but declined. 'Tastes better from the bottle, does it?'

Cooper shook his head. 'Last-minute thing, this, no time to get glasses.'

'Every day's a celebration, eh?'

'Yeah. Every day.' Cooper wiped his mouth with the back of a silken sleeve. 'Y'know, I used to spear cobbler under this jetty. There's a sunken boat down there in about twelve feet. Couldn't ever see a bloody thing, but stab a gidgee in any gap of that boat and you'd come up with a cobbler. Used to sell them to the fish-and-chip shop back there. Door to door too. Fifty cents a fillet. Made a bit of money over the years selling 'em, but now I can't stand eating 'em. Probably a lesson in that.'

Cooper didn't look drunk, which told Swann that his preamble suggested something else. 'About what you were saying this morning,' he began.

Cooper shook his head. 'Don't know what you're talking about there.'

'Bullshit.'

'Seriously, I have blackouts. I woke up this afternoon with my head near the porcelain altar. Seems I didn't make it in time. Shat myself in my sleep. You don't want to know the rest.'

There was no point pushing him on what he'd said in his phone call – the Mancusos would never corroborate it anyway. Better to chip away where Cooper was really vulnerable.

'After that pretty picture, Cooper, I will have some of that champers.'

'No hard feelings?'

Because if Cooper had covered his tracks, why had he contacted Reggie to arrange the meet? The answer was obvious: he was worried about the federal taxman, thousands of kilometres away in Canberra, who, unlike the local coppers, couldn't be bought. Whether Cooper admitted it or not, remembered it or not, what Swann had heard in his voice this morning was fear, and misery.

The bottle was nearly full and Swann drank the shoulders off it. 'Thought you were in the red?' he said.

'I won't lie to you, Swann, I'm in some serious debt to some serious people.'

'Explains the champagne and oysters.'

'Got to keep the morale up. My dad taught me that.'

'Let me guess, Cooper. There was a break-in at your offices and all the paperwork relating to Ruby Devine's investments was pinched.'

Cooper laughed, pleased with himself.

'And,' Swann continued, 'a backdated police report on the theft has been subsequently filled out, to the letter.'

'To the letter,' Cooper agreed.

'Anything else?'

Cooper looked at him speculatively. 'I called my good mates at Crown Law; they've never heard of any tax investigation into me.'

'According to *my* mate in Canberra, they don't trust the local Crown Law prosecutors with shit. Over here, only the bottom of the barrel end up working for the state.'

'Well, that's true, if nothing else.'

'It's all true. They don't give up, those boys. Once they get a sniff. Look what happened to Ruby.' Swann took another long draw before passing the bottle back.

'For old time's sake then, Swann. Lest old acquaintances be forgot.' Cooper toasted the glittering yachts out on the dark river, the sounds of laughter and music on the wind. 'You tell your taxation mates they should be looking elsewhere instead of wasting their time on me. And that if they can see their way past my minor indiscretions, then I'll point them towards some very big fish. There's no shortage of the bastards, either. Half the Liberal Party are into this shit, they're getting greedy and fat. You seen how many new houses are coming up in Dalkeith, Applecross, City Beach? New money, all of it.'

The way Cooper said *new money*, his mouth puckered in disgust, told Swann what was coming next.

'There's a new boy in town.'

'I know about Solomon Sands. Perhaps you could get on with the specifics.'

Cooper laughed, spraying champagne over his shining bonnet. 'And there we were getting all nostalgic. Okay, if you're that impatient.'

'No need to pretend this is about anything other than bloody-mindedness, Cooper. If you're going to stick it to Sands, do it good. Then I'll finish with a little word of my own.'

'You aren't taping this, are you? Because I'm just telling you so you know.'

'Get on with it, Cooper. I've got other places to be. And I want time to explain to you that the only reason you're not dead already is because then you wouldn't be able to pay back the people who want to kill you.'

Cooper stared, suppressed a shudder. 'Ease up, Swann. I've already shat myself once today.'

'Get on with it, I said.'

But Cooper didn't. Instead he bent forward and held his guts. When he finally spoke it was in an eerily quiet voice. 'No joke, mate, I've got ulcers. These bastards, the new types, they make me sick.'

'So I see.'

'Good-time charlies, every one of them. Most are dumb micks who've got it in for people like me. Bloody cowboys acting like they already own the place, trying to take what my people built up over a hundred and fifty years.'

'Where's the money come from? Drugs?'

'Damn right it's drugs. Drugs and share-market scams. Tax rorts and gold cons, real-estate swindles and other miscellaneous rip-offs. But yeah, plenty of it's drugs. Ruby Devine used to pay Donald Casey five hundred a week to keep her brothels running. That's a lot of money over a year but it's got to be spread around, right up the food chain. You know how much a kilo of heroin costs in Kuala Lumpur and how much it sells for here, wholesale?'

'These new-money types are smuggling?'

Cooper laughed. 'No, they're investors. You wouldn't have learnt it in cop school, but it's basic share-market capitalism. It shares around the risk. Suppose I want to bring in heroin, for example, but I don't want to invest any money myself; I want to keep my financial exposure to zero risk. So I find five investors who want to make some quick money but don't want to risk direct involvement, have reputations to protect, et cetera, and I get them to put in ten grand each. Then I pay a few grand to a couple of couriers who bring me back five kilos within the week. I pay the investors triple what they put in, and if I sell it wholesale to the Italians I'm up almost three hundred grand. Not bad for a week's work. Then those investors put in another ten grand and off we go again.'

'I've heard rumours that the Mancuso brothers —'

'Yeah, well, that's the other alternative, and even more lucrative. Instead of wholesaling it, assuming I'm a certain detective inspector with the power to do whatever the fuck I want, I can set up people like the Mancusos, or Dom Franchino, Leo Ajello, someone with a respectable business face, pillars of the church and community, give them the green light and take an even bigger cut. So everybody's making money. Detectives are happy. They in turn make judges and politicians happy.'

Swann wondered how many of Cooper's ancestors had done exactly this – developed a conscience and a loose tongue right about the time the competition was getting the upper hand.

'And all the investors are happy,' Cooper was saying, 'and of course the really clever ones go to a bloke like Solomon Sands.'

'I get where he comes in, recycling the money, asset stripping and the rest, but what are these investors using the money for?'

'Influence. That amount of money can buy you a lot of authority, a lot of protection with certain people. These investors have already started to make donations to the political parties. Even the Liberal Party's taking their money, no questions asked. It's like the colony's starting all over again, like we're right back at the beginning. It's the future but it's all been done before.'

'Except this time your mob's on the outside.'

'In a few years nobody's going to remember that these cocky

bastards were once heroin dealers. Their start-up capital's going to buy them companies that get preferential contracts awarded by their new mates in government. It's only a matter of time before one of them opens his own bank to finance everything. Then they'll get the really big infrastructure projects. They'll start to make the old money look small-time. They'll buy the newspapers and the television channels and the pollies will love them even more. And the north's opening right up. All that iron ore. All those diamonds. All that gold. Who do you think will get the green light there?'

Cooper's voice had grown shrill but now it tailed off as he pressed the bottle to his lips and drank, long and deep this time.

'Ruby didn't know any of this, before you ask. But she always took their money if they were paying customers. At least prostitutes aren't hypocrites, unlike our pollies.'

'Never had you down as a moralist.'

'You got me on a bad day.'

'The trust-fund money you hold for your clients, the money you've been using to pay off your debts – some bad people are watching. And not just the taxman.'

Cooper peered down into the bottle, held it up and shook it around. 'This is nearly empty. You feel like some more? I've got credit behind the bar at Steve's.'

'You want to stick it to Sands and the people he's rorting for? You want the taxman to take it seriously, back off a bit? Put it all down on paper. All the details, all the names, on paper. We clear on that?'

Cooper nodded, lifted a forefinger into the air like an antenna. 'Hear that? Boz Scaggs. I met that bastard once too. He's even shorter than me.'

Swann knew something was wrong as soon as he got out of the car, but by the time he saw the men rise from the shadows opposite his hotel it was too late. There were three of them, wearing balaclavas and carrying revolvers. One of them looked like Sherving but it was hard to tell in the dark. They had the draw on him and he didn't reach for his .38. He didn't shout for help. He was conscious of this moment being preordained, right down to the ritual movements, the ritual fear.

There was nobody else around. There was all the time in the world.

The men spread out along the length of the Holden, one on either side of him, aiming at his chest. When the third stepped towards him Swann launched himself and punched, landing a right on the man's jaw, punching again as he doubled back. But he was pistol-whipped on the side of his neck, and the back of his head. He had his hands around the other's neck now, reaching for his eyes, but felt a numbness in his arms and then was paralysed, letting go but not falling, being held up. He took the blows to his stomach and ribs, was slung to the ground and kicked, stomped on. They worked him over methodically. The first time he heard a voice was when he was kicked in the back of his head: 'Not his face.'

Then the beating stopped and someone knelt over him and spoke in his ear. 'Little message from Casey about your lovely daughters. The two that are left. We're gonna fuck 'em, Swann. We're *all* gonna fuck 'em. Hard, like they like it. And you're gonna be there to watch.'

Laughter, as the speaker put a hand into Swann's jacket, pulled out his revolver. 'We'll be keeping this for down the track. When it all gets too much. We'll be right there to help you. See you down the track then, Swanny.'

So this wasn't to be the end of him, just yet. The kicking started again, and amid the flares of black and red inside his head he thought of his stepfather, who had taught him how to take his punishment, using fists and boots, and his mother just standing there watching.

He was parked in exactly the same spot as the brothel madam's Dodge on the night she was murdered. The rear of the Valiant faced the freeway, its lights cut, windows down. Behind him was the river, the caving-lights of prawners and people spearing catfish, the faint strains of the Raffles house band blowing up from the south.

One block in front of him was the zoo. He listened to the howling and whooping of the monkeys and thought of the animals who must have heard the four shots from the .22 on that rainy night. The bears and the great cats and the other carnivores who'd smelt her blood on the wind.

He knew from Marko that there were numerous rumours about who'd pulled the trigger and why. There was the diver who crawled out of the river and killed her and then went back in. There was the country cop from Merredin who came up for the day on his motorbike then buried his gun in the wheatbelt. Another story had it that the murder was linked to an armed robber currently doing a lag in Fremantle prison. Others claimed that a colourful racing identity, a silent partner in Ruby's brothels, had shot her, or that Ruby had threatened to name some Chinese who'd invested in her business.

Or DI Casey had done it, while sitting on the bench seat beside her. Or a couple of uniformed rookies, on Casey's orders, for the promise of a yearly payment for life and their kids' school fees looked after. Or a Sicilian gangster by the name of Franchino. Or Abe Saffron, on behalf of one of his local madams. A Painters and Dockers hitman who'd shipped in on a merchant vessel called the *Iron Yampi* the day before and shipped out the following day.

There were so many rumours he had stopped listening. From his experience the deliberate mixing of fact with fiction always worked in the interests of the killer: it reinforced the message intended by the killing while obscuring the perpetrator.

The rumours did tell him one thing, though – how much Perth had changed in the decade he'd been away. Growing up the son of a copper hadn't meant the people he met ever bothered to hide their loathing of the police. But tinged with that loathing was a kind of respect, an understanding of the way things had to be. In his father's day, the same police who were on the take from bookies and brothel owners would yet have dragged a bloke like Leo Ajello out into the bush and made him dig his own grave. They wouldn't have let someone like that get bigger than the law, even if he was an informer. Taking money off bookies and brothels did nobody any harm, that was the old way. But those days were gone. He knew better than most how it worked now. The brothel madam's murder was a sign of the city looking into its future, although the historians would probably see it differently.

He looked across at the empty passenger seat and it wasn't hard to put himself there. If things had been different it could have been him who pulled the trigger on the woman. Even as a junior cop he had still been out there stealing cars and moonlighting as security on the doors of clubs in Perth and Fremantle. He hadn't been the only rookie to know both sides of the street, although he wasn't like the others.

He hated the uniform, all the saluting and yessirs, nossirs. And when his father died, while he himself was still in the academy, and he went to the funeral and saw all his father's purple circle mates looking straight ahead, heard the speeches full of lies, he'd hated it even more.

But it wasn't his hatred of the rules and hypocrisy that got him out of the force. His first kill had been an accident. He was working the door at a club in the west end of Fremantle when a drunken stevedore wanted for murder came at him with a metal pipe. He'd pulled his knife and stuck it into him.

It was one of his father's detective friends, a man he'd always called uncle, who kept him out of jail on the manslaughter lag. The detective sergeant suggested he do a bolt east until things calmed down, join the army in the meantime; the guy had even pulled the arrest sheet out of the register and opened the cage at the Fremantle lockup.

Not a soul in Sydney knew he'd once been in the uniform, or that his father had been a detective, not even his wife.

He leant under the dash and brought the ignition wires together. The Valiant started with a jolt and as he turned on the headlights and put the shift into reverse he glanced once more at the passenger seat, saw not the ghost of the dead woman but the spectre of himself as he might have been.

Swann stared at himself in the bathroom mirror. His eyes had a hideous intensity in the morning light, brought on by the pain, but his face was unmarked. He pressed his ribs one by one, working down from his collarbone to find the source of shooting pain. There was nothing broken but his ribs were heavily bruised. The painkillers he took when he woke had helped, as had a mouthful of vodka from a near-empty bottle.

Twisting carefully in front of the mirror he saw that the flesh around his spine was crosshatched with boot marks. The area around his kidneys was the colour of blood. There was asphalt ground into the palms of his hands.

Crawling into his room last night he was glad they'd taken his revolver – it would have been too easy to drive it under his chin and end the pain, which was coming in waves, causing him to break out in a sweat. He had vomited then, and felt better for it. Had lain on the tacky carpet in the foetal position and taken slow control of his breathing. The nausea rose again as the pain subsided. He spent the next hour in the bathroom, curled inside the shower stall, face pressed against the tiles, cold water on his head when the pain got too much. When he made it to bed he dreamt he was in court. His hands folded on the table before him like a schoolboy, waiting to be told to stand and speak, not knowing what he was meant to say.

He put on a crisp white shirt, tucked it into clean trousers, tightened the belt. He had lost weight. The shirt too sagged a little. He had to sit on the bed to tie his laces.

Outside, an easterly was blowing and it was too hot for a jacket, but he wore one anyway to conceal his empty .38 holster. Taking his gun was insult on top of injury, and he needed to get it back. The likelihood that they'd use it to frame him was high. That they would use it to shoot him was even higher.

He felt like escaping. He wanted to be with Marion and his daughters, wanted to lie down among them and hold them safe, but he knew that once home he would never get up.

Gingerly he put his damaged hands on the wheel of the Holden, headed through the quiet streets. The suburbs were like a silent dream – a family packing the car for a trip to the beach, towels slung over shoulders, dog scampering between sunburnt legs; an old man on his verandah absorbed in the paper, sunshine wreathing his nut-brown head. Swann pulled onto Stirling Highway and headed west towards the prison.

Hergenhan turned the polaroid of Michelle over and licked it, then stuck it to his forehead. 'Can I keep this? It's always nice for a fella to have a snap of his girl.'

Swann stared at him, but there was nothing in his face. 'You know, Ray, what Michelle proposed to Jacky, it's still possible.'

'Hard to spend money when you're locked up, not to mention when you're dead.'

'I can do something there.'

'Hard to do things if you're dead yourself, detective.'

Swann shifted his aching body. 'All we need is a signed statement. Something I can take to the royal commissioner. If it's good you'll be looked after.'

Hergenhan whistled sarcastically but his eyes were interested.

'And I'll get you out of here, like I said. You can make a new start.'

'And how do you propose to do that? Gonna hoist me out in a helicopter? Dig yerself a tunnel? Buy the head screw a new house?'

'That depends on what you give me, Ray. The royal commission's got the power to get you moved somewhere safe, if you turn witness. And immunity if you follow through. A new face. A new life.'

Hergenhan frowned, thought about it. Both of them knew he'd be the same fuckup wherever he went, but the offer was clearly worth considering.

'Why didn't you tell me Michelle was babysitting for Ruby the night she was shot? I could've helped. It might have saved her life.'

'Don't know what you're talking about there. I don't know about Ruby Devine, but I wouldn't trust Michelle around my kids. She wasn't the responsible type.'

'Did she say who she saw at the house on the night?'

'Wouldn't want to fib now, would I?'

'We both know Casey had Michelle killed. And you're next – sooner, when he finds out you've approached me with a story.'

'Nah, mate. See, that's where you've got it wrong. Michelle approached you with her story. And now she's dead she can't talk no more. Got nuthin' to do with me.'

'You think Casey will see it that way? You're no better off than me. Soon as you're no more use you're finished.'

'Oh, I'm a useful kinda fella, detective. Always have been, always will be. Lucka the Irish, mate.'

'Something my father-in-law once told me, Ray – how it all works. Everything you can see passes away, everything you can't is permanent.'

'What? What the fuck is that supposed to mean? He some kind of fucken preacher or something? You're madder than they say, you know that?'

'You know what it means. And you know exactly why I'm saying it. Casey's screwed up. He reckons he's bigger than the game. That's why you're so afraid of him. That's why everybody's afraid of him.'

'I ain't afraid.'

'No, *I'm* the one who's not afraid. I know about Pat Chesson's girls muling, some of them washed up on beaches – another one just yesterday. And Michelle put down like a dog. You know Casey was behind that, and I know who's been protecting him, higher up.'

'Yeah? Well, maybe you do, but I don't know anything about any of it.'

'You know that once all this hits the media you're a loose end. You're history.'

'Nah, I was just mouthing off, trying to liven things up.' Hergenhan's words were hollow and he knew it. He sat back and stared at his hands. When he looked up his eyes had lost their heat.

'Tell you what, detective,' he said at last. 'Supposing I *was* interested, how about I made you a deal? If you're still alive one month after the royal commission, and you've got the readies, *and* you've got me a new face, I'll tell you what I know.'

'That's not much use to me right now, is it? And without me you won't last that long.'

Hergenhan nodded gravely, with the kind of face he might use in court. 'You could be right. But if I help you now and then you're dead next week, I'm in the same boat, aren't I? It's a gamble either way.'

Swann shook his head and stood to leave, but Hergenhan was up off his bunk and blocking the doorway.

'Get out of my way, Raymond.'

Hergenhan didn't budge. He tried to sneer but there was desperation in his eyes. 'I look under that shirt, you're all black and blue, right?'

It was instinct for Swann to hide his injuries, instinct for Hergenhan to notice.

'Last time I'm telling you. Get out of my way.'

Hergenhan loomed over him, fists bunched. 'You know why I ain't backin' you, detective? Cos I don't trust you. You used to have a reputation, man. I heard you'd gone all foreman material, but fuck me.'

Swann stepped into Hergenhan, could smell him now. On a good day he could take him, but not today. Hergenhan was right about that. He put everything he had left into his eyes, but it wasn't going to be enough.

'Times have changed, Hergenhan. So have I.'

'Not in here they haven't. Law of the jungle, mate. No *way* I can trust you to protect me. You've lost your touch. Truth is, I miss the old Swann. The one who would've had me up against the wall by now, goin' the bash. Where's he gone? I heard what you did to Mitch Davey, the dobbin' bastard, but it don't seem possible looking at you now. What about me? You haven't showed *me* the respect I deserve. Haven't even laid a hand on me.'

Swann felt the power in his arms, his body telling him what to do. Left jab to the ribs, grab the hair and bring up his knee. But first he needed to step back.

Hergenhan made it easy for him, took a step away. Swann saw the guard at the same time as Hergenhan sensed him, billy club turned out, eyes on Hergenhan's neck.

'I'll see you in a month,' said Swann.

'See ya before then, I reckon.'

Swann had always hated hospitals. Entering one was like entering a bad dream – the pickled smells and strip lighting, the eerie comic undertones.

Jacky was in the smallest room in the farthest corner on the highest floor of Fremantle hospital, the room usually reserved for wounded criminals under guard. Swann showed his badge to the nurse at the desk, but the guard's seat was empty. There didn't appear to be any plainclothes around either. No guard and no detectives meant that Jacky was no use to the police.

He closed the door behind him. Jacky lay propped up on a wall of pillows. She'd been beaten to the point of death; her face was like a demented sunset. Oily red ridges and violet knots overlaid the dark grain on her cheeks and jaw. Her scalp was stitched like a baseball; her left ear looked like a gnawed bone. One of her eyes was an exploded red marble, the other swollen and closed.

He could see she was doped to the eyeballs – Reggie had made sure to tell the doctor about her habit, to up the regular morphine dose. He could feel the remnants of violence in the room, an invisible threat that fed into his own bashing the night before. It made the palms of his hands itch and his shoulders tense. He felt the blows still raining down on both of them. He had taken a savage beating but it was nothing like this.

He pulled a chair up to the bed, in line with her good eye.

She had watched him come towards her. 'Give me a ciggie, Swann? They won't let me.'

He looked down at her wrists, bandaged where the bastards had opened her veins, and shook his head. 'You don't look like you can manage one.'

She blinked like a lizard. 'Then help me.'

He lit a cigarette and put it between her mangled lips. She manoeuvred them around the filter but couldn't form a proper seal. Somehow she managed to smile. 'Lot to be said for a finger in a dyke,' she croaked.

'Heard that one before, Jacky.'

She tried to laugh, made a keening sound instead. 'One of Ruby's sayings.'

'Yeah, it was.' He reached into his shirt pocket. 'You up to looking at a few pictures for me?'

'Sure, if I can see 'em.'

He held one up level with her eye. 'You know this girl?'

She looked, then closed her eye. When she reopened it she nodded, swallowed. 'That's Debbie. Debbie McGinnis. What happened?'

'She was washed up on a beach twelve months ago, still a Jane Doe. They're cremating her tomorrow.'

'You set that *straight*, Swanny. She's Debbie McGinnis, North Shore girl gone mental. She one of the two I told you about?'

'Looks like it. You know when she came west?'

'Yeah. A bit after me, but I didn't see her much. Her airs and graces put plenty of us girls offside, plenty of blokes too. Makes some blokes uneasy, using girls from their own class.'

'She have any family who need to know?'

Jacky tried to shake her head. 'She was never a runaway. But she didn't have anyone who cared.'

'What about this one?' He held up the polaroid of Michelle's roommate.

Jacky didn't react at all. She lay perfectly still, silent. Barely breathing.

'Jacky?'

When she exhaled it was with a hard sob. She bit down on it. '*Jesus*. That's Trace. An old mate of mine. We're the same age. Started out together, even locked up together for a while. Redfern girl. We was lovers for a bit there too.'

He reached for the box of tissues beside the bed and spoke gently. 'Last night she also washed up on a northern beach. Just like the others.'

'Christ, you've got to *do* him, Swanny. *You've* got to do him.'

He made no reply. But he squeezed her hand, a kind of promise. Her skin was cold and dry, and she appeared to have shut down completely, mid-breath. Jacky was about as tough as they got, but she was frightened.

Swann felt so tired he wanted to put his head on the bed and sleep. He placed Jacky's hand back on the blanket and left.

He found Mitchell Davey in a public ward in the southern wing. The beds around him were empty and Davey was shirtless above the tucked sheets, his ribs strapped. Tattoos flowed red and green and blue over his shoulders. A painted bird up one arm, a shark across his chest, naked dancer down the other arm. An Iron Cross on his neck. One of his wrists was plastered and over his head he wore a gruesome steel frame, vice stems pressed into his skull, bolted into his jaw.

It was cool in the ward but Davey was sweating with the pain, his forehead beaded with silver. When he caught sight of Swann his eyes widened and he grappled for the call button on the sheets. The exertion forced his tongue through his missing front teeth.

Gently Swann flicked away the call button and put his finger to his lips. Smiled. His own ribcage and back were aching, making it hard to hold the smile. He put his gravel-rashed fingers on Davey's throat, which was unshaven and cold, and felt the rapid pulse there. The raised veins. There was froth on Davey's lips.

Swann held the carotids down and counted to ten. When Davey started to struggle he pressed down with his elbow into his broken ribs, felt the legs kick then settle. Just as Davey started to pass out he lessened the pressure and let him gasp for air. Then he did it all over again, taking Davey right up to the point where it would end, lessening the pressure and bringing him back.

He removed his fingers and leant right over him, face to face. Davey gasped again. There were tears in his eyes.

Swann held up the polaroid of Tracey. 'There she is, you *see*?' he hissed. 'Look at her. Look at *Tracey*!' Keeping his voice low.

Davey looked. A minute passed.

When Swann spoke it was in a whisper, right at Davey's ear. 'Who did you give Tracey to? Where did you take her?'

Davey tried to speak but no words came out.

'What? Didn't quite get you.'

Davey spluttered through his broken teeth, nasal and whiny. 'Casey, and Shervo. I took her to Casey's yacht club.'

'You go out with them on the launch? You see what happened?'

'No, I swear. I —'

'But you knew what was going to happen, didn't you?'

Davey closed his eyes. 'Yes.'

'The heroin – they still using your girls?'

Davey kept his eyes closed, whispered, 'No.'

'So how's it brought in now?'

Davey clenched his broken jaw, body twitching with the pain. Swann put his hand back on the man's throat, found the carotids and began to press. Watched the eyes open wide and fade to black. Brought him back again.

'I'm still here, Davey. Never going to leave you now.'

Davey fought to catch his breath. 'I don't know,' he got out finally. 'Something to do with Mick Isaacs, the horse trainer. And a vet. Importing Indo furniture. But I'm not involved.'

Swann leaned closer. 'Who did Ruby? Give me the name. And don't say Ray Hergenhan.'

The sweat made Davey's face shine like plastic wrap. The spit on his lips had turned pink. 'I'm not fucking suicidal. I'm not gonna ask – they'd have to kill me.'

'Who'd have to kill you?'

'You know who.'

'Say it.'

Davey swallowed and closed his eyes again. 'Casey.'

'Louder.'

'*Casey.*'

'You're on tape now, Davey,' Swann lied. 'I own you, you understand? I'll be back later, let you know what you can do for me.'

By the time Partridge had completed the short walk from his hotel to the ferry terminal his shirt was drenched in sweat. He wiped his handkerchief across his forehead, noticing with alarm the number of flies attached to the shoulders of the woman before him in the queue. He could see blue and green tints in the black mass.

He reached a tentative hand over his own shoulder and cringed as a cloud rose above him. He was tempted to return to the comfort of his hotel, but the queue had moved and it was his turn at the counter. He bought his ticket and clambered across the rocking walkway onto the Swan River ferry.

He took a seat on the starboard side, away from the sun, but this meant that the hot easterly wind was in his face. The river was the colour of beer, its surface creamy with bubble-shaped jellyfish. There were hundreds of them, the smaller ones on the froth, the larger ones drifting in the murk.

The commentary started when the engine did. Tourists in floppy hats and shorts and sandals listened to an acne-pitted man with one hand on the ceiling rail, the other wielding a microphone. His eyes scanned the audience and lingered rather obviously on the bare legs of a teenage girl. When the man's eyes met his own Partridge looked away to the foreshore, receding now in the sculpted wake.

It was time to take his medicine. Partridge felt in his shirt pocket for the jar of nitroglycerine tablets, loosened the cap and tipped two onto his palm. He swallowed them, tasted the residue in his mouth, carbonate and something bitter. The rocking of the ferry made him sleepy and he dozed for a while, before the microphone roused him.

When he opened his eyes again they were far upriver. The white light over the water and trees seemed to have yellowed. The liver spots on his hands seemed to glow against his skin. The fervent commentary plugged his ears.

He didn't know whether it was because he hadn't slept well or because of the lingering effects of his illness, but there was an unreality about the weatherboard houses crowded together on the narrowing banks. They were identical, painted the same pale green. On the bank a group of children were swinging on a rope and playing in the mud. Their egg-white chests contrasted with their nut-brown arms, scabby knees and sunburnt noses. They stared dumbly at the passing ferry as though it were an expeditionary vessel and not an hourly venture.

The yellowed light had taken on a distinctly orange pall, and smoke shrouded the water ahead. The ferry lurched, then began to ease towards a small jetty, their destination of Guilford, according to the commentator, an old settlement now part of the eastern suburbs. Children fishing drew in their lines and pulled their feet back from the edge. The commentator threw a rope and leapt enthusiastically off the ferry, followed more slowly by Partridge and the other passengers.

Then his lunch host was at his side. 'Your Honour?' Bill Standard was the National Party MP for Wagin, a large seat in the wheatbelt region. He was tall and rangy and his handshake was firm. 'Great to meet you. Thanks for coming out here, know you're busy. Car's this way.' He waved an arm.

'Sorry about the smoke,' he continued as they walked across to a Ford LTD parked illegally, engine still running. 'The kids are always lighting fires on the weekend. It's not my suburb this time; it's away at Lesmurdie, thank God. Though the damn easterly's got hold of it. We're all hoping the sea breeze will come in early, push it back into the hills. Anyway, got air conditioning, hop in!'

Partridge eased himself onto the chilled leather upholstery while Bill Standard made his half-circuit around the car.

The Fremantle cemetery was a short drive from the hospital. Swann bought an iced coffee at a deli on the way and swallowed two more painkillers. He didn't realise he was headed to the grave of Marion's father until he found himself there.

George Monroe was buried in the Anglican section. He hadn't been a religious man but when he was dying he and Swann walked down the cemetery hill to have a look at the place. Swann held his arm as he puffed and wheezed his way between the rows of graves, through the Orthodox section with its ornate plots, inverted-looking crosses, Cyrillic writing and large headstones. The Catholic section was just as well tended – a great deal of money had been spent on the graves there. Marble headstones and tombs, gold and silver inscriptions, pictures of the Virgin Mary.

They came to the Protestant section. The area was not cared for. Low cement headstones, many fallen or cracked. Not a single flower or sign of remembrance on any of the graves. A rusted sprinkler lay on its side.

'All right, here's me,' George chuckled. 'This is where I belong.'

He paused under an old gum tree where no grass grew, which

seemed to comfort him. 'Get me under a tree if you can, otherwise it doesn't matter. But tell Marion no fancy coffin. Just a pine box.'

On the way back to the car George tried out epitaphs. 'How about "I'd rather be here than in Bunbury"?' he suggested, and wheezed with laughter. Bunbury was his first posting as a young constable and he'd hated it. Bunbury was where his wife had died.

And there, now, was the inscription, at Swann's feet. It had been a large funeral, with bagpipes and kilts and some funny speeches from friends. At the wake the priest got drunk and disgraced himself by touching someone up. The bagpipe player squawked in the suburban backyard as the party went on until dawn.

Swann stood looking down at the grave, his fists clenching. George Monroe had guided him, back when he was wild and needed a guide. He'd explained to Swann the difference between justice and the law, had told him that the law was merely force translated into words. That beyond this frontier of words there was only terror and fear and the purity of the decisive act. That murder was itself the truth, beyond the frontier.

The bastards had threatened Swann's family. He had no idea whether Louise was alive or dead.

He remained standing there, at his father-in-law's grave, head bowed. He sought the protection of a ghost, but that did not make him feel vulnerable. On the contrary, he felt a fierce strength grow inside him, locking his heart and mind and body together.

The crematorium was tucked away just behind the cemetery gates. People were milling around outside, men in black suits and plain ties, women in dark skirts and hats. Swann lit a final cigarette before he went in, concealed from the mourners by a stand of tea-tree.

He checked the listing at the entrance. There was a blank space where Debbie McGinnis's name should have been, alongside the allotted time, which allowed only fifteen minutes. After that the schedule was full for the rest of the day – fifteen cremations in all.

Inside, within the panelled walls of the crematorium, Swann was the only person there, except for Debbie in her unvarnished box. He took a seat as a young woman in a grey suit entered from a side door. She seemed surprised to find him there; was about to say something then thought better of it. She stood by the coffin and waited, hands crossed in front of her. Then she checked her watch, looked across to where the flowers for the next service had been piled on a table. She glanced back at Swann and checked her watch again, impatient to pull the silver lever.

It would have been more honest to give Debbie to old Abraham and his hospital incinerator, he thought. Let her pass into flames with all the other garbage. The empty crematorium seemed crueller. The organ silent by the wall. The woman in grey scratching her nose.

Swann saw Donovan Andrews even before he came in. He was peering through the stained-glass windows behind the altar, talking to someone standing alongside. His companion entered first. High heels clattering on the tiled floor. A strong smell of Juicy Fruit chewing gum. Both Andrews and his girlfriend lifted their sunglasses when they noticed him. Marcia from Dubbo was caught with her mouth open, gum flattened on her tongue. In her mini-skirt and heels she looked exactly like an off-duty prostitute. She closed her mouth and began chewing again.

Andrews came towards him but Swann shook his head and the pair moved on down the aisle. The woman in grey stared at them as Marcia broke loose from Andrews and took some flowers from the table to place on the coffin.

'Can I see her?' Marcia asked.

The woman frowned. Shook her head solemnly.

'She was my best friend. You don't even know who she is, do you?'

The woman blushed and bit her lip. She looked like she wished they'd leave. Checking her watch a final time she moved her hand closer to the lever.

'Do you want to say anything? About your best friend?'

'Yeah, sure.' Marcia turned back to the coffin. 'You sleep well, sister. Leave it up to me an' Donny. We'll get the bastards —'

'Babe,' Andrews urged, 'just say goodbye.'

Marcia bent and caressed the coffin, kissed it. The woman pulled the lever and the coffin dropped down, began to trundle away on slow rubber tracks towards the furnace.

Swann intercepted them outside the main door. 'What the hell was that about?' he asked Andrews.

'Jus' paying our respects. Marcia and Debbie was mates, is all.'

She pushed him in the side. 'That's *not* all. Debbie was the reason I come over here. She looked after me back east. I've been looking for her everywhere. Thought she'd moved on again. Nobody told me she was dead.'

'How did you find out?'

'This morning's paper, of course. Picture of a girl who drowned yesterday identified, picture of two others. I recognised Debbie as one of them right away. Didn't give her name, but said where she was going to be cremated. Front-page story. *You're* in it too. In the headline.'

'Don't believe everything you read.'

'I don't. I believe Donny. Says you're no pervert.'

Donovan Andrews was fidgeting, looking nervously over at the front gates. As far as Swann was aware, Marcia was the first person Andrews had confided in about his relationship with Swann.

Andrews was understandably anxious about being seen with him, but there was more to it than that – he looked like a bashful son bringing home his first girlfriend.

'Don't look so surprised, Mr Policeman. Donny told me all about you this morning, when I told him I knew Debbie. He told me how he knew you. How you've been helping the girls. Looking out for us. Putting it on the line for Ruby. That time you came to the kennel and bashed Mitch, I didn't know who you were. If I did I would've talked to you.'

'I appreciate that, Marcia. But don't be talking around other people.'

Andrews took her arm. 'Babe, let's go,' he said.

'No, I ain't goin' anywhere. You didn't have to come, I told you that. But I've made my decision. Mr Swann, I wanna help, maybe some of the other girls too. There's Michelle done in, and rumours about Trace now. I can tell you about the pigs at the kennel, what I heard them say to Mitch, what I seen there.'

Donovan Andrews was so desperate to leave that his keys were shaking in his hand. Swann looked around at a new crowd of black-suited mourners. One of them, he had no doubt, had been watching out for him, watching the front gate.

Marcia was waiting for his response, looking at him with the wide eyes of a defiant child. Swann was afraid for her, proud of her, ashamed of himself. This was what it had come down to – a teenage girl and a drug-addled snitch.

The milling crowd parted for a hearse. 'You still have that money?' he asked Andrews, who nodded, tapping his pockets.

'Then if you two really want to help me, don't go back to the boarding house. Get on the BSA and head to Darwin. I'll find you when I need you. And most important of all, in the meantime keep your traps shut, and I mean shut.'

Whatever it was in Swann's voice, the urgency, the care, the anger, made Marcia grab him by the lapels of his jacket, pull him down and kiss him on the cheek. A daughter's kiss, and he didn't want her to let go.

'Now, get lost. Quick.'

Donovan Andrews didn't need telling twice. He took Marcia's hand and they strode off like lovers eloping.

Partridge yielded to another slice of sweating cheese from the platter. He was being force-fed by Bill Standard's granddaughter and he didn't have the strength to resist. Four-year-old Melanie had him in a stranglehold. Her knees dug into his thighs as she leaned back to test his expression.

Standard's house was in Kalamunda, in the hills overlooking Perth. While the exterior was impressive – architect-designed, no doubt – the interior was a little too garish for Partridge's taste, and he'd immediately agreed to lunch on the balcony.

'Mmm, delicious. Thank you, Melanie. That's enough for now.'

For the hundredth time Standard said, 'Leave his Honour alone, Melanie,' but she reached immediately for another piece of cheese while Standard glared at a fly in his beer.

Partridge shifted in his seat and repeated, 'It's probably about time I was getting back.'

'They won't be long now.'

Having offloaded Melanie on the men, Standard's wife and eldest daughter had taken the car into town. Standard wouldn't hear of the judge taking a taxi to the ferry; to allow that as a host would be rude, he insisted.

Partridge had turned down several other invitations from politicians in Perth, but had accepted Standard's because his was one of the names the PI had lifted off the radar. His bluff manner and cheery smile, his large gestures and loud voice were part of the naïvety he projected, the lack of guile. He appeared to talk off the top of his head, even as Partridge was aware of being measured, lured into some kind of response.

Then suddenly Standard changed tack. 'You know,' he said, 'my friends in the police are furious. Their reputation has been dragged in the mud by this fellow Swann. It's bloody ugly, to say the least. You can imagine how it is in a place like Perth – everybody who matters knows everybody else. But that doesn't mean we mind our own business. On the contrary, here the common good means an awareness of what is in all our best interests. Troublemakers tend to stand out for that reason.'

On the surface of it, Bill Standard was an undistinguished backbencher, but the PI had described him as a muckraking facilitator who worked both sides of the fence. What both sides of the fence had in common was the economic prosperity of the state, as Standard himself put it, a bipartisan merging of official and private interests wherever possible.

'This great state,' he told Partridge without irony, 'is wide open for business.'

According to the PI, Standard was the go-to man for people who wanted something done, or not done. People who had the money but lacked the means. It seemed that Standard could, on behalf of his cronies, get motions passed in parliament; he could get projects fast-tracked or shelved with a single phone call. He could arrange for journalists to undermine or shore up reputations. He could guarantee blocs of council or party votes, get branch members elected or disendorsed. His power was entirely the result of the relationships he cultivated and the information he collected.

Standard refilled his beer and topped up Partridge's glass. 'There have been rumours, unreliable I'm sure, that you're considering complaining about the scope of the royal commission to the governor, in effect going over the premier's head.' He ploughed his balding scalp. 'Now, I know this is unlikely, after all the evidence undermining Superintendent Swann's credibility as a witness, but the uncertainty is taking its toll.'

Partridge could scarcely believe what he'd just heard. The man looked like he'd merely asked for the time of day. He drew himself together. 'Beyond the fact that the governor is on holiday in Europe and therefore unavailable, I'm sorry, I can't possibly discuss —'

'Of course, of course. But it would be reassuring to hear your position on the matter. My friends would be very pleased to hear what you have to say. Very pleased and grateful. Like I said, this state is wide open — Ah, look who's here.'

Partridge made to stand, believing Standard's wife had returned, but his relief turned to dismay when he saw Police Minister Sullivan appear from the kitchen, wearing shorts and thongs and grinning over the top of a freshly opened stubby. His entrance onto the balcony made Melanie finally desert Partridge's lap and run after the dog.

'Des, how good to see you. Take a seat.' Standard shook Sullivan's hand with mock formality and the minister rounded the table, holding out his hand to Partridge.

'Your Honour.'

'Minister.'

Sullivan gave Partridge's hand an effete squeeze, a sarcastic gesture. 'Don't worry, your Honour,' he said brightly, 'this isn't an ambush.' He turned to Standard. 'Didn't know you had company, Bill. Thought you might be up for some fishing on the river. Got some you-beaut Jap lures. Drives the flathead crazy. Pity the blowies don't mind them either. You like fishing, your Honour?'

'On occasion. But not for many years.'

'Probably just as well. That black mud can get a wee bit stinky this time of year. Doesn't rain much, of course, the river doesn't get flushed.'

Sullivan sat down and swigged on his beer, smiling. He put on a BBC accent. 'And how do you like our little burgh, your Honour? First impressions?'

'Beautiful, thank you.' Partridge didn't believe for a moment that Sullivan had merely dropped in. He was enjoying himself too much, as was Standard, looking out over the view now, but alert. Both of them were putting on a show. They were too clever to be direct, but there was scorn there in the playing up of the class differences, the fake curiosity, the schoolboy mockery, and now the deliberate crudity of Sullivan's gestures, scratching at his stomach, which was threatening to spill out onto the wooden seat.

'Well, here we are,' Sullivan said in his normal voice, but Partridge heard an edge in it.

He let the silence build. Sullivan's eyes took on a subtle malice, reading Partridge with the knowing stare of an ex-policeman.

It was the minister who finally broke the silence. 'I'm aware you had a meeting with the premier recently,' he said. 'And that you requested he broaden the terms of reference of the commission.'

'That's correct. He refused.'

'Of course he did,' Standard put in, the contempt in his voice taking Partridge by surprise. 'This is *our* state; we shouldn't even be in the bloody Commonwealth. Our state, our business. And our money.'

Partridge observed him calmly. The acidity of Bill Standard's manner was offset by the comical puffing up of his lanky body. He looked like an aged schoolyard bully.

'What Bill is trying to say, your Honour, is that you're not half the man the premier is. You didn't serve in the war, did you?'

'No, I didn't see any action.'

Standard and Sullivan laughed together. 'I can tell,' Sullivan said. 'I can tell that just by looking at you. Bill and I were on the Kokoda Trail.'

'I lost a brother-in-law and a cousin in PNG, but I fail to see the significance.'

'They some of those coward Victorians they had to force to go up there, were they?'

'What's your point?'

The minister smiled again but his eyes were set hard. Partridge knew that look all too well.

'It was tough up there, wasn't it, Bill? We didn't take prisoners. We didn't take a single one. You understand what I'm saying, your Honour?'

Partridge gave them nothing beyond his placid courtroom face, curious to see where this would go.

'But back to the matter in hand, your Honour, irrelevant as it may be. Now that the premier has said no to your request, now that Superintendent Swann is, shall we say, fucked, may I inquire as to your intentions in seeking a widening of the terms of reference?'

Partridge was surprised by how well he was feeling. The imperative of not showing weakness before these two carnivores overrode all else. He cleared his throat. 'Were they to be broadened, I'd most likely start by bringing in a team of my own investigators, impartial and experienced.'

He ignored Standard's snort of derision and locked himself deep into Sullivan's stare. 'Having done this, I'd requisition the financial records of all serving detectives, past and present, who have worked in the Consorting Squad, those who have had dealings with the madams of the larger establishments. And once my teams are out working, why not have them look at the financial records of the fraud, armed robbery, drug, liquor and gaming squads too?'

Bill Standard was silent now, matching the stillness of Sullivan.

'But why stop with an examination of the financial records? Bookies and stockbrokers would need to be interviewed, as potential money-launderers. Land deeds would be searched, along with private and commercial deeds and trusts taken out in the names of family members – and leases taken out for mining purposes too, of course. Directorships of companies would need examining to see whether or not any detectives had diversified their interests into that realm of private enterprise. Assuming that anything had come of the investigation thus far, I imagine that I'd also want to speak to the heads of interstate and international companies, to determine whether kickbacks had been solicited for the right to operate in this state – you see the model I'm working with here? The same model the Consorting Squad has allegedly used over the years to regulate but also profit from illegitimate business. I'd have to see how it might have spread into other areas.' Partridge stopped, looked in turn at the two men facing him.

Standard laughed viciously. 'You're fishing in a dry river there, son.'

'Perhaps.' Partridge smiled at them both. 'Perhaps,' he repeated, 'but that would be just the beginning, I can guarantee you. One thing leads to another, as they say. Another area I'd be focusing my attention on is taxation, seeing as it was the unfortunate Mrs Devine's tax bill that seems to have started this whole affair. Personally, I'd be interested to see how her murder might have been related to the current investigations into these Bottom of the Harbour tax rorts I keep hearing about – a loophole first discovered in Western Australia, as I understand it, but now part of a much larger system of fraud. With links to the more nefarious sectors of the national banking system, shonky government investment, organised crime . . .'

The combative postures of Sullivan and Standard had fallen away now. Both of them were sitting back in their seats, eyes afire. Partridge had seen that look in court many times over the years – the calmness that comes over the violent man who's been exposed, condemned, brought low, but who preserves his dignity by a belief in certain revenge. Partridge had been partly fishing, sure enough, but now had little doubt that the insult he'd done these two was felt deeply; his bluffing had cast light on the truth.

The silence endured. Beneath the balcony a crow moaned.

'Leaving us, your Honour? Or has a woman walked into the room?' Sullivan sneered. But he had the look of an animal who'd lost its prey.

It was always three times round the track with someone like Ray Hergenhan. Not until Sunday morning did the significance of his invitation to bash him become clear to Swann.

It gave him no pleasure to see that he was right. In twenty-four hours Hergenhan had changed from proud crim to something the prison system was designed to make of him – a broken man. All his defiance was gone and he could barely meet Swann's eye. He sat on his bunk and stared at his feet, cradling a small contraption that Swann had hoped never to see again.

'You really going to use that?' he asked.

Hergenhan closed his hand around the mousetrap – a device consisting of two nails wrapped in a tightly wound elastic band, the whole fixed by a second, thinner band. Once swallowed the thing worked its way down into the stomach, where acid ate away the weaker band until the trap sprung and the nails cut into the stomach wall.

The mousetrap was a brutal and potentially deadly means of getting out of prison and into hospital, requiring an operation to remove the nails and staunch internal bleeding.

'Where's your cellmate?' Swann asked when he got no reply.

'They moved him for good. Back to 2 Div where he belongs.'

'So you're all alone.'

'Yep.'

Swann lit Hergenhan a cigarette, handed it to him. 'Talk to me,' he said.

Hergenhan grunted. 'How about this? Not *one* fucker on this planet's gonna miss ol' Raymond when he's gone.'

'Come on, Ray.'

Hergenhan tried to mock his self-pity but only frowned. 'You know how it is – you're in here long enough, you can see the future in every bastard's eyes. That mongrel head screw of 4 Div has been lookin' at me funny. Yesterday he walked past with one of the other screws, joking how it's nearly time to take out the garbage. Pair of fucken dogs.'

'I know you want to get out of here, Ray. And why you need to. So talk to me.'

Hergenhan nodded slowly. 'I'm gonna tell you the truth, detective. Out of respect, you understand? But for fuck's sake, treat me like a man in return. None of that shit about getting me out of here. That's just salt in the fucken wounds. I've gotta make my peace, okay?'

Swann agreed by remaining silent.

'So, the truth. The fucken truth, detective, and nothing but the truth. I'm only telling you this outta respect, like I said. All those other bastards saw me for what I was – stone-cold, man, stone-cold. Just tried to take advantage, use me, never tried to change me.'

'I get it, Ray.'

'The truth is I had nothing to do with the murder of Ruby Devine. And I don't know who did it either, beyond the fucken obvious.'

'So you were played, Ray?'

'Fucken oath I was. But you know, a killing like Ruby's – in here, it's good for the rep. I never said I *didn't* do it.'

'Go on.'

'We had a falling out, Casey and me. We were tight for a while there, but all things must end. Not that it's gonna do you much good. My word against his and all that.'

'What was the thing you had going with Casey?'

'The fucker good as green-lit me. I've been doing armed robs for him for years. Everything was sweet. But then he came up with this new bullshit idea. Wanted me to *deal* for him. Never has trusted the dings, has Casey. Can't control them enough. Wanted me to distribute for him instead, as the front man, in weight too, but I refused. Front man in that business is always the fall guy. He thought I was stupid enough to want the cash and take the hit when the bust came. It don't mean much to a mongrel like Casey, but I'm armed robbery, not fucken drug dealing – that stuff is for dogs and curs. Specially after I seen what it did to my dad. Got a back wound in the Korean War, never got off the stuff. So I told Casey to stick it up his arse and next thing I know I've been fitted up for an armed robbery. Wasn't even one of the ones I *did*. Then he's spreading rumours that it was me who knocked Ruby. And here we are.'

'No disrespect to your reputation, Ray, but I never figured you for Ruby.'

'Course not. Any bastard knows you do a hit for the cops, you're next. And I liked the woman, anyway.'

'When did you last see her?'

'When she was mouthing off, just before they got her. She wasn't involved in the heroin. Not her style. Some other stuff about Sullivan that I didn't want to hear. She was always worked up about something, was Ruby.'

'Worked up about what?'

'Last time I saw her it was about a dodgy cheque she got passed. From some john.'

'That sounds familiar. When was this?'

'Few weeks before she was done in. I've done debt collection for her in the past. Ruby asked me to track the fucker down. I did but I took my time and meanwhile she asked someone else.'

'Was it a company cheque?'

'Yeah, it was. Only reason I took the job on. The cheque was signed by a John Stewart. Know how many John Stewarts there are out there? But it had a company name on it.'

'Which was?'

'I dunno . . . began with C. Carmichael, something like that. Carmichael Enterprises, Pty Ltd, maybe. I told Ruby it was goin' to be a fucker to track down, but I was lying. Easy as, that kind of thing. Every company's listed in Company House, over there on the Terrace. So one day I come back to Perth from where I was hidin' out from Casey, I needed money, right? Went down to Company House, looked it up, there was John Stewart listed as one of the company directors, so I wrote down his address, went after him, but there was no sign of the fucker. Some Chinese grandpa answered the door. I went through him, knocked him about a bit, had a poke around, but there was nothing there to link the address with a John Stewart. I still needed the money, so I went to Ruby to tell her to follow it up with her madam friend.'

'What friend? Who are you talking about?'

'Easy up. Annie DuBois. She was also listed as one of the company directors. Not just that company but a couple of others too.'

'Did Ruby know about that before you told her?'

'Nup, don't think so. Not from her reaction.'

'What kind of companies were they?'

'No idea. Doesn't tell you that, the list. Anyway, like I said, I'd taken too bloody long by then, Ruby reckoned, and she'd already gone to a mate instead.'

'And who was that?'

'Annie DuBois' boyfriend, some Jew calls himself a tax agent. Scam-artist, more like it.'

'Solomon Sands.'

'Yeah, him. But when I told Ruby about Annie's name on the list of company directors it made her angrier than shit for some reason. Dunno why.'

'And that was the last time you saw her?'

'Too right. I didn't like that big sign on her back saying shoot me. I even told her to shut her trap. She got stuck into me then – boy, was she mad. I left. Not that I got far. Casey got me. Waited until after she'd been knocked to shanghai me back in here. That's when the rumours started about me doing Ruby.'

Out on the mesh walkway, steel doors began to slam, vibrating along the length of the block.

'Fucken lockdown. Here we go.'

Swann stood up and tossed his cigarettes and lighter on the bed. 'Give me the mousetrap.'

Hergenhan passed it over. 'Wasn't gonna use it anyway. Found it slid under the door this morning, one of my caring mates looking out for me, eh? Wouldn't make any difference if I did use it. Bastards aren't gonna let me go to the infirmary. They want me here alone.'

'I hope you're wrong, Ray.'

'Either way, I'm not gonna give the bastards the satisfaction of doing it meself. See you in hell, copper.'

When Swann first started out as a policeman it struck him as strange how many crims believed in hell. It didn't seem strange any longer.

Swann took the chalky path down the limestone hill from the prison to the hospital.

Jacky seemed better this morning, although she still looked like she'd been dragged a mile behind a car. But her good eye was clear and fierce.

Swann sat down beside her bed. 'Anybody been to visit you since yesterday?' he asked.

'Apart from the doc? Just Annie DuBois. That girl's not afraid of anything. You go to the funeral?'

'I did.'

'You come to tell me you done that other thing?'

'No,' and he put his hand up before she could interrupt. 'About your friend Annie – she's the one who suggested you come back to Perth, isn't she?'

'Yeah. She was cut up this morning when she saw me, let me tell you. She's hard but —'

'She's not just hard, Jacky, I think she's the one who arranged this.'

Jacky fell silent. Then, '*She* did this to me?'

'I believe so, yes.'

'But why, for fuck's sake?'

'Same reason she wanted you back in town. To find out what you know.'

'What I know about what? I don't know anything!'

'That's why you're still alive. Though anybody can see they went too far. Maybe Annie didn't plan it like it worked out.' He filled her in on what Ray Hergenhan had told him, and when he was finished she made a sound in her throat like a stick breaking. Her right hand started to spasm.

'I don't know if what Michelle said about Cooper dipping into Ruby's trust account was right,' Swann went on, 'but I think Annie would have wanted her to say it. Sands and Cooper are competing for the same business.'

'You think it was Annie had Ruby done as well?'

'I doubt it. If she thought Ruby was onto her she'd have buried her in the hills. Made her disappear. But whoever killed Ruby left her body in public as a message for others. Meaning she wasn't the only one to know things. A warning to all the mugs in all the other scams the cops are running. To keep their mouths shut, or they'll know what to expect.'

The tears in Jacky's eyes had begun to fall. Swann took her hand, which was still trembling. Electric jolts coming down her arm.

'Do you reckon Annie put Michelle up to claiming she was the babysitter?' she said.

'Might have. Maybe she gave her the idea as a way to tap some money. We'll never know now.'

'I don't get it. Why was she killed, then? If she was doing what she was told?'

'No idea. But she must have known something . . . seen something.'

'How're you gonna make this right, Swanny?'

'I've got enough, I think, to pass on to somebody else, somebody who I reckon will follow up, just in case those rumours about me are true.'

'Don't talk like that. You get him before he gets you. You gotta live. For your daughters, your family.'

'Yeah.' He stood and looked down at her. Jacky was going to be badly scarred but she was already on the mend. She passed him her hand, which he squeezed a final time. Then he leant and very gently kissed her forehead.

She closed her eyes to hide her tears.

'I have to go. But if Annie DuBois comes again, not a single word. The only reason you're alive, remember?'

'Yeah, I should be grateful to the bitch.'

'She'll get hers.'

'She'd better, Swanny. Ruby was my life. This is what's left.' She indicated her broken body. 'Annie's gotta pay. Otherwise I don't think I can . . .'

'Next time I come it's to get you out of here, okay?'

She nodded, the tears streaming down her face now, daring to believe him.

He had no trouble finding the launch. It was said you could map the rising fortunes of Donald Casey's career by tracing the yacht clubs he'd joined as things got better. The Royal Perth Yacht Club, where he now moored his monstrous vessel, was the pinnacle of a long social climb. It sat right alongside the University of Western Australia's sandstone buildings and snapping pennants.

He found Casey cut-polishing his beloved boat. He was concentrating so hard he didn't notice Swann clamber on his pain-sharpened joints from the dock to the bow and then edge around the cabin. The jetties around them were quiet, most of the moorings empty.

Casey had his back turned to him. Swann saw the heavy shape beneath the towel on the padded seat and picked it up, cocked the hammer of the single-barrel Remington.

Casey jerked round, then stood up slowly. 'Well, well,' he said. 'I've been expecting you. How you feeling?'

Swann inspected the weapon in his hands. 'Sawn-off 12 gauge – bit dramatic. You alone?'

'I kick the tarts out at dawn, before they start to stink.' Casey wiped the sweat from his top lip. 'What can I do for you, Swann, you fucking delirious idiot?'

'Where is it?'

Casey laughed, chin-nodded at the cabin. 'By the galley, in the oilskin.'

'Come in with me.' Swann pointed the sawn-off towards the open door, followed him in. On the galley table and the seats around it were baskets of long-life groceries. Crates of canned food and cartons of beer were stacked against the cabin walls.

'Planning a holiday, Casey? Enough food here for a month.'

'We're all due a long holiday, come tomorrow. Some of us longer than others.'

He ignored the threat. Indicated to Casey to sit, then reached into the oilskin on the bench and extracted his service .38. Still loaded. No bullets missing.

But there was something else there too, on the floor by the bunks. A pyramid shape with a plastic shower curtain draped over it.

'You're shitting me.' Swann backed deeper into the cabin and lifted the curtain. A stack of gold bars, three by two wide at the base, pressed deep into the carpet. Each one a London Good Delivery Bar, weighing 12.5 kilos.

'Thought she was sitting low in the water. You going to make a deposit somewhere on your holiday, Casey?'

'Fuck off, cunt.'

'Crank her up. Let's go for a ride.'

'What for?' Casey's eyes fixed on the gold, not the gun pointed at him. 'You fish-brained fucking moron.'

'Keep it up, it'll make it easier.'

He followed Casey upstairs onto the console. The key was in the ignition. Casey turned it and the engine throbbed to life.

'Where're we going?'

'Downriver.'

Casey stood with as much dignity as he could muster behind the wheel of his launch. Swann could tell he was hung-over – an alcohol sweat was coming off him. The DI eased back the twin sticks and reversed into the channel between the empty jetties, then nosed out onto the wide brown water. He stayed under the speed limit and waved obligingly to other boats.

Swann kept out of sight of potential witnesses. As long as he didn't move, his bruised body caused him no great pain. His chief discomfort was the weight of the shotgun in his hand. A dull ache had settled into the bones of his wrist and spread up into the strap of muscle over his shoulder.

Casey was refusing to answer any questions but that didn't matter. It wasn't Swann's questions that were important, or even Casey's answers. There could be only two reasons why Casey hadn't had him knocked off yet. Either he wanted Swann to sit out the royal commission in fear of his life, or he wanted him to come at him beforehand, to confirm that he had nothing.

Swann manoeuvred a cigarette from his packet one-handed and lit it. The silence suited the moment. The sunlight, the breeze, the pleasure boats on the water all mocked him. The wheeling seagulls in the wide blue sky were ridiculous and unlikely. He felt like a child with a toy gun in his hand.

Even so, he would have to go through with it. Today was Louise's seventeenth birthday.

'Straight ahead?'

'Go right.'

They had breached the harbour mouth, passing a US aircraft carrier and a cruise ship docked at the wharf. Casey opened up the throttle and the boat lifted in the water. Salt spray flecked across Swann's face as they picked up speed around the mole.

'You should have finished me off when you had the chance,' he said.

He got no reply.

He and Casey had started out the same but had gone different paths. Swann didn't regret their falling out, only what had happened beforehand. Working together, they'd put dozens of crims away. Some had done long stretches, one or two hadn't made it. Knowing what he did about Casey now, they couldn't all have been guilty.

'All right, that's far enough. Turn her off and leave the keys in the ignition. Go downstairs, nice and slowly, into the cabin.'

Swann took the keys and followed. They were settled a good distance offshore. He could see the Norfolk Island pines above Cottesloe Beach. The coast was clear of other vessels.

In the cool darkness below, Casey stood with his hands on his hips, staring at Swann. There was no hint of fear in his eyes. Swann pulled open a bureau drawer, rummaged around. Bundles of dollars, American. He took out a passport, flicked through it. Hong Kong immigration stamps. He replaced the passport and stepped up to Casey, put the sawn-off under his chin.

'How many of them were innocent?' he asked.

Casey sneered as if he'd been expecting it. 'Need to work yourself up, eh?'

'How many?'

Casey looked down at the gun, back up at Swann. He snorted, spat on the floor. 'Ancient fucken history. Do what you came here for.'

That smile on his face. Swann struck him with the butt of the gun, grabbed a handful of hair and dragged him to his knees. 'Where's my daughter, dog?' He thrust the sawn barrel into Casey's eye. The other eye burned with hatred, and something else – a knowing.

An answer.

'Here's how it's going to be,' Swann hissed. 'I'm going to sink your gold – out there.' He pointed across the ocean to Rottnest Island, its dozens of back bays and secret beaches. 'Dead or alive, I want her back by tomorrow. Or you never see your bars again.'

He dragged Casey up by his hair, pulled him out onto the deck.

'Get over,' he said. 'Before I change my mind.'

Casey spat blood from his broken mouth and backed away. He climbed up onto the gunwhale, blew more blood out of his nose, wiped his hands on his legs. Then he bent his knees and dived, and didn't come up until he was far away from the boat, where he stopped to tread water and watch.

Swann went back to the wheel and keyed the ignition, felt the dual inboards rumble before pushing forward on the twin sticks. The nose of the *Lucy* lifted as he surged towards the islands. He had a long afternoon's work ahead of him.

He had witnessed some strange behaviour in his time but this took the cake. He hadn't expected the boat to take off after seeing Swann go aboard. He followed in the Valiant on the road that circled the river, watching from Point Resolution as the launch cut around the sand-spit at Point Walter then passed under the Fremantle Bridge. After that he had no choice but to drive to the northern mole and wait.

Soon enough the boat rounded the mole and headed up along the coast. He parked at Leighton Beach but the launch kept going. He parked again at Cottesloe and saw it anchored offshore.

He had a clear line of sight to the men on the upper deck, until they disappeared downstairs. Then one of them was in the water, the other watching from the boat.

The launch lifted her nose as she headed out into the ocean. The man in the water swam to shore, emerging among the bathers on the crowded beach.

He drove back to the northern mole, saw the wind change on the surface of the waves, the Fremantle doctor setting in. He got out of the car and sat on the bonnet. Fishermen cast off the rocks and reeled in herring, gardies, the odd snook. A US aircraft carrier passed through the channel and headed north, gigantic even on the horizon. Sailboats raced a course out on Cockburn Sound, the victory horn coming to him clear on the southerly.

The number of herring fishermen dropped off as the day wore on. By mid-afternoon others started arriving, longer rods strapped to their roof racks. Many of the men waited in their cars, drinking and smoking, listening to the cricket, getting out and preparing for the evening tailor run only when the sun sank closer to the ocean.

Stretched out on the bonnet of the Valiant, he felt the sun lose its heat on his face. Boats started returning from the islands, the smaller craft pitching about on the swell and the larger ones cruising through the harbour mouth, cutting back on their engines and sending waves against the rocks. Most of the tailor fishermen were down there now, casting upwind into the chop.

He sat up and looked through his binoculars at the line of yachts and launches that stretched right back to Rottnest Island. There it was, following in the wake of the old ferry.

He got off the bonnet and yawned and took his seat again behind the wheel, put the binoculars away in their case. The scalloped sun cast a bronze net as it slid beneath the waves. He brought the ignition wires together and pumped the gas, rolled back across the gritty road.

Partridge entered the converted courtroom on Monday morning with a tight smile. The place was packed with spectators and journalists, who rose to their feet amid whispers and the scraping of plastic chairs. The Sunday paper had reported a 'leak' that the royal commission was being shut down, and supported it with comments from Sullivan and Barth. Both men stated that the commissioner had exceeded his brief. They made mention of unauthorised investigations, the possibility of defamatory action being taken by the police union on behalf of three officers, all charges of corruption being unsubstantiated.

Partridge had called Carol from his hotel room, the last call he would make on this phone, which, it occured to him now, was probably bugged. She confirmed the rumour: the governor was on a plane back from Europe, due that afternoon. It was within his powers, albeit unprecedented, to order the commission to cease its inquiries. He simply had to sign off on his order and the commission would be disbanded.

Partridge took his chair and adjusted his microphone. 'Please be seated.'

He looked across the rows of rubbernecks and saw their morbid curiosity and could not bring himself to begin. He looked over at Sullivan and saw the smugness in his eyes and could not bring himself to begin. Then he looked at Superintendent Swann and saw not the shamed man he'd expected but someone determined to see the verdict through. A look of understanding passed between them as Partridge took up his gavel.

On his return to Melbourne, Partridge intended to sue for a follow-up royal commission, this one at arm's length from the local-mates club that passed for a government here. A commission that had the power to seize documents and subpoena witnesses, a commission that was genuine in its endeavours to investigate Superintendent Swann's allegations. Since those allegations involved cross-border criminality, there were sufficient grounds to argue for an interstate commission of inquiry.

Wallace stepped up and announced Helen Tempest as the next witness. Her name sent a squall of whispers around the gallery. Partridge saw Swann close his eyes as she passed by him, open them again when she took the oath.

'Yes,' she said in response to the first question, 'I was a close friend of Superintendent Swann's for a period of a year, in Albany, when I was posted there for my first duty. In the beginning it was a very pleasant . . .'

Swann looked a little shocked by what he saw. The woman was turned slightly away from him but seemed to sense his gaze. Her honey-gold hair was long enough to sweep across her cheek but did not conceal her eyes, which were full of regret. It was clear to Partridge that she didn't believe what she was saying.

'Mr Wallace,' she said. 'This is difficult for me.'

'Go on, Miss Tempest. You're doing very well.'

'One day I was in the station staff room when Superintendent

Swann came in. We were alone, and he . . .'

Her story was perfunctory and brief. Once excused by Wallace she immediately walked out of the room. The QC's job was done. He returned to his table, shuffled some papers and placed his hands on his lap.

Partridge cleared his throat. 'Do you have anything to add, Superintendent Swann, before I commence my remarks?'

Swann nodded and stood up. He looked up to the ceiling, down again, and spoke clearly into the silence. 'I would just like to remind you all that Ruby Devine was the mother of three children. I hope that one day they will know justice.' He sat down again, his hands flat on the table before him, ignoring the whispers from the gallery, the hum of surprise that the man hadn't tried to defend himself.

Partridge drew his robes about him. His heart beat steadily in his chest. For what it was worth, he would take his lead from Swann's example. He had no intention of letting them close down his commission. He would finish on his own terms.

'Depending on the events of the coming day,' he began, 'my official report will be handed to the governor in due course. Needless to say the following remarks will be expanded upon therein.

'This royal commission is at an end. According to the terms of reference that define it, I can only find that the reliability of Superintendent Swann's testimony and good character has undoubtedly been called into question in this courtroom, by his colleagues, by expert witnesses, and most damningly today, just moments ago. And yet, despite the weight of that testimony, I remain unconvinced that this unreliability diminishes the necessity, as I see it, of relieving the public of their fears regarding official corruption in this state. Certainly as long as the murder of the unfortunate Mrs Devine remains unsolved, public anxiety as to the nature of the rumours currently circulating will continue to grow.'

He paused to catch his breath, his hand steady on the gavel. 'Before I conclude I would like to place on record the fact that I have asked the Premier of Western Australia to widen the terms of reference of this commission, and he has refused, without satisfactory explanation. Such an unwillingness to address the extremely narrow, one might even say obstructive, terms placed on this commission – terms which in my mind have impeded my ability to carry out my proper duty – will, I expect, only add to the public perception that the government of this state is reluctant to get to the heart of the matter.'

He raised his gavel in the eerie quiet and brought it down.

At the sound of the judge's gavel the shooter stood. He waited patiently for the line of people along his row of chairs to drain into the aisle. He enjoyed his frustration at their bovine indecisiveness. He enjoyed the smells of armpit and hair oil, the egg-sandwich breath of the man next to him.

Out they ambled, into the brightness of the morning, silent and unsettled, witnesses to an absurd spectacle which they plainly hadn't appreciated. Nothing in their world had changed, and he could see from their faces that they hadn't understood.

At the doorway he turned and looked back into the hall. Already the judge's bench was being dismantled – the black tablecloth had been removed and the table legs kicked down. Extension cords were wound fist over elbow towards the ports in the wall. The PA amplifiers came next, off their shaky legs, up-ended onto a trolley. A milk carton filled with the cords was placed on top and wheeled out behind the folded-up tables. Soon a boy in shorts and sandshoes, soles squeaking on the linoleum, began hefting the first row of chairs, one on top of another, and carrying them out in piles of five.

For a moment he was the only one in the hall. He felt like shouting, if only to hear his echo. He had been in many courtrooms, but this was one to remember. He reached across and flicked off the lights, one by one. Who was there to stop him?

Horizontal slabs of grey shade marked the glass bricks near the ceiling. He heard the squeaking sandshoes returning and closed the double doors behind him, moved on silent soles out into the sun.

Soon he would be in Marko's GT Monaro and driving north. Soon he would be out on the ocean. Soon he would be getting a good night's sleep. But first he had a job to do.

Swann sat on the vinyl couch in his hotel room, waiting for the phone to ring. His hands were shaking. He was breathing too fast and had already vomited twice. The room reeked of his desperation and failure.

He had taken the map of Australia down from the wall, packed away the red and blue thumbtacks, stowed the letters in the same bag. He kept one of the flyers out on the coffee table, Louise's face looking up at him, smiling and innocent, the one bright point in an otherwise bleak view. How beautiful she was. How perfect.

He made himself look away from her and at his watch. Nearly twenty-four hours since he'd put the word on Casey, sunk the gold bars in twenty metres of water at the back of Cathedral Rocks, off the western end of Rottnest Island. He made himself do the maths again, the numbers that he knew would bring on Casey's call: 4375 ounces at a hundred and forty dollars an ounce – more than six hundred thousand dollars. Sixty years of the average copper's salary. Too good to leave on the ocean floor.

But the phone sat silent on the table. He could feel his pulse thumping in his head, the nausea rising in his stomach again. He lit another cigarette, poured himself a finger and tossed it down with shaking hands. The silence in the room fizzed in his ears.

He shouldn't be alone right now, didn't trust himself if things went wrong, but he couldn't be with others. He'd never been in more danger. Either Casey would deliver Louise's location in trade for the gold or they'd rush the door, torture the bars' whereabouts out of him. His revolver was loaded and sitting by the flyer. It took all his strength to avoid picking it up.

When the phone finally rang he stared at it stupidly. Then made himself pick it up.

'It's me, Frank.' Helen's voice. Small, uncertain. Then silence. He sighed, nearly broke down. It had hurt to see Helen perjure herself. One day he would find out why. But not right now.

He forced himself to speak. 'Helen, I . . . Look, I'm sorry, but . . .'

He heard a deep breath on the other end of the line, a sigh like his own. When she spoke again she sounded like a different person, her voice freighted with determination. 'Listen to me, Frank. Louise was at Ruby's house on the night she was killed. You understand what I'm saying?'

Oh, Christ. He felt tears come to his eyes. His *daughter* was the babysitter. Doubled over, he began to rock, couldn't breathe. What that meant, for Louise.

'Frank, she isn't dead. She's alive.'

Shaking his head. Still not breathing.

'She's in Queensland – I just spoke with her. Louise is safe. She's coming home.'

So this was what Casey had over Helen. What had made her speak against him in court. She'd done a deal to protect his daughter. When he tried to speak, only air came rushing out, keening. The unreality of it all. What he hadn't dared to dream.

'Casey told me to call you,' she was saying, and then her determination faltered. 'He's here now.'

Swann clenched his jaw, swallowed on the surge of anger. Helen was still in danger. Louise was still in danger. He covered the phone while he controlled his breathing, but could still barely manage a whisper.

'You tell him this. When I see Louise myself, in person, I'll let him know. Where it is.' He took in more air. 'And Helen . . . thank you.'

'Frank, I'm so sorry —'

The phone went dead in his hand. The knot in his stomach turned to water. He sat on the couch holding the receiver as if it were a hammer, the cord wrapped around his wrist, weeping through his shouts of joy.

The river smelt of seaweed and black mud, just like it had when he was a kid. Every now and then a crow moaned from down by the water. And just like when he was a kid he felt the excitement of lying in wait.

He had scoped out the house and learned there was no security. The Valiant was parked in the dirt alley at the back, where the night cart used to collect the dunny can through a hole in the outhouse wall. The outhouse was gone now but the alley gave him a good means of escape, unseen. All he had to do was open the gate down the side fence, climb the back wall and drop into the alley.

Protected from the neighbours' view, he had been standing under cover of some eucalypts for two hours now, but that didn't trouble him. It felt good to stare into the dark-green foliage with its tints of blue. Behind the screen of leaves he could see the marks left by borers as they worked the trunk. He looked closer and saw the spitfire larvae that had colonised one of the branches. Spider webs were laced about the leaves. He couldn't see any spiders but there were ants massed in the webs.

He inhaled the ancient decay off the riverbank and imagined

the sepia shallows of the foreshore where the mullet spawned and the flathead lay in wait and the water became progressively cooler the deeper you walked. He pictured the bleached sand at the banks where old rope and jellyfish and chunks of polystyrene lay tangled in the matted paperbark roots and where the tracks of feral cats and pelicans and seagulls spotted the darker sand below the tide line.

He heard the low-revving engine long before the car turned into the driveway and stopped. A door opened and the driver got out. The hinge on the mailbox creaked.

He thought of those other occasions when he'd pulled the trigger, the faces of those untouchable mongrels he'd shot for his own reasons and not for money, because they deserved to die and nobody else was going to do it. When he killed like that he was the nightmare of every evil bastard, because he couldn't be controlled, he couldn't be bought, and he couldn't be understood.

He thought of the bagpipes that would be played at this man's funeral, the speeches from the politicians and senior colleagues, the newspaper headlines that would tell nothing of the truth.

He thought of the man's secrets that would go to the grave with him, and of those who would hate him for the loss of those secrets.

He thought of the fear and confusion among the man's friends, who would never know who'd pulled the trigger, or why.

He thought of the ancient fear of the lone assassin, who was nameless and numberless and haunted the dreams of the powerful.

He thought of the detective sergeant he had always called uncle, who had allowed him to escape and who would never have wanted this for him, because he was a good man and would be ashamed. The same detective sergeant who'd told him it was easy to force a man to eat his gun and make it look like suicide. Who told him that the law was just violence translated into words and that his father had always lived beyond the frontier, where things like that happened.

George Monroe had told him that what was unclear now would one day become clear, and only then should he return. He told him these things just before he shook his hand and reminded him there was a war on, that he should go over east and join the army, and then he opened the door and set him free.

The shooter thought of these things as he scraped the mulch with the toe of his shoe to cloud the impressions he had left. He thought of them as he withdrew his pistol and chambered a round and slipped out the clip and pressed the 9mm shells with his thumb before returning the clip and weighing the pistol heavy and cool against the palm of his hand.

The Statesman whirred in first gear up the slope of the driveway and jerked to a stop in front of him. The handbrake was ratcheted up and as the door opened the shooter got a whiff of saltwater and stale tobacco. He took the breath that would last him until the moment he decided and stepped out from behind his cover. He saw the scuba tank on the back seat of the car and he noted the suit the man was wearing and the half-carton of beer he was carrying under one arm, and he walked on silent rubber soles up behind him.

He felt the need to breathe but swallowed down on the name of the face that he would never see. He took a final step inside the range of the man's instincts and leaned closer and pulled the trigger, once, twice, three times.

'For my father,' he said, and he walked away.

*Acknowledgements*

Some of the events in this novel are based on a true incident; however, all characters in it are fictitious, and any resemblance to real people, living or dead, is entirely coincidental.

I'd like to thank Ben Ball for taking this on, Meredith Rose for her incisive editing, and Mary Cunnane for her representation.

I'd also like to thank Terry McLernon, fifth-generation West Australian copper – something of a record, as I understand it – for his advice and efforts. And Frank Scott, ex-detective sergeant in the WA CIB, who suffered the usual fate of police whistle-blowers – marginalisation, harassment, forced retirement. Thanks also to Shane Finn, Rose Black, Archie Marshall, Juliet Wills, Marty Saxon, Avon Lovell, Joseph Fernandez and Quentin Beresford for sharing their knowledge, and others who helped but prefer not to be named.

Thanks also to those who offered advice on the manuscript: Deborah Robertson, Mark Constable, Perry Middlemiss and Hilary Bonney.

Finally, for your heart – Bella.

ALSO FROM PENGUIN

OLD SCHOOL

P.M. Newton

Sydney, 1992. Nhu 'Ned' Kelly is a young detective making her way in what was until recently the best police force money could buy. Now ICAC has the infamous Roger Rogerson in the spotlight, and the old ways are out. Ned's sex and background still make her an outsider in the force, but Sydney is changing, expanding, modernising, and so is the Job.

When two bodies are found in the foundations of an old building in Sydney's west, Ned is drawn into the city's past: old rivalries, old secrets and old wrongs. As she works to discover who the bones belong to – and who dumped them there – she begins to uncover secrets that threaten to expose not only the rotten core of the police force, but also the dark mysteries of her own family.

P.M. Newton worked in the New South Wales Police Force for thirteen years. Her debut is both a gripping crime novel and a brilliant portrait of Sydney's recent past.

> 'As authentic as a .38 bullet wound. File between D for Disher and T for Temple.' ANDREW RULE, AUTHOR OF *UNDERBELLY*

> 'The writing is razor-sharp and the dialogue sizzles with tough-as-nails authenticity. Newton is a writer to watch.'
> MATTHEW REILLY

> 'Relentless . . . what a multi-layered, powerful piece of writing. This novel puts P.M. Newton in the company of Gabrielle Lord and Peter Temple.' GRAEME BLUNDELL

GENTLE SATAN: MY LIFE WITH ABE SAFFRON

Alan Saffron

Abe Saffron was Australia's most notorious underworld figure, for decades known as Mr Sin and the King of Kings Cross. His wife called him something different: Gentle Satan. This fascinating memoir by his son Alan tells us why, for the first time revealing the truth about the man and the crimes – both professional and personal.

Alan counted the money from Abe's brothels and hotels, and frequented his illegal bars and strip clubs, including the famous Les Girls, The Roosevelt and The Pink Pussycat. He describes Abe's corrupt deals with premiers, police commissioners and a prime minister – many of whom he met – as well as the real-estate deals that 'legitimised' Abe's fortune.

But Alan's most compelling stories are about his own highly volatile relationship with his authoritarian father, and his mother's struggle to deal with Abe's affairs, including the attention he gave to his 'second family', up till his death and beyond.

Gentle Satan is an incredible story of family loyalties, betrayals, illegitimate siblings and contested inheritance, all in the powerful grip of a flawed millionaire patriarch.

'This book reminded me of *The Sopranos*.'

SYDNEY MORNING HERALD

CRIMS IN GRASS CASTLES

Keith Moor

In the 1970s Robert Trimbole and the Calabrian Mafia ruled Australia's marijuana trade from their castles in Griffith, New South Wales – dream homes built with drug money. The business expanded to heroin when Trimbole joined Terry Clark and the notorious Mr Asia syndicate, and then to murder when anti-drugs campaigner Donald Mackay blew the whistle.

Walkley Award-winning journalist Keith Moor learned the truth about Mackay's disappearance from those involved, recording candid interviews in the late 1980s with the hit man, his contact, and the infamous supergrass Gianfranco Tizzoni, as well as a top cop. His classic account now includes excerpts from the unpublished memoir of Mackay's widow and a dossier on the involvement of controversial federal minister Al Grassby.

Moor questions how Trimbole's Griffith Mafia bosses – Australia's true Godfathers – are today able to maintain their links with the global drug trade as they continue to enjoy the view from their grass castles.

'Painstakingly researched . . . an absorbing read.'

ROSS FITZGERALD, WEEKEND AUSTRALIAN

MOSQUITO CREEK

Robert Engwerda

Under ceaseless rains, the Murray has burst its banks and engulfed the remote Mosquito Creek goldfield. Life on the diggings just got even tougher. As disease adds to the camp's miseries, a suspiciously abandoned tent suggests frictions have turned murderous. The experienced Sergeant Niall Kennedy knows that things are not always as they seem. But if the missing digger is on the run, what is he running from?

Another group of miners is feared stranded somewhere amid the raging floodwaters. The troubled young Commissioner Stanfield orders the building of a boat for their rescue – and perhaps that of his reputation back home. His drafting in of special troopers behind Kennedy's back betrays other, more shadowy interests.

In a new country where trust is rarer than gold and everyone's past has a question mark, seeking answers is dangerous. Can Kennedy uncover the secrets of Mosquito Creek, and live with his own?

Mosquito Creek is gripping historical fiction that richly evokes life on the margins of colonial Australia, where crime touches upon everyone and everything.